The Buddha in Malibu

The Buddha in Malibu

New and Selected Stories

BY WILLIAM HARRISON

University of Missouri Press

COLUMBIA AND LONDON

Copyright © 1998 by William Harrison
University of Missouri Press, Columbia, Missouri 65201
Printed and bound in the United States of America
All rights reserved
5 4 3 2 1 02 01 00 99 98

Library of Congress Cataloging-in-Publication Data

Harrison, William, 1933–
    The Buddha in Malibu : new and selected stories / William
Harrison
        p. cm.
    ISBN 0-8262-1170-4 (alk. paper)
    I. Title.
PS3558.A672B78   1998
813'.54—dc21
                                                97-51351
                                                CIP

∞ ™ This paper meets the requirements of the
American National Standard for Permanence of Paper
for Printed Library Materials, Z39.48, 1984.

Text Design: Elizabeth Young
Cover Design: Mindy Shouse
Typesetter: Crane Typesetting Service, Inc.
Printer and binder: Thomson-Shore, Inc.
Typefaces: New Baskerville, Aladdin

"The Warrior," "Roller Ball Murder," and "Down the Blue Hole"
appeared in *Esquire;* "The Arsons of Desire" and "The Makeup Man"
appeared in *Playboy;* "The Good Ship Erasmus" appeared in *Paris
Review;* "On Location" appeared in *The Lowlands Review;* "Stuntman"
appeared in *Antaeus;* "The Magician of Soweto" appeared in *The
Southern California Anthology.*

This book is dedicated to special friends and old cronies:

BOB DOUGLAS

SKIP HAYS

JACK MARR

ROY REED

DON TYSON

Contents

The Movies and Malibu

The Rocky Hills of Trancas *3*
Yes, I've Bought a Couple of Options Myself *23*
The Buddha in Malibu *38*
The Cockatoo Tower *57*
Stuntman *77*
Pretty Girl and Fat Friend *83*
The Big Bang Theory of Love *93*

Africa and Anarchy

The Magician of Soweto *111*
The Warrior *126*
On Location *134*
Sun City *139*

The Future and Forever

Roller Ball Murder *151*
The Arsons of Desire *166*
Down the Blue Hole *177*
The Makeup Man *187*
The Good Ship *Erasmus* *195*
Weatherman: A Theological Narrative *208*

The Movies and Malibu

The Rocky Hills of Trancas

⌐ Setting

We lived far out in Malibu on the wrong side of the highway. In those scraggly, rocky, desert hills above Trancas—which is really just a crossroads with a seedy supermarket, a gas station, and a bar and grill that constantly changes ownership and names—there are a number of shabby, low-rent houses and tiny ranches. Many of the places feature eccentric gates: the residents' names fashioned out of horseshoes, an arch of used tires painted in reds and yellows, mailboxes adorned with the bleached skulls of animals, seashells in tacky patterns on the gateposts. Our gate was composed of two stone columns: desert rocks stuck together with too much mortar so they resembled fountains of lava that had exploded upward and dried in place above the surrounding dust. Our forlorn house had the same look: a melted mass created out of my father's labors. When he wasn't writing another unwanted screenplay, he did rock work. Either behind the typewriter or behind his wheelbarrow, he trapped us inside the crafts and dreams he never mastered. He was also a womanizer who often left home, calling to say that he was staying in the city for script conferences or making other lame excuses. The world was filled with gullible women and girls for him to charm, and the lies he told them became part of the arid spaces in my early teenage years.

Not a mile from that monstrosity we called home, just across the Pacific Coast Highway, was Broad Beach: rows of seaside mansions and exquisite beach houses where the movie stars and famous producers lived. One could cross the parking lot at the Trancas Market where all the migrant workers gathered in hopes of getting day jobs, wait at the traffic light there at the far end of Zuma Beach, then enter the infectious dream that makes our coast so seductive. Go along the main road and you pass Dustin Hoffman's place, then, further on, Spielberg's. Go down a lane toward the lower beach and there's Mel Gibson's. I could never fault my father for being so susceptible to the movie business at this close proximity to success. Broad Beach was newer and even more potent than the old Malibu Colony behind its closed gates; there was gold dust in the air, the heavy pollen of talent and money, and it was always real enough if just beyond one's own capacity to breathe it into the lungs.

⌒ Backstory

One day when I was barely thirteen years old I came home early from school to find my father in bed with another woman. I stood in the doorway watching their copulation and the strange prop they shared, the old Hasselblad camera that had once belonged to my grandfather. A curious and irrational thing happened inside me as I stood there watching: I assumed, suddenly and without the least doubt, that my mother—not just my father carrying on before my eyes—was having an affair, too. My mother in those days was an assistant to the dean at the nearby university, a hardworking woman who provided the family's means of support, and she was always in the company of the dean, a tall man with gray skin and silver hair, and so my adolescent assumption had its basis in odd pieces of evidence. The two of them often went away to academic conferences or my mother frequently went back to the university in the evenings for seminars or cultural activities at the dean's side. He was the distinguished father figure in some of my odd fantasies, the successful Dean Havens who somehow enhanced my mother, Jenna, with his attentions.

Standing there in the doorway, then, watching my father hold the camera at arm's length, snapping off photos as he thrust himself into this anonymous young woman, I assumed that my parents—both of them—were into free love and open marriage.

These intuitions ultimately proved wrong. Dean Havens was a gentleman of the old school: a family man, a community leader, straight-arrow all the way, if somewhat lazy. My mother did most of his work—and hated his laziness, I learned, while taking pride in

her work for the university and for our family. I knew, finally, without having to ask her, that there was nothing remotely intimate
between them.

My father eventually caught sight of me in the doorway.

"Roper," he called to me. "Hey, fella, would you mind going out
on the patio? I'll be with you in a minute."

I waited on the unfinished patio—the eternal project with bags
of cement mix lying around—and kept my eyes on a Ford Mus-
tang, red, parked at the top of our driveway. At last my father
came outside, fully dressed, and began an elaborate and hollow
explanation about taking photographs, art pictures, a hobby of his
until that time unknown to me. He talked loudly and too long,
punctuating his words with short bursts of embarrassed laughter.

"Nudity, you see, well, it's controversial. Some people don't understand the difference between, well, art and smut. Your mother,
for instance, probably wouldn't understand."

"I won't tell," I promised, and as he talked on, relieved, I
watched the young woman hurrying out the back door and getting into her car. She wore leotards and rolled double socks: the
standard uniform of girls who worked out at the gyms in those
days.

⌐ Storyline

I met Mirelle, the love of my sixteenth year, at Malibu High School.
We both lived in absurd houses up in the hills—more about that
in a moment—and among our wealthy and wildly spoiled classmates we would've been outsiders except that she was beautiful
and, although I never played on the team because of my part-time
job, I was probably the best tennis player in school.

I learned to play on the school's courts. Few others wanted to
be seen on them. Surrounded by a cheap chain-link fence that
curled at the bottom so balls constantly went through, made of
grainy concrete scarred with hideous cracks, they were regarded
as an eyesore. After all, half the kids at school had tennis courts at
home: the newest hard surfaces, well-kept clay courts, even one
grass layout—neatly trimmed by a battery of gardeners—up the
winding road at Las Flores Canyon. My time off was usually spent

at these private tennis courts—Mirelle, eventually, on the sidelines sipping cola and cheering me—and because I rarely lost a set, and because a few of the snootier players hoped to beat me, I kept getting invitations.

Mirelle's beauty intimidated everyone. Tall and thin with hardly any breasts, she had a look of icy cool and had already made money as a model when we first became acquainted. I owned an old junker, a battered Chevy Nova that cost less than three hundred dollars. I drove it to school and to my various assignments for Creative Caterers. Mirelle didn't have a car, so suffered the indignities of the school bus. Occasionally, since she lived up a canyon road not far from our house, she allowed me to drop her at her gate after school—never allowing me to venture up her driveway. Then one day she saw our rockpile. She stopped off with me to borrow a library book I had checked out. When she saw my house she broke into laughter. Embarrassment flooded over me.

"No, you don't understand," she assured me, and after we located the book she allowed me to drive beyond her gate for the first time.

She had a rock house, too, studded with seashells, chunks of crude ceramic, pieces of colored bottles, and metallic strips: a terrible stucco heap decorated with the shiny artifacts of bad taste.

"Your dad should meet Stella," she said of her mother, smiling at me with those perfect teeth and touching my hand as I steered us into the carport. A big Persian cat jumped on the hood of the car. Cats everywhere: perched in windows, strolling the slate roof, lounging around a dry fountain and pool adorned with glinting ceramic and shards of glass.

Stella, her mother, who wasn't home, had been a soap opera actress, but now, according to Mirelle, she drank too much and stayed on call for a battery of ex-husbands. She was also a mystic and the world's worst potter, Mirelle said, whose bowls and ashtrays could be lifted only by musclemen.

"Stella says that she helps me through life by serving as a bad example," Mirelle added, sighing.

We sat in the kitchen with mixing bowls and plates heavy on the shelves around us, drinking orange juice. In some miraculous way we talked about our parents' sex lives—about which we had very few actual facts—then about our own and those of our classmates.

"I'm a virgin and mean to stay that way," Mirelle announced.

"In spite of all my efforts, I'm a virgin too," I admitted, and thankfully she laughed.

"Every girl I know does it," she confided.

"What about Karen Highsmith?"

"You don't know about her?"

"No, what about her? She doesn't go steady with anybody."

"That's because she bangs anybody who asks."

"Karen? You're kidding."

"If you want her, just ask. She likes the direct approach. And I guess you'll ask if you're all that interested."

"It's not Karen I'm interested in, not at all," I said, giving her a look that made my meaning clear.

Mirelle studied me over the rim of her glass. In an enormous mixing bowl above us on a shelf, a cat lay curled in sleep.

"I guess we both have promiscuous parents," she finally began, thoughtfully. "We love them, I guess, but we don't want to be like them. You know, we could possibly go together. I mean, you're perfect for me because you get invited everywhere to play tennis."

"You get invitations, too."

"No, I don't, that's the point. The boys seem to be afraid of me and the girls know I'm poor and can't keep up with them. I mean, guess where Anna and Susie went for their summer break? The Himalayas. To see the Dalai Lama or something. Ginger Dickinson says she only skis in Switzerland these days. Half of them have new convertibles. Look at their clothes, then look at mine. When they heard I had a modeling job, they considered me a working girl. And except for the tennis it's probably the same for you. I mean, you work for the catering service. They see you at their parents' parties wearing a white jacket and serving the hors d'oeuvres, don't they?"

"Sometimes I even have to wear white gloves," I admitted. "But let's get back to you and me."

"We're perfect, but no sex," Mirelle said, putting the deal straight. "I like you, I mean, but this is for the social situation. Because our parents have these god-awful houses. And because I'm miserable, but I'm twice as pretty as Becky or Ginger or any of them."

"You're ten times more beautiful," I added. "So what about kissing?"

She smirked and placed her empty glass on the rough kitchen table. "Just kissing?" she asked, again thoughtfully.

"I believe we should kiss each other all the time," I suggested, trying to sound rational about it. "In front of everybody. At tennis matches. In the hallway at school. You know, to keep up appearances."

She considered this argument. Then she moved over and sat on my lap, sighing and saying, "All right. Let's see how it goes."

The kiss she gave me, open mouthed, slow, wet, deep, filled with the subtleties of arousal, ignited all my hopes.

She liked it, too. "Goodness," she said afterward, and she got up and walked to the window where she stroked a fat little Siamese who sunned himself there. "Goodness, you have strong arms."

Strong arms. It was a compliment I've remembered all my life.

She came back to me, shoved her kitchen chair against mine, sat facing me, pulled closer, placed her long legs over mine, and kissed me again. In pleasure and in misery we practiced kissing that whole afternoon. Afterward, everywhere, just as I had suggested, we were considered ardent lovers, kissing on the mouth, the neck, the cheek, constantly, in a conspiracy against those around us and in the turmoil of our own early confusions.

⌐ Close Up

Unlike my father, Tally, who never went on walks, my mother and I enjoyed strolling along the beaches. At low tide we sometimes walked from Broad Beach up toward the Ventura County line, passing all those elegant houses and the raw cliffs filled with wildlife. We saw a bobcat, once, and often ran across rattlesnakes, the small dark ones that hunted for rodents and rabbits beneath the gorse and windblown trees. Out at sea windsurfers turned their bright sails into the breeze, making sharp cuts at the edges of our thoughts. Overhead, gulls called to one another and rode the wind. Surfers in their black wet suits waited for the waves, adream, like a special species of ocean creatures.

During those walks I often wanted to talk about my father, about the demanding dean, about Mirelle, or all the restlessness inside me, but somehow didn't.

In a rocky cove one day, sheltered from a fierce afternoon breeze, we ate apples and slices of cheese as my mother's silken scarf billowed softly in the air. She had a soft look, a serenity, and used her scarves to dress up a modest wardrobe bought on sale far from the fashionable shops. At Christmas or on her birthdays I usually gave her a new scarf, something expensive bought out of my wages—a Fendi or a Picasso—and I always promised myself that I'd someday buy her a new car, a new house, or a new life.

We talked about my Grandfather Roper that day in the cove. "I know he was a cowboy and an atheist and I've heard all the stories about how tough he was," I said. "But can you remember anything else? Something about him you've never told me?"

She bit into her apple, looking at the ocean horizon where, far offshore, an oil tanker passed. I was my grandfather's namesake, and she knew I loved the old anecdotes.

"He once told me that he just loved revenge," she said slowly, grinning and remembering.

"Getting even, you mean?"

"Exactly. Payback. He was even a little cruel about it. He said it was one of life's wicked pleasures. He beat up that deputy sheriff, the one who stole the antique saddle."

"You told me that story. You said grandfather almost had to go to jail himself."

"When he thought he was in the right, he was terrible. He sometimes overdid it with my brother and me. But you're not like that. You're gentler. More like your father, I believe."

I didn't want to hear that and she sensed it.

"Let's finish the walk," I suggested.

"Throw your apple core up on the cliffs for the little animals," she reminded me, and we set out again.

Not only did I consider my mother wrong about how I was like my father, but the mystery of her marriage to Tally always nagged me. How could she love this philanderer? This typewriter bum? It was far beyond me. Angry in this uncertainty, I threw my apple core high onto the cliff as we walked on.

⌐ Panning Left

Back when my father temporarily had an agent—not a good one, of course—he went to a script conference with a producer who was guiding the career of young Tom Cruise. It was the most important meeting of my father's writing career.

He spent the morning dressing himself, getting the casual outdoor look: sneakers, black jeans, a crisp white shirt, and the old black leather jacket with the little dangling chain. He noted for us later that the actor's producer, the assistant, and the recording secretary all wore essentially the same costume: jeans and fancy new shirts. They drank Diet Pepsi and spoke his name in a litany of friendliness: Tally Jones, yes, Tally old pal, Tal, Tally this and that. They were doing a boxing movie, he told us, and already had the storyline. He sat in that studio office, he said, turning his Diet Pepsi in his fingers, excited, trying not to say the wrong things. Too much, he told us: sitting at a real studio, sound stages just beyond the window, talking to real producers about a possibly real movie for which he would really get paid.

The story was about a crude southern boy who had been in prison and his new black manager. It was about racial prejudice and how the two become friends. In the last act, the young boxer, Tom Cruise, wins the title.

"You have the storyline already," my father says he told them. "So what can I do for you?"

The crucial moment of the meeting had arrived. All script meetings are actually auditions, and the writer is supposed to have a good idea or two if he expects to land a writing assignment.

The second act is the problem, the assistant pointed out. You know, the part where Tom and his manager—Morgan Freeman, say—become pals. Characterization. All that.

At this point, Tally told us that he had an inspiration. The black manager, see, reads Miss Manners, he said to them. The manager believes in courtesy the way some people believe in the Bible. So he carries around this big book of etiquette by Miss Manners and reads passages to Tom Cruise. While he's teaching Tom to box, he reported telling them, he also teaches him table etiquette and how to talk to women. And Tom discovers that courtesy works. Tom even learns to quote Miss Manners himself, using some of her arch diction, in a reverse bit when Morgan Freeman loses his cool.

The producer, assistant, and recording secretary laughed, my father told us, and slapped him on the back. Wonderful stuff, they said. Softens the movie with humor. Terrific. As the last handshakes began, my father said he knew he had the assignment.

On the freeway driving back out to Trancas, my father said he felt clever and successful. It was a day clear of smog in Los Angeles, he said, and some distant Filipino volcano provided a vivid sunset, as if God had used the right filter.

We heard the details of this meeting for a week. He took me aside—we went into the bathroom where he sat on the edge of the tub—to tell me that his dreams could come true, they really could, and that everything would be different. He loved both my mother and me, he said, and he would give us everything he had failed to provide in the past. He meant it, I knew, as an apology for that time I caught him in bed with that strange woman—and for all his shortcomings.

A week later the second-rate agent phoned. The producer had decided to go with another writer, a former black boxer who wanted to try his first script. Later my father learned that the producer had asked a dozen or so writers to stop around, writers looking for work, picking their brains in a flurry of first names and Diet Pepsi, so they could provide the novice screenwriter with material.

I felt sorry for Tally. The world out there was cruel to him even when he was allowed to briefly touch it. And I suppose, even now, if they ever make a movie about a boxer and his black manager with Tom Cruise, Morgan Freeman, or the next incarnations of movie stars, whenever such a movie goes into production, at whatever studio in this decade or the next, Miss Manners might be part of the story. Sadly, my father did give them something nice, a little thought to be ground up, along with some of his supply of hope, in the machinery of the business.

⌐ Racking Focus

We were at the Spencer house in the Colony playing on their clay court. Mirelle flashed her smile, sipped lemonade, and hung around with us talking about colleges. Craig was going up to Stanford, while Charlie was waiting on Harvard but would probably end up at Berkeley.

Charlie and I had just started a game of singles when Mr. Spencer came out. Craig's father had an unruly mop of dyed hair, hunched shoulders, and a pipe in his mouth. He concentrated on Mirelle and soon asked her to go into the house with him to look at his paintings. Mr. Spencer's seascapes featuring young women in diaphanous lingerie strolling among the sand dunes were in some of the galleries up in Santa Barbara, but in my opinion they were silly, amateurish works. Besides, Mr. Spencer remained one of the few men in Malibu living off alimony payments from a famous wife, a singer, and we all knew that both Mr. Spencer and his son Craig were braggarts and fools in spite of their clay court.

"Be right back!" Mirelle sang out, waving, and as I watched her stroll away with Mr. Spencer I had this odd, sinking feeling.

I liked playing with Charlie Beringer well enough, but that afternoon I made quick work of him: passing shots, a lob here, a dropshot there, my whole repertoire. He became a bit surly, but I couldn't give him points as I usually did. I beat him in two love sets, so we could get indoors.

We found Mirelle and Mr. Spencer seated at opposite ends of a big leather couch in his studio. I went over and sat between them, pretending to admire his most recent surf-and-dune epic perched on an easel before us. The house, by the way, had a pulse in it: with each wave breaking on the nearby beach, the windows shook and the floors gave us a definite tremor. Mr. Spencer said it was soothing. Anyway, Charlie and Craig turned on a TV set in another room and Mr. Spencer wanted to know if I appreciated art.

Guarding against a sarcasm, I gave him a humble no.

"I'd think you'd be turned on by the arts," he replied. "Isn't your father a writer?"

"My father's a failed writer," I corrected him, and that ended the discussion. Mr. Spencer probably fretted that I might have artistic standards, and he was a painter who certainly didn't want to be drawn into a discussion of those.

After smalltalk, a last lemonade, and a moment in front of the oversize TV screen with Craig and Charlie, we said our good-byes. Suddenly, Mr. Spencer, acting wildly formal, grabbed Mirelle's hand and kissed it, and for a crazy moment I thought Craig might do it, too.

As I was driving us back home in my rattling Chevy, Mirelle told me that I had been rude to Mr. Spencer.

"He's a nerd," I said. "Who can like that guy?"

"Also, you were jealous," she accused me, and she seemed proud of herself for making me feel that way.

"I'd be stupid if I wasn't," I told her. "You're gorgeous and you drive us all crazy."

She liked that, so pulled her legs up and encircled her knees with her arms. Smug and beautiful, her future assured, she closed her eyes against the oncoming western sun. My own future in comparison was far less certain. Others spoke of college and what lay ahead, but all my hopes were vague, poorly defined, even though I sensed that I would soon be expelled from Eden and should worry about it all.

⌐ Jump Cut

A family dinner up in Oxnard at Sal's.

My parents called one another by their names that night, Jenna this and Tally that, stiffly, so I suspected they were making up after an argument and taking me along in order to remember why they were still married.

We talked about Tally's screenplays—which at this time must have numbered about thirty—and they tried to draw me into the discussion.

"Which one do you like best?" my mother wanted to know.

"I haven't even read them all."

"Of those you've read, which one?"

"Maybe the science fiction epic."

"Really? You like that one?" my father asked, biting into his taco. "I thought you told me it was over the top. Too weird, you said, remember?"

Sal's served my mother's favorite Mexican food. It was a big noisy place with checkered tablecloths, families, enchiladas, and beer, and if we went out to dinner it was the place my mother felt we could afford. Of course the whole question of family money remained a mystery to me: How could Tally afford, at times, to disappear for a couple of days? Did Grandfather Roper leave us anything? We were poor, that was always made clear, and my own money, hard-earned, went for Mirelle's pleasure and mine—we usually dated in packs—and even when we drove over Kanan Road and went to the movies in Agoura we often ended up eating at places like Fettucine's because the others were oblivious to what things cost.

My father that night insisted on analyzing the sci-fi script while I tried to concentrate on my steak asada.

"The wizard shouldn't be the main character," I finally told him. "Otherwise, the whole thing's a good idea. Original."

"So who should be the main character?" Tally asked with sarcasm, his taco stopped in front of his mouth.

"Not the wizard because he's too old. A young audience won't identify with him. Maybe a new character, a kid, like his apprentice."

"Listen to him," Tally said to my mother. "The script doctor."

That ended the conversation. They had little to say to each other after that, and we drove home in silence.

Later that evening Tally asked to borrow twenty dollars.

"You didn't pay me back last time," I reminded him.

"Yes I did," he argued. "And, look, I'm driving Ellis Kerry's car up to Ventura tomorrow. I don't even have gas money. He's paying me for the favor and I'll pay you back right away."

"Ellis Kerry, the producer?"

"We've known each other for years. He almost bought a script from me once."

"And you do what for him now? Errands?"

"Roper, c'mon, don't make me ask twice. I'll pay you back with interest. Promise."

⌐ Quick Take

The next day while my father was supposed to be driving up to Ventura I laid out of school to work a big catering job at a new house on Broad Beach. The staff had to arrive early to set up tables, get the food into the ovens, stock the bars, and receive assignments. Once again, I wore the white jacket and was ordered to circulate among the two hundred guests serving champagne and picking up empty glasses.

Built on the side of the cliff, the house had six floors and two elevators. From the main road, like all the other houses along that stretch, one saw only the garage doors and a modest entrance, but above the garage, tucked behind a row of barred windows, a battery of security guards monitored everyone who approached. Beyond the entrance and garage, the house became a jewel of spacious salons, open decks facing out to sea, white stucco passageways, game rooms, and vaulting glass windows. A crystal waterfall trickled down a series of artfully arranged boulders in the middle of the house, opening up into hidden pools, alcoves, hot tubs, and a sense of flowing splendor.

The businessman who owned it, I was told, referred to it as his little seaside cottage.

At one of those hidden pools, discreetly tucked away in a nook beside the waterfall, I found my father holding hands with a striking woman who wore a string bikini. Both their bodies were sculpted and perfect. Tally's tanned physique, I wanted to tell her, came from hefting big rocks into our oversize wheelbarrow and from basking in the hot sun of our ugly patio and garden.

But I said nothing, even when she called after me asking for a glass of champagne.

She might have been the wife of the owner or Ellis Kerry's secretary or a porno star, but I didn't want to know. It might have been an innocent interlude, but I saw Tally's face and knew it wasn't.

He caught up with me at the elevator, beginning another weak explanation, stammering, but I didn't let him get started.

"Now that you're back from Ventura you owe me twenty bucks," I told him. My face must have twisted with disgust because he turned away and padded barefoot back toward his little cove.

⌐ Wide Angle

It's a dreamcoast, sure, but the false optimism and elusive hope that resided in my father's deepest core, that gets into so many others out here, becomes a poison. The climate is warm and sunny; everyone hears success stories, gets glimpses of celebrities, and it's a palm-tree world, a halter-top world, where phrases like *Malibu* or *development deal* roll off the tongue, but one lives on a personal fault line where everything is shaky and terrifying.

As I began to sense this, I wondered why Tally didn't.

One evening I accompanied my mother to a university picnic up in the canyon near the Hindu temple. A soft evening in an arbor of eucalyptus: tables covered with white linen and adorned with hurricane lamps, strolling musicians with guitars and flutes. I danced with my mother, our feet shuffling over the bare earth, and found that she seemed very small in my arms. Afterward we talked for a while with Dean Havens and his wife, then sat on the ground with our backs against one of the trees. I thought of saying that I'd like to get away early so I could drop by and see Mirelle, but then I realized I couldn't hurry off.

"You okay? You seem sad," I said to her, and since I was sixteen years old it was hardly precocious of me, yet it was that rare first moment when one asks about a parent's feelings.

"Oh, I was thinking about your father," she mused, reaching over to touch my arm and reassure me. "He'll never be a writer, I sometimes think, because so much of his life is, well, physical. Like his rock walls. He doesn't read much. He doesn't have—oh, I don't know, a very strong inner life."

"He doesn't have any talent," I said, then wished I hadn't.

"Maybe not," she said, sighing, and accepting that. "But where does talent come from? How does it develop? Poor Tally. He wants to be in the mainstream so much, yet he needs to live a secret life, doesn't he?"

For me, everything about my father had become too painfully

important to be discussed further. In silence, then, we sat looking up through the dark branches of the trees at the greater canopy of stars. My mother gave my arm a gentle squeeze.

"You're worried about college and money and what will happen to you, aren't you?"

"Sure," I answered, "I guess so."

"Things will become very clear. You'll see. You know what I've been thinking recently? This is odd. Don't laugh. I've been thinking that you'll do something very big. You know, famous."

"C'mon," I said, giving her a nudge. "Not me. That's scary talk, anyway." In our house, I thought, we've had too many big dreams, and my mother, my steady and practical mother, should know that.

An evening breeze rustled the leaves above us.

The musicians played "Red Sails in the Sunset."

➤ Plot Point

Mirelle and her mother, Stella, came to our house for bean soup. Stella wore a tight-fitting black sheath dress, black boots, and about ten pounds of assorted jewelry that dived into her cleavage. Her hair was teased into a lopsided bird's nest. Purple lipstick. She brought a gallon of cheap red wine, two Tarot decks, a crossword puzzle in the event she got bored, her cell phone, and a Doberman pup named Coco who didn't get along with the cats, very docile because she had given it Valium. She flirted shamelessly with Tally, clomping around in her boots like a flamenco dancer while he stirred the soup at the kitchen range. Then she swept away the magazines on the coffee table and sat down cross-legged on the floor to read fortunes. Through all this, Mirelle gave us her famous smirk and rolled her eyes.

"Oh, my, dahling!" Stella cried out with each card she turned up, wildly pretentious and aware of it. Our fortunes, thankfully, were all bright and happy, although one of my cards she called "troublesome" and said we just wouldn't think about it.

My mother, slightly tipsy after two glasses of wine, put on a Dixieland CD while we ate supper. At the table Tally became the centerpiece of the evening, telling stories and doing impressions. He did a great Jack Nicholson: the nasal voice, yet back in the throat in the bass range, reciting those famous lines from the restaurant scene in *Five Easy Pieces* when the character was trying to order a chicken salad sandwich that wasn't on the menu.

Stella stood up at the table and gave him an ovation. Her dress by this time had slipped off one pudgy shoulder and a white bra strap had appeared.

After that Tally did the Godfather with pieces of French bread in his cheeks. As the women nodded and laughed, I watched his effect on them. His shirt was open to his waist, exposing the hair on his chest and his hard flat stomach. When he gave them his crooked smile it provoked all of them to smile in return. I couldn't have won their attention if I had set the room on fire; I was a boy just getting my bearings and he was a man of fearsome charm, worldly, oddly confident, in command, and it occurred to me—how old was he that night? maybe forty-three?—that he should have been an actor, not a writer, and that he possessed a special physical grace that I had never fully understood.

He drank off a glass of wine, did Cary Grant, and then, in an amazing transition, did both Bogie and Claude Rains in their famous exchange from *Casablanca*—dialogue that Mirelle liked yet didn't quite understand because she admitted never having seen the movie.

With everyone under his spell, he quit. Perfect timing.

"I'm going to make us a dessert," he announced, and went back to the kitchen.

My mother and Stella retreated to the sofa together, clasped hands, and fell into an earnest conversation like old friends. Mirelle gave her attentions to the dopey dog. I decided to help finish off the wine, so poured myself a glass and quickly drank it down.

With the evening performances ended, the five of us wandered through the house and outdoors for idle conversations. Tally made brownies. Overpowered by that single glass of wine, I stood at the bathroom mirror taking stock of my unremarkable features. A definite new pimple. Too much. When I emerged, I found Tally and Mirelle in the kitchen playing a game of slap: his palms turned down and extended, hers turned up underneath as she attempted to quickly turn her hands over and slap his. She scored on him every time and they both laughed at every twitch, feint, and success.

"Hey, you're too good," he told her, and she bit her lower lip with pride, grinning.

Alarm swept over me.

Their touching, however slight and quick and violent, was worse for me than anything that had happened with Mr. Spencer. They both looked over at me occasionally, smiling, both of them natural and having fun, yet I felt put in my place. I was a losing competitor, I knew, and I added up my assets against Tally's. I can beat him at tennis, I assured myself, and I get paid when I work. On all other counts, clearly, he had me: he was bigger, stronger, more handsome, and most surprisingly of all, more alive.

Later we ate the brownies and drank strong coffee.

At the end of the evening we stood outdoors and pointed out the constellations to one another; Stella knew them all because she was also an astrology freak, a Scorpio, and because our hills, she reminded us, sheltered the glare of lights from Santa Monica, giving us a superb view of the universe.

She and my mother hugged goodnight. Mirelle embraced everyone, too, giving Tally, I thought, a bit more enthusiasm than necessary.

"Your dad's cool," she whispered when she hugged me, then she left me without a kiss.

They almost forgot the puppy.

⌐ Wildtracking

The following Saturday I agreed to roll out cookie dough with the bakers for extra pay at the catering service. At noon, though, we had the job done, so I drove home to find my mother sewing. She was no better at stitching than she was at cooking, so we made conversation while she stuck needles in her fingers and swore under her breath. I asked where Tally was.

"Gone off on a hike," she said, shrugging her shoulders and shaking her head because this was definitely something new for my father. "Took the old Hasselblad with him," she added. "I guess he's going to photograph the cactus and maybe take up a new art."

My alarm went off again. I hurried to the car and drove up to Mirelle's place.

On my way I invented several excuses about why I was dropping in unannounced, then decided I didn't need any. I wondered if Stella was home, if I'd catch anybody doing naked photos, if I was going insane. Then, forgetting caution, I pressed the accelerator. In less than a minute I roared up Mirelle's driveway and skidded to a stop in a cloud of white dust. I hurried inside, running, seeing nothing except all the cats, finding no one, then with long strides I went down a hallway toward the back bedrooms.

Mirelle sat on her bed, fully dressed, eyes wide. Yet for a moment we didn't speak and I suddenly knew that all my worst fears were true. Glancing out the window, I saw Tally hurrying over the hill, making his escape, and without thinking I went after him.

He was in full flight and I couldn't catch him. Not knowing what I'd say if I did, I stood at the crest of an arroyo and hurled rocks after him. They fell around him in little white puffs of dry dust until he was finally out of range.

Back inside the house I found Mirelle still on the bed, sobbing.

"Goddammit," I said, and walked out.

⌐ Slow Fade

That was the last time I saw my father.

I drove all around, cooling off, trying to find the right words to say to him, yet they were all wrong. Under the circumstances and because I was still so young and generally inarticulate, the phrases were all moralistic, even righteous, and I knew that just wasn't the right pitch and tone for this latitude. I drove up the PCH as far as the county line, then crossed over toward Thousand Oaks, then looped back and cruised along Broad Beach. All the celebrity houses glared at me. I had only kissed Mirelle, I kept telling myself, and I certainly didn't own her. And Tally's such a bastard. So grow up. Get used to it and get over it. And don't say anything to mother.

By the time I reached our house, though, Tally had thrown a

few clothes in the back of mother's car and without saying anything, embarrassed beyond recovery, slinking away like a dog, had left us. He left his pile of scripts on the shelf and the oversize wheelbarrow filled with stones. A week later he phoned and told Jenna that he was living in an apartment in Pasadena, giving her a phone number and arranging to send back the car.

These days he lives in San Bernadino, a million miles away. He's with a young stewardess, my mother told me, and doing what for a living nobody knows.

During my last year at Malibu High School, I fell in with the son of Ellis Kerry, the producer, and he started taking me to screenings at the studios. When we weren't playing tennis over at his place in Corral Canyon we hung out at the movie houses on Third Street in Santa Monica. Bosco was a quiet kid, serious, and thoughtful about money—for instance, he tried to stay within my budget when we did things together—and he helped me with dates after Mirelle. We took a few girls out, mostly for burgers but sometimes to the screenings—which they went crazy for—and Bosco did a strange thing: although he drove a new Nissan, he bought an old junker like mine, a beat-up Escort, and said he felt better in it. When I told him he was crazy he reminded me that he still had the Nissan, too.

From Bosco I learned about the student film competition, so entered in the screenwriting category. I dug out Tally's old sci-fi script, the one with the Wizard who was the Leonardo da Vinci of the twenty-third century, and I added the new character, the kid who was his apprentice, and a half dozen new scenes. I scanned the whole manuscript into Bosco's computer, then worked at his house, spending a month on it, and incorporating all his suggestions. After revising it again, I sent it to the student competition— which included college students, even grad students, so I knew I'd never win.

After that I considered claiming Tally's abandoned office as my own, but it didn't feel right.

I did steal his scripts, all of them. Turnabout was fair play, I decided, and, besides, that career of his—such a long indulgence— was over.

For a few weeks my mother drank too much, then, abruptly

and rationally, she stopped. I never saw her cry. That summer she went to Italy with Dean Havens, his wife, and a group of faculty members.

The wheelbarrow filled with stones was never touched.

Stella married again, and Mirelle, the model, signed some sort of contract.

⌐ Trailer

The screenplay, *Lords and Masters,* won the competition, making me the youngest writer ever to win.

After that Bosco and I began trying to get jobs in the story departments of various studios. If this happens, I tell him, I'm going to buy my mother a new car and tie a beautiful new silk scarf on its antenna.

She sold the Trancas property—left to her by Grandfather Roper, I learned—then bought a new condo down near the old pier. The investors who bought the old place tore down the house, bulldozed away the unfinished patio, the wheelbarrow, the columns at the gate, and finally auctioned off the barren land.

When I won the competition my picture was in two or three newspapers, but I suppose Tally didn't know that because he never phoned.

Yes, I've Bought a Couple of Options Myself

Manny, his boss from the escort service, phoned and instructed him to have his Givenchy suit cleaned, told him that his date for dinner would be at the Bel Air, and asked him to drop by the office to study the file on Hazen Wilson. She was an ex-model who had become president of World Mansions, a real estate firm out of Seattle, and she was flying into LA to close a big deal. Her requirements, both intellectual and sexual, he was informed, were very specific.

All this on Cappy's answering machine. Manny's voice was up an octave.

Cappy had heard of Hazen Wilson. The other male models, would-be actors, ski bums, brutes, and handsome waiters who worked from time to time for Manny at The Male Slot, who took the bejeweled crones and truly ugly widows of the world out to dinner or sometimes to bed, spoke of this female tycoon with awe. They longed to be seen with her, to receive the big tips she dropped on her hired dates, and to satisfy, if called upon, her kinkiest needs. By Manny's standards, a legendary client: cool, demanding, beautiful, and a spendthrift. At first she had insisted on a Latin type, then a blond muscleman. Until now, according to Manny, she had also insisted that the escorts keep silent—not a word, not on any subject—but this had obviously changed. In this town, after all, Cappy knew, the intellectual life, like the spiritual life, was part of one's general status and ambition, a commodity like cars, cigars, shoes, or cocaine, items to be purchased then shown off and bragged about, so intelligence was only bought when needed, if only a bit of educated table talk. In this case, Cappy figured, since he had only one modest area of expertise—

the movie business and all its trivia and nuance—the client must be trying to sell a mansion to somebody in the business.

He drove his battered Ford Escort into Brentwood, went up the garage elevator to The Slot, and read the file. A photo of Hazen Wilson was included—maybe from a few years back in her modeling days, he assumed—along with her account sheet and business card. She had used the service twice previously, dating none of the guys currently on the hunk list.

"Okay, tell me about the sex part," Cappy said to Manny.

"I only know what Stevie told me," Manny confided, and his voice dropped off into low, intimate notes of perverse gossip. "First, a rubdown. Then cowboy enthusiasm. Just remember you're paid to do all the acrobatics. You look good, but I hope you've been going to the gym on a regular basis."

Stevie, a legend himself, had married and moved to Rome.

"And she wants someone to talk movies?"

"Somebody who reads *Variety* and who knows the names of directors and producers, all that. I told her you had some acting credits and that you'd written a couple of scripts. Drop the names of some TV shows that've been canceled."

Manny stood close while Cappy read the file, a hand resting on Cappy's shoulder. Manny was an old fag, but married with children who were already divorced. He lived in Toluca Lake, had a cabin up in Arrowhead, raised Siamese cats, and adored his stable of young men. All of them permitted him to touch them, but all of them also regularly said no. He didn't seem to care. "Liff und let liff," he said every day, enunciating the phrase like Emcee from *Cabaret.*

"Here, a present," he said. "Wear it tonight."

Cappy unwrapped a shirt with a flared collar, ivory in color.

"Her instructions were also no neckties," Manny explained. "Dark suit, no tie, no jewelry of any sort including a wristwatch."

"Nice shirt," Cappy managed.

"No fancy cufflinks, either, I'd say. Little black studs at the very most. I'll have the limo pick you up at seven. He'll wait all night in the Bel Air parking lot if you stay in her room. And, please, Cappy, take my advice, don't talk too much. She says she'd like a bit of chitchat, but I know this bitch well enough and she really doesn't want much."

That afternoon Cappy ate a chicken salad over on San Vincente, then looked into Rudy's gymnasium on his way over to Dutton's Bookstore. An aerobic class of groomed housewives occupied the gym, and he stopped to watch Debbie, the instructor, as she put them through their paces. He longed for a nice, lanky tomboy like Deb: savvy, young, a girl with real laughter. But the city seemed to be built on a debris of hopes like that one, as if below every street the fault lines opened, the tar pits lurked, and the bones of hopeful actors and players like himself filled a waiting netherworld.

He perused the overstuffed shelves of his favorite bookstore trying to ignore these little twitches of depression. He was still handsome, he knew, but that was all: a mop of hair, solid features, blue eyes, the deep tan, yet he was also a speck of glitter wanting to believe that glitter was something more meaningful.

Later, after a shower and a nap, he waited for Gus, the driver, to pick him up. Gus kept a small leather pouch of male cosmetics in the booze compartment of the limo: three varieties of cheap cologne, a hot aftershave, and hair mousse. A couple of years ago one of the escorts, Gus told him en route to the hotel, maybe Stevie, drank all of the bay rum after a particularly harrowing date.

Everything at the Bel Air was the same: the white swans on the pond, the sturdy wooden bridge, the silent rows of bungalows, and, far off, the tinkling glasses of those raising toasts to a night as black as exposed film. Cappy made his way to a large bungalow engulfed in bougainvillea and jasmine at the end of a covered pathway. He took a deep breath, moistened his lips, and knocked.

She came to the door wearing one of the hotel robes, her hair still wet. "Cappy," she said, pronouncing his name slowly, then appraising him for a long beat as he stood there. He tried a smile.

"You're beautiful," she said. "Come inside. Mix the drinks."

Compared to the photograph Cappy had seen earlier that day, Hazen Wilson's beauty had badly eroded. Her smile was a manufactured effort in a face that didn't want to do that anymore. Her shape beneath the terry-cloth robe, he noted, appeared to be stick-figure thin. But the terrible things were her hands: sad little claws bent by arthritis.

"Gin and tonic and not much booze in it," she said, waving at the bottles on the coffee table, then strolling into the bathroom, where she resumed her efforts with the hair dryer. She left the door open.

The room featured white lilies in two arrangements the size of funeral sprays, white roses in three vases, and her white business suit laid out on the bed. Cappy stirred the drinks as she finished her hair and came out. Her gnarled fingers accepted the tumbler.

"My clients tonight are Lou and his wife, Victoria," she began. Her voice struck an occasional low note, sort of Lauren Bacall, as she got down to business. "Lou makes millions and can't seem to stop. He recently bought Victoria a major share in a cosmetic company and she looks like she's trying to wear all the makeup at once like a fifty-year-old Kewpie doll. They want the biggest available house in either Beverly Hills or Bel Air and they want to produce movies."

"They know anything about the business?"

"They attend their local movie house in Davenport, Iowa."

Cappy grinned and tasted his glass of pure tonic water.

"And what are you?" she asked, her voice low with sarcasm. "Some sort of actor?"

Cappy gave her both hard facts and embellishments: reared in Texas, worked in the oil fields around Beaumont, disliked manual labor, liked the girls too much, came looking for a modeling or acting career without benefit of training, played two parts in failed TV pilots, became a night watchman, went to work for The Male Slot. "I'm a reader and a moviegoer," he added. "English major type. Analytical."

"Then keep the wife talking about movie stars while I sell Lou a house," Hazen said, knocking back her drink. "I can make a million-dollar commission on this. Win yourself a bonus."

He didn't ask how much. One is promised snowflakes and one usually gets sandstorms.

"Do my back," she ordered, and she turned around and dropped the robe to her waist.

"Rub it, you mean?"

"If you don't know how to give a massage, then just give it your best. Wait. I'll stretch out here on the bed."

She lay beside her white business suit. The rest of the robe came off—so much for preliminary modesty—and he began to knead her shoulders and spine.

"Hang the suit in the closet," she commanded him.

He followed orders, then returned. She was terribly skinny, unappealing, and he hated what he feared might be next, but took a deep breath and asked to make sure.

"Want anything else before dinner?"

"Just the rubdown. That's it, hm, good."

Her bony shoulder blades stood up like bat wings.

"Relax," he suggested. "There." He worked on her until his fingers began to tire.

"Get some lotion," she growled at him. "The blue bottle in the shower."

Entering the bathroom, he gagged. A sour perfume. The toilet hadn't been flushed and the lavatory—why?—was filled with pubic hair. He staggered into the shower, retrieved the blue bottle, then made his way back to the bed, where he began, slowly, to apply the lotion to her flesh.

"That's it," he encouraged her. "Let yourself go." Those words, so often spoken, sounded like an echo.

Then, quietly, she fell asleep. He continued to stroke her back after she nodded off, then slumped beside her, his hand touching her, as hope seemed to ebb out of him: a meltdown at his core, so that he wasn't himself anymore. He wasn't the kid from Texas or a potential performer or even a guy who often took refuge in bookstores and dark movie houses.

Get real, he finally told himself. Pull out of it. Sometimes we use each other. This woman rented me and I became a willing mannikin again. Lust, need, opportunity: we all do it, we all use each other. With luck, nobody gets hurt and everybody gets wiser. It's the lowlife trade. It's working for a living.

After twenty dead minutes she woke up, then suddenly became petulant and said, "You're just sitting here looking at me, aren't you? Looking at my naked body?" What did she expect? Yeah, sure, he wanted to say. Her breasts were two little sad apples and as she hurried out of sight her tiny butt, he noticed, was beginning to fall into her thighs.

After she dressed they walked down the lighted pathway to the patio where candlelit tables sat beneath wide umbrellas. The evening had cooled, so waiters were lighting the heaters. From the surrounding gardens the scent of jasmine drifted in, mixing with a faint odor of garlic from the kitchens.

Lou was short and animated, waving an unlighted cigar around, nodding and grinning through all the introductions—during which Cappy received only a first name. Victoria, on the other hand, possessed an elegance: softly coiffed, gently smiling, and with none of the extravagant makeup Hazen Wilson had described. Victoria gave Cappy a direct, inquiring gaze, the sort his mother might have given him, as if she worried about his health.

"Metal boxes," Lou told Cappy as they started with white wine and a medley of seafoods. "Fuse boxes. Containers for electrical switches. All sorts. Started the goddamn business in my garage in Iowa, then moved to an old warehouse on the river. Added employees. Got government contracts. See, every goddamn building in the world has metal fuse boxes—maybe dozens, maybe hundreds. Now I got reps in Europe. A new one in Belgium. I own tool-and-die companies. And a silver mine. And I'm over sixty and selling out. For millions. The time comes, see, when you go another direction. Has to happen."

Hazen listened with elaborate attention, although she had heard all this before. Her wineglass warmed in her poor bent fingers.

"Now he wants to do movies," Victoria added softly.

"I love movies and every goddamn producer out here makes bad ones these days. There's only money or talent! You produce or you perform, right? And you don't want to enter the business looking lowball, right? You come with flash. You buy a goddamn mansion with rooms you'll never walk into. You make contacts. I'll bet you've a few contacts, haven't you, Cappy?"

"Some," Cappy replied. "And what's mine is yours."

Victoria smiled warmly as Hazen smirked and ate a shrimp.

"Hear that, Victoria? What Hazen has brought along tonight is a contact. So tell me, Cappy, how would you begin?"

"I'd probably option a best-selling novel."

"You mean buy the movie rights?"

"Exactly. Something everybody wants. You come with more money than the author can resist. Then you hire a screenwriter, get a script, and shop the project to top directors and actors."

"That's a very delicate process, I imagine," Victoria put in.

"Lots of time, many lunches, a thousand phone calls," Cappy told her. "But it can be done. Even by outsiders." Hazen waited through all this, wanting to talk about the right addresses, floor plans, swimming pools, and decor.

"We have friends in the business," Victoria remarked. "Some high up in the studios. Some of them say the same things."

"The boy knows what he's talking about," Lou added.

Victoria placed a hand on Cappy's sleeve. "I think he does," she told her husband.

The waiter came and they ordered. Hazen took the opportunity to start selling the place on Ladera Drive, but Victoria's attention remained with Cappy. Meanwhile, Cappy tried to guess Victoria's age and decided that she had a remarkable presence and serenity about her, a confidence and true poise that everyone in the business faked but didn't possess. Her eyes wrinkled at the corners when she smiled and listened to him. Was that a face job? No, the mouth was perfect.

"So what exactly do you do?" she asked him.

"I'm a producer, too. Just starting out."

"Lou," she said, interrupting Hazen's flow. "Do you hear this?"

Lou turned away from Hazen, scooped up a bite of fish, popped it into his mouth, and said, "Say what?"

"Yes, I've bought a couple of options myself," Cappy lied, and he swore to himself that it would be the last lie he'd tell them, the last, fate willing, that would be necessary.

"Tell us about the stories," Victoria urged him.

"Oh, a little science fiction short story," Cappy went on, inventing more in spite of himself. "And a novel. Literary. It was written by an author named Dick Yates, a fine writer hardly anybody out here knows. I optioned it from his daughter, who runs his estate. It's about a guy who wants to get his kids into a good school."

"I could tell you were a literary type," Victoria stated softly, smiling as though he were her gifted son. "Lou never reads, you know, and I've told him this is what the business is really about: stories."

"There's actually two houses on the property on Ladera," Hazen said, trying to win back the conversation. "The pool house has three bedrooms and a huge game room with a wet bar."

"Could it serve as an office?" Lou asked.

"It's perfect for your headquarters," Hazen answered.

"No, that wouldn't do," Cappy said, disagreeing. "You don't want to start out working out of your home. I'd say rent something in the Wilshire corridor, an office with a view."

"I see your reasoning," Lou told him.

"Do we even need a big house in Bel Air?" Victoria asked.

In the slight pause, Hazen Wilson sucked in her breath.

"If you can afford it, sure, that's good," Cappy said thoughtfully. "But maybe you should let it be known that you have a lodge in Aspen, too, or a villa—an old family place—in, say, Tuscany."

Lou and Victoria nodded, leaning closer.

"I haven't even told you about the English manor on Bellagio Drive," Hazen said, still trying. "It's very near this hotel."

"One of the famous studio heads lived here at the hotel for more than a year," Cappy told them. "Talk about a man with flash. He's got a place now filled with more paintings than the Getty Museum. Several Monets. A whole room filled with Hockneys."

"You know a lot of stuff," Lou observed.

"Sure, but everybody out here talks about people in the business. Most of it's rumor or gossip—and not very useful. My barber, for instance. He's written a couple of bad scripts and he knows how to get to some of the studio development people. He tells me about actual meetings he's been to. All information is golden, Lou, but getting into the pipeline is tough. I mean, this is impertinent of me, but how many millions are you willing to put into the effort?"

"That is impertinent," Hazen said in a low groan.

"We don't know exactly," Lou admitted. "But lots."

The entrées arrived in a flourish of waiters, servers, stewards, and a Latino kid with a basket of breads. Cappy ate heartily while the others poked around with their forks and watched him.

"The thing is," Cappy said, chewing, "you shouldn't even have to invest much money in the actual business of keeping an office and shopping scripts. For instance, I paid very little for the options I currently own. To tell the truth, I put my money into my image. I live very simply. Drive a modest car. But I came here tonight in a limo—always do when I come to one of the big hotels. My driver is waiting out in the parking lot. And little things. I don't hang out with midlevel studio types. I try to be at the right parties. I make the right donations to charities. It's an art, this game, and you two are obviously shrewd enough to play and win—with a bit of help. You just have to worry about who to trust."

Victoria, taking her first bite of veal, glanced over at Hazen, clearly wondering if she could possibly trust her.

They ate in silence for a while, the music of faraway mandolins moving across the evening chill. Hazen's crippled fingers had difficulty holding a fork, trembling slightly, possibly with rage at Cappy's opportunistic performance. Soon the plates—with only Cappy's cleaned of all its food—were swept away. They talked about how the movie industry patrolled the lists of forthcoming books from New York in hopes of discovering good material months in advance. Hazen Wilson sank into a melancholy silence during all this.

"Finding your best-seller—assuming you decide to make that move—would be troublesome," Cappy went on. "The agents and studio people learn from publishers what books will get the big play. These days novels often sell in Hollywood—in manuscript—before they're sold in New York. It's like insider trading. It's like buying futures in the grain market and only the sharp players—with information—win."

"Cappy," Victoria said slowly and carefully, "why don't you consider coming to work with us?"

"I think I'd love you two," Cappy answered. "But I have a lot of freedom on my own and you probably couldn't afford me."

"Let us be the judge of whether or not we could afford you," Victoria said with a little laugh, and the gaze she now gave him seemed different, mildly lustful, as if a mysterious and womanly gear had altered inside her. Cappy, experienced in detecting such change, wondered if Hazen or the husband detected it, too.

Clearly, Victoria was the major partner here, not Lou. And why didn't Hazen see that, if she was so smart? As if underscoring her ignorance, Hazen rested one of her clawlike hands on Lou's arm as she asked, smiling, "How about coffee or a nice glass of port?"

She was ignored.

"Tell you what," Victoria said. "Lou and I should talk. About you, Cappy, and also about the matter of the house. Why don't we break this up for an hour or so, then find each other in the hotel bar around eleven? Would that suit all of us?"

"Good idea," Lou said, nodding and poking the air with his cigar.

"Fine with me," Hazen managed, offering a weak smile.

The head waiter stopped by as Lou signed the check. "That salad," Lou told him. "I love it chopped up that way. You know, so I don't have to slice up the goddamned lettuce leaf to eat it?"

"Very glad, sir," the man replied.

Cappy and Hazen strolled back to her bungalow. His nerve ends were singing, and after all his recent humiliations, all his many disappointments in himself, that familiar sinking feeling every time he took out a client, he dreamed of becoming transformed. The hope of immediate transformation—sudden success—fueled everyone in the business here: barbers with scripts, bellboys who wanted to dance, truck drivers who longed to be stuntmen, everybody. Yet he felt close to a score. So close.

"They like you," Hazen said with disgust. "They'll do anything you say and you know it, don't you?"

He made a snorting noise in reply.

"All that shit about buying options. They actually believed you. And they're going to offer you some sort of partnership."

"Shut up, will you? I'm trying to think."

They reached the bungalow and went inside.

"That house on Ladera Drive is worth 15 million," she went on. "You know what my commission is on that? Plenty. So if you want part of my deal, you've got it. Just help me close it."

She was stripping out of that white suit. Her frail body once again confronted him and he started to object, but didn't. The lace on her panties looked old and soiled.

"Anything you want," she offered. "Anyway you like it. Look, I'm on my knees to you. Just walk over to me."

"Sex isn't necessarily a part of the escort service, you know. If it happens, it happens by common consent."

"I know that," she groaned. "But here. Walk over here."

"You don't just order it up like room service," he went on. "When a client makes demands in advance, that's—well, demeaning."

"I'm very sorry," she said, and she appeared to be at the edge of hysteria. "One percent of whatever I get on the house," she went on, her chin trembling. "Or more. You call it. But I've got to have this."

"You've never sold a damned mansion in your life, have you?" he asked suddenly.

"One," she admitted, her voice going strangely high. "I've sold one before. In Seattle."

"Then let me coach you a little. Don't be dumb. Don't bring up the subject of real estate again this evening. Damn! This is movie night! You've got to act like you don't even want to sell them a house!"

"You're right," she whimpered.

"And for god's sake don't cry!"

"I won't," she said, and her voice was a sob.

"Did you hear what I told them? That they probably couldn't afford me? Did you look at Lou's expression when I said that? It was fear. As though he thought, wait, maybe I can't."

"You were brilliant," she admitted.

"Get off your knees, for Chrissakes."

All around them the white lilies and roses looked wilted and alien.

"This isn't tied down, yet, you know. They might not buy your house or my deal. When we go back to the bar they might be checked out of the hotel and headed back to Davenport, Iowa."

"I know it," she said, recovering her deep growl.

"Get your clothes back on."

She went toward the bathroom, dragging her white business suit behind her.

"Do your face. You look wired," he said. "Get yourself together, then we'll go talk to these nice people."

"They're suckers," she called to him, and he went to the door of the bathroom and leaned on the frame.

"If they mean to do all this, yeah, they are."

"They're not nice in any sense. They're showing off their money. They're bopping in from the Midwest to show off. They want the glamour—like a new Cadillac. And they're so stupid they might actually option somebody's lousy best-seller."

"Maybe with my help," he allowed. "That's why your house sale is important to both of us. I'll take 5 percent and I want it in writing. Tomorrow. With a lawyer. If you stick with me, they might even deal for another house in Aspen. And I'll use my part of the house deal to get those options I talked to them about."

"How much money do you think they have?" she asked, stepping into her clothes again.

"Who knows? Not enough. Nobody has enough for this business. That producer I told them about with the Monets? He's real. I don't imagine they could afford to buy one from him."

"Probably couldn't," she agreed, turning around for his inspection. "How do I look?"

"Skinny. What are you, anorexic?"

"I suppose you like the buxom Victoria? She certainly likes you. Don't think I haven't noticed the subplot."

"There's no subplot. I want 5 percent. A lawyer gets involved and we sign a paper."

"I might be a little in love with you," she said, getting her growl back.

"What we have is a collaboration, that's all."

"Hell, that's what love is. Before I do my lip gloss you should probably kiss me."

"No kisses," Cappy said, and he moved toward her and took her grim little hands in his. Then he kissed her fingers. "Life's hard," he said, his voice almost a whisper. "An ordeal."

"It sure as hell is. And I'm tired of being a loser."

"We're all losers," he said, and she ran her bent index finger across his cheek.

Toward midnight, deliberately late, they arrived at the bar, both of them tense yet laughing their way toward Lou and Victoria. Behind a thicket of potted palms a trio of drunks tried to keep their vulgarities to themselves, but failed. After a round of greetings, Lou poured out additional glasses of an ancient port. "You said you wanted port, so I bought a good one," he said, proud of himself.

"Are we having a toast?" Hazen asked hopefully.

"Lou went out to the parking lot and had a talk with your limo driver," Victoria announced.

"Oh? With Gus? Is that right?"

A brief silence gathered, and for a moment he was on the freeway again, breathing exhaust fumes, in the deli buying the special he didn't really want, back in Beaumont asking his uncle for his old job back.

"Your driver," Victoria finally resumed, "told Lou that he drives for you all the time."

"Yeah, a bit," Cappy managed to reply, and he waited for the film to snap in half and for the theater to go dark.

"He said you were pretty goddamn mysterious," Lou added. "And that you prefer older women."

"Guilty," Cappy confessed.

"And he didn't know jack shit about your business."

"He wouldn't. I don't talk about it with limo drivers."

"Lou and I want a production executive," Victoria began again, slowly. "Why should we choose you when you don't have any screen credits?"

"For that very reason. I haven't made enemies. Yet I've been around and I know the ropes. And I'm handsome, good mannered, and people like me. You liked me yourselves from the very start. Most important of all, I'm younger than either of you—and the whole town's suddenly young. There are vice presidents at the studios and networks who look like paperboys and girl scouts. Also, I won't work for pennies, but I won't cost all that much. You both know that, if you know anything."

"You're very direct," Victoria allowed. "Charming, but direct."

Hazen Wilson, quietly hysterical, drained her glass.

"Give me something to write on," Victoria told her husband.

He produced a linen napkin from the stack on the bar. Victoria took out a gold pen, wrote down some numbers, then slid them over to Cappy.

"We pay you that every year on a three-year contract," she explained. "You throw in the properties you currently own, we buy others together, then your share is 10 percent out of any producers' fees we earn."

The amount oozing into the cloth napkin was far less than Cappy had hoped, yet far more than he had ever made. He quickly calculated what he might make additionally from Hazen Wilson's dealings with these two. Even so, he played his hand without expression.

"Leaving my options off the table, this suits me."

Hazen's eyes glazed, as if the port was a mortal head wound.

"Your properties really ought to go with this," Lou stated, yet without conviction.

"No way I can let you in," Cappy repeated.

"Maybe we can negotiate a price for them," Lou said, surrendering.

"Well," Cappy said. "You're a tough businessman, I can see that, but I think you're both fair. I trusted you both the first second we met."

"We're completely fair. And generous," Victoria promised, and she looked at Cappy as though he were completely delicious. "And I think we should take the rest of this wonderful bottle, go out to our bungalow, strip down, and get in the hot tub. The four of us."

"Sorry, I can't possibly do that," Hazen put in. "I'm a member of the Church of the Exodus."

"Isn't that some goddamn cult out here?" Lou asked.

"We believe in the spirituality of the human body," she explained. "No nakedness among strangers. We're conservative that way. You know, integrity in business and bodily, uh, spirituality."

"But you're allowed to drink?" Lou wanted to know.

"Oh sure, I'll go along for the last of the bottle."

Together, then, they strolled down a flagstone path through a garden redolent with flowers, passing the pool where the white swans slept, their graceful necks tucked in. They also passed the small bungalows where other guests slept, the far less lucky ones; then, with nightsounds all around them, they passed beneath the stars wheeling across the sky, beneath the planets in their fateful orbits, and passed out of their old lives into some new and waiting cosmos. Cappy allowed Victoria to cling to his arm while he entwined his other hand in Hazen Wilson's brittle, aching fingers.

He was someone else now, but he didn't know who. He had a pleasant suspicion, an exciting one, that it didn't matter who or what he was, and that in this distant coastal land where so many lived—who said this? the philosopher Cecil B. DeMille? who was it?—change itself was the thing of great importance.

The Buddha in Malibu

Brock worked for Westec, the big private police force on the west-side, but the low pay and long hours on patrol in his squad car through neighborhoods and shopping centers prompted him to look for other work. He responded to an advertisement for a job as a bodyguard—it included an apartment out in Malibu—and got an interview. On a Sunday afternoon he drove out beyond Zuma, then turned off onto Broad Beach Road where the oversize houses clung to the cliffs looking out to sea.

He wore his khaki officer's uniform and drove the squad car adorned with blue lights and siren, hoping this might impress somebody. Brock was twenty-nine years old with a twenty-one-inch neck, big arms, a shaggy head of blond hair, and a ready smile.

Like all the houses along the row the one he faced showed only three garage doors to the street and a modest entrance off to one side. He found the bell and rang it. A mounted camera looked him over and a voice on the intercom asked him to state his business. Only after his identity was determined did the door click open so that he could enter.

He strolled across a redwood catwalk into the main house, where he met Ennis, a smallish man with thick, expressive eye-brows, black and bushy. The eyebrows rose in skepticism, fell into a frown, or went one up and one down when he smiled—which wasn't often. Ennis was well enough known—although not really a celebrity—so that Brock recognized the name. Years ago he had produced two movies that made him wealthy, but had done nothing since.

For about an hour Brock told his prospective employer all about himself: football and ROTC in college, a stint in the army, more criminology courses in night school at Santa Monica College, weightlifting, a breakup more than a year ago with a longtime girlfriend. Brock concealed what he knew about Ennis. Although he was something of a movie fan, he didn't want to say anything wrong and wanted the man to talk.

"See, I don't want anybody kidnapping Sonny," Ennis began, the eyebrows going up. "He's four years old and I get him every other weekend. I don't want his mother—Velda is her goddamned name—coming into the house, either, and taking my shit, then saying it's hers. I don't want any Muslims, racial types, strangers, or fairies in the house. My accountant, Carlyle, be courteous, but don't let him through the door unless I'm here to watch him. I fired my cook for lying and stealing. I'm gonna fire the maid, too, and I want you to screen a new one for us. Give her a full security check."

"Wait a second," Brock put in. "Am I hired?"

"If I didn't like you, you'd already be gone. You're perfect, my man. Blond. Right outta central casting. Can you by any chance shoot a pistol?"

"I'm a crack shot. I carry my own Sigma."

"Fine, we can shoot together. There's a soundproof practice range in the basement. Okay, let's see: the schedule. I'm at the studio weekdays, but we'll have our beepers and phones. You'll have most of that time off. Nights I sometimes go out. About half the time, say, you go with me. Naturally, we have to buy you the right clothes. I mean, you'll be on call. My man. See any problem with any of this if the money's right?"

"It's okay if the money's right," Brock agreed.

"Write your current salary on this pad. Here. Don't make it out to be more 'cause I'll check. There, write it down."

Brock obeyed. The sum looked paltry.

In full view, then, Ennis turned the pad around and did a times three, tripling the amount. Brock struggled against grinning, but couldn't help himself.

"The house is rigged with cameras, lasers, and intercoms. You live above the garage: big rooms, two baths, bars on the windows, and the TV monitor that watches every room and space. Even looks in on my bedroom unless I turn off the eye. This house drops off six floors all the way down to the beach. Two elevators, nine bedrooms, decks, an outside pool, and everything gets a sharp security check constantly. Money's no problem if you need anything to do your job. Just tell me what we need: steel doors, more laser stuff, anything. What's your name?"

"Last name's Brock. Everybody calls me that."

"I like it. There's a rock in that name. Now one last thing: my last bodyguard. I had to fire him."

"What'd he do?"

"Scared hell outta Sonny. Jake. A big hairy guy. Eyes like a dragon. But I think Sonny'll like you because you're, well, so normal looking."

—

Lonely in the big cliffside house during the weekdays while Ennis was at the studio, Brock tried most of the Malibu lunch places. He went to the sushi bar at Bambu, then sampled the pasta at Tra di Noi and the fried platter at Malibu Fish. At Coogie's, though, a waitress, Luanne, kept stopping by his table to give him refills and smalltalk.

"I'll bet you're really an actress," he said, using the familiar line.

"Not anymore. I'm looking for something a lot more permanent."

She was impressed that he was a bodyguard, but when she heard he worked for Ennis she smirked. It was a reaction he often witnessed, and she could only say, vaguely, that Ennis wasn't beloved around the neighborhood.

Luanne was a long-legged girl, twenty years old, tall and cocoa brown as if she might be a professional volleyball player. When Brock spoke, she tilted her head to one side and smiled with radiant sympathy as if he were a poor waif, a lost soul in need. That look actually convinced him that he did need her, although he wondered if it might be a clever trick she picked up in acting school.

He wanted to ask her out, but somehow just kept going there for lunch, not getting the words out, feeling confused around her.

The first time Brock met Sonny, Ennis's kid, the child strolled over, put his arms around Brock's thick leg, placed his head softly against Brock's khakis, and pointed out to sea.

"That," Sonny remarked, wiggling his fingers.

Ennis, Brock, and Sonny stood on the upper deck in a particularly warm autumn sunshine. He was a beautiful child with a winsome look, not at all like his father, probably favoring the infamous Velda, who had full custody.

"What are you pointing at?" Brock asked gently.

"That," Sonny repeated.

"Oh, I see. Porpoises. Look, Ennis."

"Daddy can't see any porpoises," Ennis managed.

"Three of them," Brock said, grinning. They swam just beyond the first breaking waves, arching their backs to catch the noon warmth as they traveled up the coast.

"One's a baby," Sonny noted.

"By golly, I believe you're right," Brock replied.

"Can't locate 'em," Ennis added, but he gave Brock a nod and a smile that confirmed everything: Sonny was completely at ease, perhaps even more than they could have imagined or hoped for.

They spent the day together, Brock and Sonny, while Ennis returned phone calls. At one point they explored Brock's rooms, examining all the monitors and security equipment. Sonny seemed indifferent to TV pictures of empty rooms.

Late that night when they had all gone to sleep, Sonny woke up, left his bed, went up the elevator by himself, padded barefoot across the catwalk, entered Brock's apartment, and crawled in beside the bodyguard, snuggling close.

Brock found that he liked it. Soon, though, he buzzed Ennis on the intercom to report Sonny's whereabouts. The father's drowsy voice came back, saying, "Yeah, good, okay, he likes you, thanks."

—

When Brock accompanied Ennis in the evenings the occasions were those where having one's bodyguard was meant to impress, like having one's Maserati or one's golden cell phone or one's baby leopard—all of which, at one occasion or another, Brock noted in the possession of other guests.

At most of the events—charity dinners, screening parties, award ceremonies—Brock also ended up alone with his boss, both of them decked out in sharp evening wear, Brock's pistol secured in the rear of his cummerbund. They usually occupied barstools or lingered at a table strewn with cigarette ashes while Ennis conveyed his paranoia.

"The studio owes me money on my pictures, but do I get any of it?" he complained. "No, they're months behind—earning interest off my money! I threaten to sue! I call in the producers' and the directors' guild, but they wimp out on me. Velda, meanwhile, screams for more alimony. I'll tell you, my man, what I really believe: she's gone behind my back with my accountant."

Ennis recited this familiar litany one evening at Ivy's on the Shore. He had a date that night, a Eurasian girl from an escort service who paid only partial attention to all his problems, so Brock was invited along for a nightcap. They walked down the way and across the street to Loew's, where Ennis and the girl proceeded to get drunk and to discuss the murder of JFK, UFOs, the X-Files, Vince Foster, and the Islamic takeover of Western civilization.

"Is what he's saying true?" the girl asked, once, slurring her words as she turned to Brock.

"He knows damn well it's true," Ennis answered. "Ask him. He's packing. Show her what you're carrying, Brock, my man."

"Here?" Brock asked, making sure.

They sat on the hotel veranda with Santa Monica Beach spread below them. Although it was after midnight, skaters with flashlights glided along the walkways. The white foam of the surf blinked at them out of the ocean darkness.

"Show her," Ennis insisted.

Brock obediently took out his shiny Sigma and held it below the table so the girl could glimpse it. Far back in the cave of her mascara her eyes glistened and Brock thought she might want to cry—either from being so impressed or from being, in general, terrified.

"Don't worry," he assured her, patting her wrist.

They soon dropped her off in Brentwood, then started for home.

"I wouldn't ever screw a girl like that," Ennis claimed as Brock drove carefully, watching the traffic. "You know, AIDS or maybe something worse. Or she could find out about me and blackmail me. They obsess on guys like me. They want my money and contacts."

"Contacts?" Brock asked innocently.

"They're all ambitious to get into the business. They want to sell me a script or act in a movie or meet some guy at an even higher level, so they can screw him outta what he's got. Everybody wants a piece of the pie. If one of us has a slice of it, we get killed for it. Believe this, Brock, my man, you're just learning."

—

On an early November day the fires came to Malibu.

Brock worked out in the mini-gym next to the practice range in the basement, talked to Ennis on the phone a couple of times, then went down to Coogie's again for lunch. Luanne greeted him with a wave as he came through the door. He took a seat facing the mountains to the north where soft brown clouds of smoke already edged over the ridges. Newscasts had already warned that a blaze across the mountains, pushed along by strong Santa Ana winds, might be heading for the ocean. Everybody in the restaurant saw the smoke, but chatted on, picking at their salads, reading newspapers, or tending to children.

"I should quit work right now and head home," a worried Luanne said, standing at Brock's table. "I live in Las Flores Canyon in this condo. Maybe I should go get my stuff in the car."

As she spoke, two fire trucks wheeled into the parking lot. Although bits of ash now blew along in the breeze, shoppers continued to wander in and out of stores.

"I'll go with you," Brock volunteered, and he counted out the cash for his bill.

"I'll tell my boss," she said, accepting.

They decided to take Brock's new Blazer, the vehicle Ennis had recently provided. Traveling along the Pacific Coast Highway toward the canyon, Brock dialed Ennis on the phone to let him know what was going on. He assured Ennis that he intended to return home soon in order to protect the house.

"This is arson, my man, and I'll tell you who it is: the Crips and the Bloods! The gangs! See, their drug business is falling off and they wanta burn us out, so they can just buy up Malibu property cheap! I heard this from a police source!"

Luanne rolled her eyes, but kept listening.

"So, yeah, you stay close to the property, my man! I'm gonna check into the Four Seasons for a few days. I figure the PCH is gonna be a traffic snarl and I got meetings. If I'm not at the studio this week, see, they're gonna cut me outta two deals minimum!"

"I'll stay in contact," Brock assured him.

"If you see any black kids with colored bandannas, shoot to kill," Ennis instructed him. "This is a coordinated effort on their part. Arson, then maybe in the confusion they come out to steal things!"

"I'll be right here," Brock promised.

"He's really wigged out," Luanne observed after the call ended.

"It's a permanent condition," Brock replied, and for the first time he heard himself speak ill of his boss.

Las Flores Canyon was closed even to residents. Standing outside the Blazer and talking to the cops before they turned back, they could hear the roar of the flames and trees exploding up in the dry arroyos.

Luanne began to cry. "I'm going to lose everything," she sobbed, and Brock put an arm around her as a big fireman with a heavy gray beard yelled at them to turn the Blazer around.

"My Buddha," she went on, sinking her face into Brock's chest. "The one my daddy brought back from Vietnam. It's gone, I know it is!"

"Come out to my place," he said, patting her shoulder. "When the fire burns out, we'll come back."

The bearded fireman began cursing at them to move on.

"There's lots of room where I live," Brock consoled her, leading her back to the vehicle and helping her inside. "Come on. I'll take care of you."

They slept together that night in the soft blue glow of the security monitors, holding one another close, entwined, her tears drying on his muscular body, his kisses in her hair. The disasters of the fires were suddenly of little consequence.

"Don't ever go back to Coogie's," he whispered. "Don't go back to any of your old life."

"It's not there anymore," she whispered back. "Not after this."

In the morning they emerged from his apartment and strolled through the elegant house. On the deck where they had watched the porpoises flash by, he told Luanne about Sonny. She looked at the artworks and the sudden surprises of the architecture. They ate fruit and buttered English muffins, then sugar cookies washed down with steaming mugs of coffee, watching television reports of the fire's devastation. Las Flores Canyon had been gutted with high winds scattering the ashes of dozens of homes. Firefighters still worked, so they made no move to go for a look. At noon they made love again on a secluded deck as the sun warmed their bodies and as that deadly breeze whistled above them. Afterward Luanne gave him that look of hers, that penetrating look of sympathy and affection as she uttered her first warning.

"This isn't your place," she told him. Her fingers traced the hairs on his arm. "It's maybe the most beautiful house I've ever seen, but it's not for you, Brock, I really know it isn't. You've got to get out of here."

He grinned at her, watching her fingers and feeling their soft caress on his arm. She was a mere girl, he felt, speaking like an oracle. He told her in reply how Sonny came from his own bedroom, up the elevator, and over the catwalk to his apartment.

"You may already love this little boy, but you've got to leave him," she went on. "And leave the money. I know you must be getting wonderful pay, but I have this intuition, Brock, I really do."

Luanne, like Ennis, he decided, had a tiny streak of paranoia, and he tried to calm her.

"I'll give you a son," she promised, kissing his wrist and palm. "Your own son. You know that, don't you?"

He did know it, but things were moving fast.

"If you want to take care of people, then take care of us," she continued. "Pack up your things and we'll find another place."

He passed his fingers across her lips, hesitating. The house, the boy, the money, and life beside the sea held him, and neither the fires in the hills nor her soft warnings seemed urgent enough to pull him away.

—

Luanne's condo—shared with two other waitresses—had been consumed in a wall of fire, they learned, that also took the giant eucalyptus trees that lined the banks of the stream, the bridge, houses, underbrush, and the teakwood Buddha brought back from Vietnam by Luanne's father.

She stood in the ashes crying over the lost Buddha, then Brock took her shopping for clothes, shoes, and bath items.

They went back to the cliffside house and during the next nights slept together in a soothing dreamworld. His destiny was somehow with Luanne, he knew, but if the job lasted he could save money and set them up very well. So, again, he waited, although she wanted to go.

On the following weekend Ennis came back to the house with Sonny and didn't want a woman in Brock's rooms.

"It's temporary," Brock explained. "Her condo burned down and she lost everything."

"I thought you didn't have a girl? Where'd you get this one?"

"She worked down at Coogie's, but not anymore."

"A waitress? Coogie's is a low-rent place, right?"

"Not so bad. And she'll have her own place soon," Brock promised.

"Listen to me. We both need a security check on her. I mean, women sleep around these days. They used to get depressed and go shopping or get fat and hate you for it, but now they're becoming serial killers. Statistics prove that out. Get her fingerprints and run them with your cop buddies."

The speech made Brock grin, but his boss wasn't kidding.

At two o'clock that morning Luanne and Brock were once again sleeping close when Sonny arrived at the bed and wedged himself between them. He told them he was having nightmares.

Luanne, meeting him for the first time, drew the blankets up to his chin and smoothed his hair.

"Don't let the dark see my hands," Sonny whispered to her.

"I won't," she promised, and she cupped his small fingers in hers and gave Brock a glance as if to say, yeah, okay, he's something.

The next day the three of them played in the pool and on the beach while Ennis went to executive meetings. They made lemonade in the kitchen. After his nap, Sonny visited a tidepool, looking for shells, taking small delicate steps among the mossy stones during a low-water period. The horizon filled up with windsurfers, their bright sails making quick turns in a hazy breeze still carrying bits of ash out to sea.

"I have a girlfriend down at Venice Beach," Luanne said while they watched Sonny searching in the tidepool. "We can move in with her until we find a place of our own. She's cool. You'll like her."

But Brock resisted. "If I leave here, I leave the job. It isn't that easy. Give it time."

On Sunday evening Luanne drove off to her friend's place without ever having met or spoken to Ennis. When Ennis returned from a long lunch and after he and Sonny had watched a video movie together, Ennis asked Brock to drive the boy back to his mother.

—

So Brock finally met Velda.

She lived on Canon Drive in one of the big Georgian houses surrounded by dahlias, gardenias, bougainvillea, and a curved driveway embraced with clusters of flowers not yet planted, still in their little plastic containers. Brock expected a hard woman, someone younger, flashier, but Velda was a soft beauty in light cashmere, maybe forty, brunette, real, and on the elegant side. Sonny flew into her arms.

Brock stood in the marble foyer saying both his hellos and his good-byes, but Sonny clutched their legs and almost toppled them forward in an embrace. As they laughed and straightened themselves, Sonny bounced away.

"Is everything all right on the beach?" she began.

"Fine, no trouble," he answered, and he didn't expect her to start talking about Ennis, but she did.

"Well, time will fix that," she said, and this came out with smiling good humor and without the least bitterness. A resignation: an admission, too, that Ennis was left to others. "Like a lot of men in the business, Ennis wants to be mature, but he just can't."

They both smiled and almost broke into laughter again.

"All his women, the shooting range, his mood shifts, his partners and their toys: it's all teenage fun, isn't it? And look at you. He's always wanted a bodyguard. You've got the physique he wants and now nobody can bully him. But I'm sorry. You don't want to hear any of this, do you?"

"I do want to protect Sonny," he managed.

"Oh, but Sonny's safe, isn't he? What would anyone get if they kidnapped him? His father's debts? And just down the street there's Spielberg and all his kids. There's the guy who should worry about kidnappings, but I don't even think he has lasers."

"We have enough for the neighborhood," Brock reminded her. "When a dog trots along the beach too close to the house it sets off alarms."

"Exactly. And I'm sure Ennis is overpaying you. And Sonny loves you. So I'm sure you'll stay on the job for a while and indulge Ennis all his current crop of fears. Want something to drink?"

"No, thanks, I'll be getting back."

"As for me, I'm looking for someone who reads books and who talks about subjects. That's not too much to ask. Here, I'll walk you out."

They strolled outside into the perfumed driveway. From the far reaches of Beverly Hills a strange sound wafted over the vesper hour: the distant and pleasant tolling of a church bell.

"Did his father spend any time with him or were you in charge of Sonny?"

"They watched a video movie together."

"Ah, terrific. He can't talk with the boy, you know."

Brock only nodded.

"I know I sound awful," she said. "But, really, there's one last thing to say about Ennis. Now that you've talked with me, well, you'll have to watch him. He'll have suspicions. You'll definitely see him get testy—not that he'll even understand why. He'll forget that he sent you on this errand, but he won't forget that we've talked together and that he doesn't know what we've shared."

"I don't think it'll come to that," Brock countered.

"Oh, Sonny told me he went up to your apartment and slept with you. I hope he didn't disturb you."

"I liked it."

"Thanks. And don't worry about Sonny. He's going to be all right. Because of me."

"I know," Brock told her. "I believe that."

—

He talked to Luanne on the phone and promised, if possible, to come down to Venice and look at places to live. She admitted that she needed money for deposits and he told her not to worry.

Ennis came home from the studio angry, making phone calls and shouting to various listeners that his bosses wanted to fire him. At his desk, later, he went into a rage over bills: too much for the gardeners, too much for the new maid, too much for the custom car wash. After that he shouted to the walls that there was nothing to eat in the refrigerator and refused Brock's offer of a sandwich.

Then he couldn't find the Brancusi.

"Little glob about the size of a fist," he told Brock. "I'll bet your girlfriend took it with her."

"No way," Brock said, trying to laugh that off.

"A Brancusi, understand? Bronze, I think. My decorator said leave it over by the window so it catches the sunset. But it's not on the goddamned table anymore, is it?"

"The new maid might've moved it."

"Don't think I don't know what's going on here with that girl you brought in! She wears sweatshirts all the time, right?"

Brock wondered what that meant, but Ennis didn't explain. Instead, he started on thieves and burglars.

"What America needs to worry about isn't organized crime!" he yelled. "Let the Mafia have its little slice! No, it's disorganized crime that's killing us! The constant petty shit like somebody just coming into your house and swiping your Brancusi!"

Brock struggled to keep a straight face. Disorganized crime.

Later, Ennis found the sculpture in the maid's pantry where it had been cleaned with Brasso and polished. This made him angry, too, so he sat down and wrote out a lengthy reprimand—in English, so that Rosa probably couldn't read it. After tacking the letter to the door of the pantry, he announced that he was going out for a meal, probably to the local sushi joint, he told Brock, where he might run into Nick Nolte or some other local celebrity.

"Go to Gelson's tomorrow," he instructed Brock as he departed. "Buy some Montreal steaks and stock up the fridge. I mean, whatta my going to do around here? Hire another goddamned cook? I'm getting bled dry with too much staff already!"

That night, again, Brock spoke with Luanne on the phone.

"I don't want to go into my past too much," she confided, "but I've known a lot of guys in the business like Ennis. They ruin their lives with big expectations. Fancy schemes that always crash and burn. You know what the Buddha says? Expectation is the source of all sorrow. I know this is true, sweet, so look: get in your own car and drive down here first thing in the morning."

"What's a Montreal steak?" he wanted to know.

"I'm not sure. A steak flavored in a certain way?"

"I do miss you," he said. "I'll come down as soon as Ennis goes to the studio."

"Know what I saw today? A handsome young cop riding his bicycle along the boardwalk. That's exactly the kind of work you should be doing. Riding your bike and helping old people and kids. And I'll be home cooking supper and we'll have flower boxes in the windows overlooking some little canal."

"It won't be long," he promised. He didn't tell her that Ennis had accused her of being a thief.

They spoke for more than an hour, then whispered their good-byes and blew kisses into the telephone.

After the call Brock made his rounds, walking the perimeter of the beach decks, checking all the outside doors, the lasers, every room, then going to bed with the blue glow of the monitors before him. He wanted to greet Ennis's return, but felt bone-tired and decided he could turn in. Just after eleven-thirty he heard the garage doors open and the sound of the car pulling in. He opened his eyes and watched the monitor as Ennis, alone, left the car and crossed the catwalk to the elevators. Satisfied, he went back to sleep.

Two hours later Ennis's voice on the intercom woke him.

"Brock, my man, you there?"

Brock sat up, drowsy and slightly addled, and tried to get his bearings. He found Ennis on one of the monitor screens: beside the elevators, again, this time dressed in pajamas and a robe. There was a pistol clutched in his hand.

Brock pressed the intercom button to answer back. "Ennis?" he asked, dumbly.

He watched the monitor as Ennis spoke again in a hoarse and rasping whisper. "Get your weapon," he said. "There's somebody in the house."

Struggling into his pants, Brock lost sight of Ennis on the monitors. He checked the magazine of his pistol: several 9 mm cartridges in place, the metal cold in his hand. After a glance at the monitors a second time—Ennis nowhere in view—he crossed the catwalk and entered the main house. Faced with the silence, he decided to call out his position, ask Ennis to do the same, and possibly scare off any intruder.

"Ennis? Speak up! Where are you?"

His voice echoed down the stairwell.

Looking up at the elevator lights—no movement there—he started down the stone stairway: six floors, darkness, not a sound anywhere.

"Give me your position, Ennis! Speak up and keep talking!"

Ennis made no reply. Stopping and listening at the first landing, he feared the worst: somebody had Ennis, choking the sound out of him, stifling his voice.

He went down another few steps, finding a bank of light switches on the next floor so that he could flood the stairwell and elevator landings with brightness. When the lights came on, he shouted again.

"Ennis!"

He knew he could easily be heard.

When he had first seen Ennis on the monitor beside the door to the elevators, which floor was he on? As he made his way downstairs step by careful step, he cursed himself for not knowing.

"Ennis! Hello! Say something so I won't shoot you!"

Only the sea answered: a faraway thud of a heavy wave breaking on the beach. Brock cleared his throat loudly, called again, and tapped the barrel of his pistol against the metal railing of the staircase. At the next level he stopped, held his breath, and listened.

"Ennis! I'm on the fourth floor!"

The salon: beyond that, two bedrooms, dark and forbidding. Adrenaline pounded through his body. He tried to keep his imagination from going crazy.

Much of the house towered above him now and he glanced back upstairs, aware that an intruder might flank him, and he considered getting to a phone, dialing for help, for backup. When he turned back around, Ennis stood before him gripping a pistol with both hands cop style, aiming right at him, those heavy eyebrows down and dark, a look of grim resolution in his eyes.

"Ennis?"

The word seemed to come from another dimension and he barely recognized the sound of his own voice.

Time stood still for a new awareness. Seconds ticked away and he still had time to raise his own weapon, but he stood paralyzed in an instant of disbelief until he knew what was about to happen. He realized that Ennis was pulling the trigger and so stiffened himself to take the blow. Even so, it came in a driving, hot needle of pain that passed through his chest, throwing him back against the stairs. He didn't hear the noise or feel himself falling and breaking his arm.

After the shot was fired he went in and out of consciousness, but for a few lucid seconds he knew that Ennis stood over him. He could hear the uneven breathing and he feared that he would be shot again, finished off, but then that anxiety passed and a shallow, painful sleep rolled over him, so that he was gone, dying, he supposed, until the sound of Ennis's voice woke him once more and he heard, distinctly, every word.

"This was an accident, Brock, my man, and if you live through it and say otherwise I'll be very disappointed in you. Remember that. It's my word against yours."

During Brock's recovery Luanne seldom left his side. She sat with him in the hospital, presenting him with a miniature brass Buddha turned green with age, and talking to him about the Zen way.

"It would really be difficult for Buddha to find the middle path out in Malibu," she explained. "I mean, the middle path is between sensuality and ascetic mortification, see, but out there in Malibu the rich man is a kind of major ego god and everything is sensuality, nothing else, it's worldly to the max. And, Brock, they're crazy. And Ennis is especially looney, everybody knows it, and I wouldn't be surprised if it wasn't an accident at all, if he just didn't shoot you for the thrill of it."

Brock listened, slightly unsure of what Luanne meant and undecided about how to respond.

The bullet had passed through his right lung, missing his ribs and spine. Prognosis was good. After all, he was in fine shape, a specimen. All the doctors agreed.

Velda brought Sonny to see him, and the child, in turn, brought another gift: a stuffed toy cat that Luanne placed on the windowsill beside the little Buddha. Sonny sat at the foot of the bed holding onto Brock's toes while Velda gave Brock an engraved business card of a lawyer in Westwood.

"Get yourself a hell of a settlement," was her advice.

"I'm trying to sort things out," he replied.

"It was no accident," she told him, echoing what Luanne had suggested.

The next visitor was Carlyle, Ennis's gray little accountant, whose clothes were dusted with cigarette ash.

"Ennis is paying for the hospital, recovery, rehab, and he's keeping your paychecks coming," the accountant announced. "He means to come see you himself when he has time. I guess you heard how all this got in the newspapers."

"When was that?"

"Last week. You were sleeping most of the time. You want me to bring you the clippings?"

"Yeah, do that."

"It was in the trades, too," Carlyle went on. "At first, you know, I thought this was gonna hurt Ennis, but it looks like in a funny sort of way that it's gonna help his career. To some people he looks more decisive. His partners, for instance, are maybe a tiny bit afraid of him. By the way how're you feeling?"

"Still weak, but tomorrow Luanne has permission to take me outside in a wheelchair."

"You kids," Carlyle said with his nicotine cough. "Health and stamina, they're worth more than gold!"

The next day Luanne guided his wheelchair along the hospital pathways and he enjoyed the pale sunlight and the movement of traffic beyond the hedges and palm trees. She went on about the Buddha: the moment of enlightenment that rises like the morning star.

"You think Ennis will come face me?" he asked, interrupting.

"That bastard? No way. And you need to put the whole incident behind you, Brock, really, it's bad karma."

She also told him about the condo she had rented with another waitress friend halfway between Venice Beach and Santa Monica. The friend would move out as soon as Brock finished therapy and was given his release. The condo, Luanne said, although it didn't have an ocean view, did have two bathrooms and a carport.

Alone, Brock kept pondering why Ennis shot him. Analysis wasn't completely possible, he decided, but a man as paranoid as Ennis looks for enemies and targets. Where, he wondered, did paranoia come from? Was it the basic malfunction in rich guys?

Two days later Ennis showed up.

Brock had been on his feet with the aid of an aluminum walker, strolling back and forth in the therapy room with its ceiling-high windows, hot tubs, and gym equipment. Brock wore a blue gown, the hospital color, and everything bore this particular shade: the walls, the barbells, even the pale blue walker itself. After his workout he made his way down a corridor to the hospital cafeteria, where he enjoyed a chocolate malt. Ennis found him there.

"Hey, my man, looking great!" Ennis took a chair at the table opposite him.

" 'Lo, Ennis. I'm surprised you came."

"You shouldn't be! Good to see you so strong, I mean that."

"I hear we're in the newspapers and trades."

"It got me a new contract with bonuses. Also the green light on a little movie I've been trying to do. I shoulda shot somebody a long time ago."

"That's not funny," Brock told him.

"Okay, but here: this is no joke, either." Ennis took the pale blue napkin beside Brock's empty glass, produced an ivory pen, and wrote down some figures. When he shoved it back to Brock, he had written down Brock's current salary times three, tripled.

"Look, you're worth it," Ennis said before Brock could respond. "The two of us are known all over town. I figure you'll get other offers, maybe acting jobs. It's like, hey, you took a bullet for me."

"Took one from you," Brock corrected him.

"Temporary lapse on my part. Don't get excited. I'll throw in the leased vehicle you're driving. It's yours."

Brock tried to imagine what the Buddha would say. The Buddha, he decided, would just sit under the tree of enlightenment with very little to say, keeping himself serene, meditative, and silent.

"There's more," Ennis went on, his eyebrows jumping around. "Hey, you notice how everything in this place is this awful baby blue? I want you to check into this spa up in the hills near the country club. Personal doctors and a private nurse, Ginger. When you're well enough, you come back to work at the new salary, but not until you're well enough."

That evening Luanne came to visit with a bag of oatmeal cookies from the new café where she worked, but Brock was gone: checked out with no forwarding numbers.

A few days later he phoned from the spa. The Zen thing, he told her, just didn't work for him.

"How do you mean?" Her voice was unnaturally high.

"Philosophically," he said, struggling to explain. "The Zen idea. Lay back, accept things, expect nothing, all that. I'm just not like that."

"What about us?"

"Maybe later, Luanne, let's just see."

"Brock, remember the deck where we made love? What we felt?"

"I just need some time."

"You're going back to work for Ennis, aren't you?"

"The shooting was an accident," he said, knowing better. "And I still have a job, yeah, except now it's more like a career."

"You know what's gonna happen? He'll shoot you again. Or maybe it'll be worse next time. You know this!"

She was crying now, talking through her tears about the simple life, common sense, wisdom, rejecting big expectations, but Brock responded less and less. Eventually he replied with only grunts and noises, not wanting to hang up on her. Maybe, he knew, Luanne was the great love of his life, and maybe he was surrendering all prospects of samsara, the gift of divine peace, but the cravings of this life had him, the seductions of the western sea enthralled him, and he was gone, lost, adream, shot through with strange visions and hopes, restless and excited beyond anything that Luanne, he felt, could ever comprehend.

The Cockatoo Tower

⌐ Lamp and Window

Corey had three jobs lined up: the bathroom for the Tolsons, the TV wheel in the McVey game room, and the cockatoo cage for Ava Dillinger. Each project was Malibu crazy—just the way he liked it—with money no object. Since he waited on the architects for his next major construction job, a hillside palace that would keep the paychecks coming for the next three years, he was happy to have these smaller and lucrative projects in the meantime.

He was lucky, too, that all three clients lived within a mile of each other in beach houses along Malibu Road facing the surf. Ava Dillinger, the widow and mystic, had also given him permission to set up his construction trailer in her vacant lot next door, so he cleared a space for pickup trucks and delivery vans among the dunes, then settled in.

One morning just after the Tolsons came back from Europe, Corey met with them to discuss the bathroom. Crystal, the wife whose days were devoted to antiques, had bought an early Tiffany lamp and wanted a window to match.

"Whatever she wants," Ollie Tolson said, and his attitude wavered somewhere between pride at having so much ready cash and fear of actually spending it.

"It just has to match perfectly with the lamp's colored glass," Crystal pointed out for the third or fourth time.

The window in question was the size of one in a cathedral, going up two floors in height and comprising the only outside wall in one of the Tolson's nine bathrooms.

"I found a glass worker in New Hampshire," Corey informed them. "He restores Tiffany pieces and also does very fine church windows. A real artist. If we ship the lamp to him, he'll match up the hues and do the window. Here's the figures on costs."

"Holy shit," Ollie Tolson said, looking at the numbers and biting down on his cigar holder, a stubby meerschaum adorned with a two-carat diamond.

"How long will he take?" Crystal wanted to know.

"About a year from the time he receives the lamp."

"Can't we hurry that along?" she asked.

"Maybe," Corey answered. "For about twice as much money."

Ollie Tolson owned two enormous office buildings in the Wilshire corridor, both debt free and leased to capacity. Since he had been in the construction business himself, he knew that Corey was an honest builder—and also a man who understood how to deal with the whims of the Malibu set. Tennis instructors, secretaries, physical trainers, travel agents, and anyone else either had the knack or went out of business quickly. Corey also wanted to make money, an admirable quality in Ollie's view, and he was good with the women, really listening to them, a trick that Ollie had never mastered himself.

"Get the window as soon as possible," Ollie finally said, heaving a sigh of resignation because he knew Crystal wanted it.

Corey made a note.

"This goddamned bathroom is going to cost a hundred grand," Ollie went on, looking skyward.

"More." Corey told him.

~ The Television Wheel

Bobby and Laura McVey had the largest house on Malibu Road: a cedar, rock, and glass edifice with a dozen decks that looked out to sea. From the topmost deck Bobby occasionally sat at his spyglass gazing over at Catalina Island and watching an infrequent porpoise or whale passing by. He had once been New Jersey's biggest used car dealer: five dealerships in four cities. He was also an arrogant, frantic man except for those rare moments alone with his spyglass, brief periods of silence and troubled contemplation. The possibility of such meditation had drawn him to this warm coast in the first place, yet he didn't like to be caught in its practice, as if his yearning for something more in life was a strange source of embarrassment for him. He tried to give up drinking Scotch during these moments on the upper deck, but so far hadn't managed to accomplish that.

The bottom floor of the McVey house opened directly onto the beach. In that downstairs game room—a space of more than two thousand square feet featuring pool tables, two bars, a mini-gym, video games, and a big Wurlitzer jukebox—an unsightly center post, iron and a foot wide, a necessary brace for the entire house, had always annoyed Bobby, so he came up with an idea for it.

"I wanta mount this big TV on it, see, and it should revolve by remote control," he said in his Jersey accent. "So's we can watch a football game, like, anywhere we go in the room. Fix it up for me, Corey, okay?"

The easier solution by far, Corey wanted to explain, would be to mount four separate television sets facing different corners of the room, but he knew better than to make this suggestion. His expression did alter, though, so that Bobby noticed.

"Whatsa matter?"

"Well, the wires will twist," Corey pointed out.

"Overcome the problem," Bobby ordered him.

"I'll talk to an engineer. About the remote, too. And I'll get back to you after the weekend."

"That's what I like to hear."

"Naturally, a consulting engineer will cost us."

"Yeah, sure, I understand. Consultants. Always."

At this point Laura strolled in. She was Bobby's third wife. The original wife in Jersey had the children, while the second wife, the model, now lived with a singer in Las Vegas. Laura McVey told everyone that she was a film producer. She was part of a tennis group of eight women who played on Saturday mornings, then went to brunch at the Marmalade Café—all of whom said they were producers. Laura wore only white: white slacks this morning, a see-through T-shirt, and spiked high heels, also white.

Corey greeted her as she approached.

"God, Corey, you are one good-looking man," she said, laughing, in her honeyed voice. "You should be an actor. Really. Get yourself an agent. I can get you a deal over at Paramount, no kidding."

"Leave him alone," Bobby told her. "We're gonna have a big TV right here in the middle of the room that, like, spins around."

"What for? We don't have friends who come over."

"In the summers we do sometimes."

"No, summers we go to the mountains."

"Then my kids use the house, don't they?" Bobby asked, raising his voice and achieving a tone that ended further discussion.

As they glared at each other, Corey took out his tape and made measurements. Afterward, Laura walked Corey to his pickup truck.

"Bobby's still ignoring me," she confided. "In case you want to know, I'm sleeping alone and without."

"Sorry, Laura," he replied, and his tone made it even more definite: tough, sorry, not my problem, I just fix houses.

Refused again, Laura pouted, then smiled big. She regarded the whole question as if it were just a matter of time.

⌁ The Birdcage

Ava Dillinger lived in the only replica of a Victorian mansion along the beach, a rambling house of cupolas, porches, turrets, and multiple roof levels. Inside it, every room was a version of the *salon de l'amour:* thick sofas, piles of brocade pillows, beds of cushions, and mounds of feathered coverlets illumined by candles or nestled beside fireplaces. The widow Ava, named by her mother, she once confided, after the actress Ava Gardner, costumed herself in scarves, beads, amulets, and rings, so that she became another bright object, mobile, gliding among her artifacts and soft layabouts.

The rooms were stuffed with an assortment of items, all of which, she claimed, possessed some mystical or magical power—and the Great Room, alone, had opium pipes, silken robes, a marble fragment with a face barely sculpted out, tins of trader beads, a stuffed falcon, a handful of gold nuggets, a dueling sword, antique perfume bottles, a teakwood nude statuette, paintings by Miró and Bacon, a big Korth .45 pistol, boa feathers, Tarot cards, a leopard-skin-covered telephone, a leather-bound copy of the

Book of the Dead, and a photograph of her grandfather, a man who had invented a special lens for movie cameras—a stern, rigid man who wore the uniform of his German panzer division.

"These things are haunted," she told Corey. "That music box? It plays on its own. My aunt, I believe, tries to speak through it."

There was a pleasant, offhand, psychopathic quality to Ava. Still sexy at age fifty, she maintained a shapely body, and as she moved through her clutter she often revealed a leg or a flash of cleavage in a constant dance of flirtation.

When she bought her second cockatoo she asked Corey to enlarge the cage, a custom-built dome of brass wire that occupied half the sunporch at one side of the Great Room.

"The ironworks that built your cage went out of business," he informed her. "I've found another one, but I've had an idea, too. How about turning the whole sunporch into an aviary?"

"Possible," she replied, thinking about it.

"I want to climb up on the roof and have a look."

"Good," she said. "Afterward we can have tea."

In the hot rooftop sun Corey took off his shirt while he checked the structural design. Looking out to sea, he saw a flotilla of green algae gathered near the shoreline, and up the beach he could see Bobby McVey's upper deck where the spyglass glistened in the sun. When he came down, perspiration covered his tanned chest.

"We could easily add space up there," he suggested. "I'd like to design you a glass turret—with screened windows that can be opened automatically."

"Marvelous thought. Sit here. I've prepared tea, but, please, don't put your shirt back on, all right? It's very warm, isn't it?"

"A tower consistent with the look of the house," he went on, taken with his own idea. It would be an expensive renovation, too, he knew, if she went for it.

"Have your way with my house," she finally said, waving a hand and manufacturing a coy laugh. "But you'll show me your plans step by step and we'll design it together, won't we?"

"Naturally. I was thinking of perches and greenery. Maybe a spiral staircase, too, so you could actually climb up among the birds, if you want that."

"Love it," she responded, gazing over the rim of her iced tea glass. "You're a real brute with your shirt off like that. I suppose you're married with lots of kiddies."

"No, unmarried," he revealed, and she drew in her breath.

"Take this any way you wish, Corey, dear, but I'm going to tell you a secret. I always have at least two men in my life. Two lovers simultaneously. Always. Since I was fifteen years old. All during my marriage. For me it has always been—well, a sensual necessity."

He nodded, keeping his calm as usual. After all, the outlandish, the cockeyed, and the inappropriate were the mainstays of Malibu reality.

"One man could never satisfy me," she went on, and he found that he was more embarrassed than he expected. "Of course it could be the drama of it all: I confess I enjoy the intrigue and all the scheduling. But I believe it's really my romantic nature. And also my mystic side, Corey, that too. I truly believe I've been many people in several incarnations. Besides, the idea of a lifetime partner is outdated. I'm trying to engage all my multiple selves, you see, in the sensual pleasures in order to—well, to intensify the spiritual adventure."

Ever more uncomfortable with this doubletalk, he let his eyes wander over the objects in the room. She talked on and on. His mind went blank, then he saw, unmistakably, an item there on her marble-topped Sheraton table, hiding among the silver snuff-boxes, tucked beside the Fabergé egg, just beside the pieces of scrimshaw: a meerschaum cigar holder with a diamond stuck in it. Ollie Tolson's cigar holder. And he knew, suddenly, the identity of at least one of her current lovers.

"Corey, I want you in my life, I really do," she was saying, getting breathy. "Those strong hands of yours. You've been a real worker and I want those fingers and hands to work on me, I admit it, and those shoulders of yours, god, do you hear what I'm asking you?"

He struggled with how to keep this strictly business, but his thoughts faltered. "Well," he managed, "I'd certainly like to build this aviary." It was a poor response to her invitations, he knew, and sounded wildly stupid.

"Yes, of course, build your beautiful glass tower and let's make it three floors high. Taller and bolder than anything along the beach. Elaborate. A monument to the birds of love. But, Corey, please, don't refuse me. At least consider it. Desire is pure, it really is."

He groped for more to say, some excuse. "Ava, any man would want you," he began, stalling.

She leaned toward him, smiling and expectant.

Then, in spite of himself, he found inspiration. "And I, ah, want you myself," he declared, inventing hurriedly. "But something's not right here. I'm getting two distinct hostile vibrations. From two objects here in the house. I've never felt anything like this before. It's so strange."

Her eyes widened with mystic alarm. "These vibrations are emanating from two distinct sources? You know that?"

"Definitely two," he confirmed.

She rose from her chair and moved through the clutter, her eyes narrowing with suspicion as she surveyed everything. She picked up the dueling sword, studying it. "Perhaps this," she suggested, showing it to him. "It belonged to my great-grandfather, the Prussian. He never appreciated the sensual pleasures."

"No, that's not it," he said, coming to her side and sliding his finger along the scabbard. "But, look, you have certain powers, I'm sure, and you'll find whatever's in our way. The ghosts, the vibrations, whatever it is. And maybe the whole thing will just stop. I'll be back in a couple of days and we'll see."

"We can have a séance," she suggested. "A hostile presence will usually make itself known in a séance."

"Good thinking," he replied, and by this time he had slipped on his shirt and fumbled with the buttons.

"If this presence is cleared up, you don't see any problems for us?" she asked, making sure.

"No problems at all," he answered, and he lifted her hand and kissed it. "Now I hate to speak of this," he added softly. "But I always get an advance while I'm drawing up building plans."

"Okay, sure," she said absently, and then giving the Great Room a final wary glance she went in search of her checkbook while Corey tucked in his shirt and finished off the iced tea.

⌐ An Old Sea Chest

Crystal Tolson asked Corey to go look at an antique with her, and
after he agreed he discovered that it was up at the Hollister Ranch
above Santa Barbara. This put him in the car with Crystal for four
hours, and she used the time to complain about her marriage.

"Ollie's having an affair," she announced as they drove along
the Ventura freeway. "He cut short our trip to Europe, so he could
get back to it. I didn't even get to see Malta."

On the evidence of Ollie's pipe holder lurking among Ava
Dillinger's things, Corey knew that the claim was probably true,
but he was courteous enough to challenge it.

"No, a wife knows," Crystal argued back. "And this time if I get
proof I'm leaving him."

So much for Tiffany bathroom projects, Corey told himself.
Sadly, if they split up, they'll put the house on the market and all
my renovations go down the drain.

The Hollister Ranch was an arid desert within sight of the sea,
yet it seemed a million miles inland. Rough terrain, rattlesnakes,
yucca plants: a barren horizon, yet dotted with red-tiled California
ranchos embraced by swimming pools and rustic fences.

The antique in question was an old sea chest: yet another piece
that wouldn't fit in the Tolson's modern house of concrete slabs
and vaulting windows. The house where Crystal bought the chest
was a monstrosity in itself, an architectural surprise that looked
like three ice cream scoops. It was filled, incongruously, with rope
furniture, horse tack, fake Remington sculptures, bad paintings
from Santa Fe, and a coffee table fashioned out of two saddles.
The seller was a plump woman in an embroidered Dale Evans shirt
who felt that the sea chest just didn't fit with the nice western decor.

People and their houses: bad taste and whimsy usually pre-
vailed. And their houses and furnishings seldom conveyed their
personalities or character, Corey knew, so that structure or decoration usually seemed like bad afterthoughts, somebody else's
idea of elegance, something erratic and wrong. They hired him,
he realized, to patch up this wrongness. They were strangers in
strange places, alienated from each other and from their surroundings, and they put him under contract to nail down their

equilibrium, to add the room that might alter their lives, to take out walls in their revolting houses and lost souls.

Driving back with the sea chest secured in the rear of Corey's pickup truck, they stopped to gaze across the green sea at the Channel Islands. Crystal pulled her cashmere sweater tight to her throat, then reached over and found Corey's hand. She was crying.

He wanted to stop at his favorite Mexican food dive in Santa Barbara, but the Superica, he decided, would be too lively for Crystal's mood, so he agreed to an upscale lunch back in Malibu at Geoffrey's.

"You know what Ollie does?" she asked, punching at her Caesar salad with a fork, yet not eating. "He cruises the aisles at the Hughes Market. He looks for Genevieve Bujold—he once saw her at the deli counter—but he hits on housewives, tourists, and the girls at the checkout counter. He's insatiable. Why are men like that?"

"I don't know," he answered quietly.

"You're not like that."

"No," he replied, eating slowly although he was starving.

"Of course not. You're the perfect gentleman. Never indiscreet. You've never made a move on me, not once."

"I predict you and Ollie will work things out."

"If you made a move on me right this minute, I'd go away with you," she told him.

"Give things time," he cautioned.

They shared an orange-and-chocolate mousse. As their two spoons clicked together inside the dish, she calmed herself and began talking about the bathroom again. She wanted mother-of-pearl tiles, she told him, but not the square or rectangular kind. She wanted them broken into odd pieces, then put back together like a jigsaw puzzle. With colored grouting, she added, that matched the lamp and window.

⌐ The Golf Priest

Corey's secret life was in the middle class: he lived in the valley, enjoyed his golf buddies, liked telling stories about the rich people he worked for, ate many of his evening meals at Hamburger Heaven, and tried to avoid emotional entanglements. Disappointments haunted him: a divorce, a friend who was his business partner then disappeared with all the assets, and a love affair of some duration that failed.

During the time he worked with Ava Dillinger, the Tolsons, and the McVeys he had embarked on a time-out, promising himself that he would enjoy his pals—a doctor, a psychologist who had quit to devote all his time to the stock market, and a guy who owned a French bakery in Agoura Hills. He had further promised himself that he would stay the hell away from love.

He and his golf buddies often played at the Malibu Country Club but also played the public courses at Camarillo, Woodland Hills, Ojai, and Ventura. One day on the ninth hole at Malibu—a sharp dogleg to the right that required a second shot over water to the green—he finally got a birdie. They celebrated with lunch in the clubhouse. He felt expansive and told more stories about his clients.

"So I hired two Mexicans to smash up the mother-of-pearl tiles," he told them. "Then my Asian tile man, Masuko, gets on a scaffold thirty feet up the bathroom wall. His assistant sends up pieces of busted tile in a basket, so Masuko can fit them together. All this will take sixty days and quadruple the cost."

"Tell us about the goddamned cockatoos," said the doctor, gesturing with his beer glass.

"The tower is now four floors high. Transparent glass with a green tint. We had to get special permits. I designed a metallic cap at the top of the tower. Push a button and the cap slides back like a gigantic foreskin, leaving a dome covered with screen so the birds can enjoy the wind and weather."

He drew a sketch on a paper bar napkin while they bellowed with laughter.

"The widow loves it," he told them, caught up in their howls.

The ex-psychologist paid for lunch.

Later, alone, little of it seemed funny. His clients lived in madness and indulgence. The swiveling TV in Bobby McVey's game room had so far confounded every engineer who dealt with it. Ava Dillinger and the wives seemed determined to draw him into their fantasies and beds. He wanted to function in a practical, helpful way, as a voyeur—nothing more than that—or as a priest: in, but not of, their world. But they corrupted all such expectation. They were made of flesh and money.

⌐ The Séance

Corey sat with Ava Dillinger across an oval table as they reached out and held hands around a bowl of steaming liquid. In the mist rising between them Ava hoped to see the faces of the dead—or at least the image of some offending item in her collection of possessed objects.

"I know that I've found and purged one source of bad vibrations from the house," she told him. "And, believe me, we'll locate and get rid of the other evil thing standing in our way."

Corey knew for a fact that one bad vibration was gone because Ollie Tolson was again smoking his Havanas out of that dumb little cigar holder with the diamond in it. But, luckily, Corey could still hold out on Ava, using this mystic idiocy to stall and delay any sexual contact until the tower construction ended.

The liquid in the bowl cooled and the mist began to fade.

"This isn't working," he finally said, and she agreed.

They abandoned the séance and each went around the house lighting even more candles. Outside, a deep twilight calmed the ocean and its outgoing tide. While herbal tea brewed, Corey settled himself on a stack of pillows and started reading the classified section of the *Malibu Times*. Then, suddenly, breathing heavily, Bobby McVey burst into the room. He had obviously been jogging headlong on the beach and didn't come to a full stop until he stood at the center of Ava's Kashmir rug.

"Who is he?" he demanded. "Where is the sonavabitch?"

The identity of Ava's other current lover was confirmed. For a moment, amused, Corey sank down lower in the cushions and thought to himself, god, the séance has produced a manifestation: Bobby McVey.

Ava, her loose gown flowing around her angrily, came striding out of the kitchen holding her Wedgwood teapot.

"This is not your night," she reminded him coldly.

"I'm in love, goddammit, so's I don't share!" Bobby yelled back. Corey rose slowly to his feet.

"I think you know Corey," Ava said to Bobby. "He's building my aviary. You know that, too. We were having a business conference."

"So he's the other guy?" Bobby demanded.

"Certainly not," she replied, clearly telling the truth.

Bobby grabbed his head with both hands and started walking around in a circle on the rug, his bare feet leaving little half footprints of sand. The cockatoos, disturbed, set up a noisy chatter out among the building materials on the sunporch.

"Sorry, I'm sorry, very sorry," Bobby kept repeating, walking his dizzying path.

"Why don't you sit down and have tea?" Corey offered gently. "C'mon, Bobby, get control." But Bobby McVey, eyes wide with the terrors of love, rushed out. Both Ava and Corey moved across the room, peered out the window, and saw him sprinting away on the beach.

Later they drank the tea with an assortment of sugar cakes. Ava gazed into the candlelight, wistfully, and spoke softly.

"Bobby has no inner life at all," she said, "Zilch. He sits at his spyglass thinking, maybe, that he ought to get one. My other lover doesn't have anything substantial inside himself, either, and he believes, sadly, that he may someday buy something to fill the hole. Their wives have daydreams, but nothing real. One wife wants to be a movie producer. The other wife just shops—and frets over her marriage. I believe it's her fourth."

Corey sipped his warm tea and listened to the surf.

"You definitely have an inner life," Ava went on. "It gives you—well, a presence. You look intelligent, like you think real thoughts. Me, maybe I'm a fake, too. All these mystic objects. They never seem to work when I want them to. Who knows if they have any powers at all? Many of them just hold memories for me. Old memories. Family, friends, husbands, and lovers."

"Memories are sometimes magical," Corey thought to say.

"You are so dear," she responded, and her voice broke.

In the candleglow that smoothed out all her wrinkles, her voice undemanding, her affectations momentarily set aside, Ava was all right. Corey gave her a smile that only real friends share.

⌒ Renovating an Identity

"What now? Go over that again," Corey said.

"We go to dinner at Giorgio's," Laura McVey explained once more. "You don't even have to talk. I introduce you as my backer from Montreal. The producer looks you over, thinks that you're Monty Ezell, and talks with me about my movie."

"Who's Monty Ezell? Is he a real person?"

"Yes, but, see, he can't be here. So you're the stand-in."

"And who exactly is the guy I impersonate?"

"Canadian mining. Big money. Sometimes he backs movies. And, Corey, please, this meeting is everything to me! This dinner, it's do or die! You've got to say yes, please!"

"Why'd you pick me? My god, Laura!"

"For one thing, you look like this guy. Better, in fact. Also, you look, well, sincere. You've got a face people trust."

"It shocks me you'd ask, though. I mean, it's so devious."

"Corey, do this for me and you can renovate the whole house. Bobby likes you, so he'll agree. You can overcharge. I'll sign a new contract this very morning. You can fix the TV in the game room so it stays in one place and the house spins around it."

"I go eat this meal and don't say anything?"

"Just be strong and silent. Just sit and eat."

They stood in the late morning sun beside Bobby's spyglass. Laura wore a white bikini with oversize mirrored sunglasses.

"You're going to say yes, I know it," she told him, and she allowed a relieved smile to grow on her mouth.

"But what if he asks me about myself?"

"He'll already know all about you. This producer, he's already researched everything. Stock exchange, net worth, taste in women, the works. Believe me."

"Then what should I know about Monty Ezell?"

"I'll give you this profile out of *Fortune* magazine. I'll tell you about the movies he backed. I'll coach you a little, then you'll wing it, and you won't be sorry, Corey, I promise you. Tear this house down and start over, if you want to. Take out that pocket-knife you always carry and cut this bikini off me. Just do this thing for me."

"What if we're caught?"

"I lose. You walk away with a signed contract to do extensive new renovations."

"And if it works?"

"If it works," Laura said, rearranging her breasts inside the skimpy halter, "I'm a producer with my own parking space at Universal Studios. And I leave Bobby McVey—who has, believe me, something on the side."

"Now how do you know that?"

"Because he goes for three-hour walks on the beach. Because he's a cheating, lying asshole and I just know."

⌐ The Tower Rises

Corey's lawyer drew up a new contract for the McVeys, but also another one-page document for Ava Dillinger that Corey delivered to her.

"What's this?" she wanted to know.

"It's a sworn affidavit concerning you and me," he told her. "If we're going to become lovers, you have to sign it."

"I've never heard of such a thing. What's it say?"

"Read it. It says I'll be your only lover."

"You're afraid of social diseases, is that it?"

"I'm a simple man, Ava, and just like Bobby McVey I don't like competition."

"This is touching," she allowed. "It makes me want to cry."

"No more two or three at a time. That stops."

"You're a jealous brute, aren't you?" she asked, and she took his pen and signed.

"Now say it. Promise there won't be any others."

"I will have no others but thee," she swore. "I'll phone the others today and call it quits."

"Good. Now take off all your clothes and climb the new spiral staircase to the top of the tower."

"Corey, darling, we haven't placed the greenery in the tower just yet and the neighbors might take an interest."

"I'll give them something to watch," he told her.

"You're kidding? Corey, listen, please, this sounds exciting, but I'm getting, well, a tiny bit baggy. I don't like to make love stripped down to nothing. I mean, I like to wear a few scarves or a bit of gown. Don't ask too much at first, darling, please."

"It's my way or no way at all," he insisted. "No more cushions and candles in your little alcoves. Get naked and climb up that metal staircase to the platform at the top."

Ava, protesting less, began to disrobe.

He followed her up the staircase. The cockatoos had fouled the railings and the platform itself, but she made not a single objection. She imagined, he knew, that this was his hardhat romantic style: raw surfaces, primitive nature, and no mystic frills. But it was strictly business. He had to dominate Ava in order to send both Bobby and Ollie back to their wives or all three of his projects would falter. He couldn't let Ava's looney sensuality threaten his job sites.

Of course, he didn't know if he could go through with it.

Ava was actually not all that attractive in the buff.

High up, exposed to anyone strolling the beach or to any neighbors who might peer over from the surrounding decks and windows, he felt like a figure on a billboard.

"I may need a little time," he said, pausing after undoing only one button on his denim shirt.

"I understand," she answered in a giddy voice.

"In fact, I may not be able to get going at all," he told her, and he regretted that he couldn't be more dominant.

"This makes me shy, too," she admitted. "But, damn, what a great idea."

Major Studio Construction

Dinner at Giorgio's was canceled.

Instead, Laura McVey and her Canadian financier, played by Corey in his only business suit, a nice enough Givenchy, were invited to the offices at Universal Studios.

"This isn't good," he said. "Now we're on his turf."

"Just keep quiet and I can bluff it through."

"Did you sleep with this guy?" he asked.

"I did what was necessary to get an official meeting."

They went down the famous lane off Lankershim Boulevard, through the studio gate, then followed the blue line painted on the pavement as the guard instructed them to do. The line went on and on. By the time they found a parking lot wedged between a row of stucco buildings and a soundstage, Corey knew they weren't seeing anyone high on the corporate ladder. As they walked toward one of the stucco bungalows, his heart went out to Laura. She tugged nervously at her white Dior suit. This producer, Saul, Corey knew, had peeled off her white stockings in some motel on Ventura Boulevard, so this was the payoff: a trip to the studio, probably to get her hopes up once again.

"This producer," Corey said to her as they walked to this sad backlot bungalow. "He can't possibly say yes to your project. I mean, he obviously works for somebody else."

"Everybody works for somebody else," she answered, being defensive. "How do I look?"

They arrived promptly at the hour. A receptionist, a gray older woman who might have been Saul's mother, told them to wait. The potted palm beside the reception desk was a fake: leaves of raw silk covered with dust.

"You think this is all wrong, don't you?" Laura whispered in the absence of the receptionist.

"I've been in the offices of fly-by-night contractors fitted out better than this," Corey admitted, keeping his voice down. "Nobody here can do much for your project."

"Then what can I do?"

"A bribe, maybe. When I deal with some sleaze in the construction business that's the only thing that works."

She nodded gravely as the receptionist came back saying they would have to wait.

"Sorry, Mr. Ezell doesn't wait for anybody," Laura responded. "Tell Saul it's right now or never."

The receptionist disappeared again and returned quickly with Saul himself. He was a bald man with a heavy tan, orange in color, who greeted them in a litany of first names. The inner office had a thin rug, shelves of scripts, two phones, and a poor Hockney reproduction behind the scarred desk. Corey felt sorry for Laura, but she seemed to have a new confidence as if she understood the game for the first time.

"Please, sit here," Saul offered, smiling warmly.

"I'll stand, thanks," Corey replied.

"Mr. Ezell always stands," Laura added, and she took a chair and crossed her legs.

At that point Saul began to talk about the storyline, below-the-line costs, and the nature of a participation deal, but Laura interrupted him.

"The only question, Saul, is how much do you want personally."

Her words hung in the air as Saul leaned forward and folded his hands atop the old desk. "Personally?" he repeated, dumbly.

Laura mentioned a large sum, "That is," she said, "if you can get our next meeting over in the big executive tower. That's just for you. Tax free. In Canadian mining stock or cash. Under the table."

"In the old-fashioned way," Corey added.

Saul turned slightly and stared into the depths of the Hockney print. When he turned once more to look at Corey, he saw a Canadian mining tycoon take a long, impatient breath.

"If the guys in the executive tower say yes, Saul, and the movie goes into production, we'll give you the same amount at each step. That's three times this initial amount if things move along."

Corey found his palms sweating as he witnessed Laura's new-found confidence. He attempted to look imperious.

"Look, I want to get started in the business," Laura made clear. "And we have other places to go, Saul, so is it yes or no?"

"I'll do my very best," Saul agreed. "But how do I know you'll pay?"

"If you get me an appointment in the tower building, the money will be there," she assured him. "Set up the meeting next week at the latest, Saul, okay?"

Saul nodded, then asked if Corey would be there.

"Mr. Ezell has to be in Tokyo," she said evenly. "Set up the meeting."

Back in the parking lot beside the car Laura tried to get her breathing under control. "God, Bobby's going to kill me for this. And he's going to have to buy a chunk of Ezell's mining stock, so these guys can see the money coming from that direction."

"He'll pay," Corey assured her. "He loves you that much, believe me, and he'll go along with this."

"You think so?"

"Take my word for it. He loves you," Corey told her, and the look in her eyes said, yes, true, that's probably so.

⌐ The Antique Shop

"What you should do, Crystal, is open a shop. Down in the market. I'm sure Ollie will lease you a place."

"He's been awfully sweet lately," she admitted. "For one thing, he used to go over to the Malibu Inn all the time, sit in the smoking section, and eat hamburgers with onions. That's because he needed to get rid of the stench of some girlfriend's perfume. You know, to camouflage the odor. Because he actually hates onions. They give him terrible gas."

"There's somebody I want you to meet," Corey said. "She has thousands of baubles—maybe even a genuine Fabergé egg— and she could really help you fill up a nice shop. You know, you find the large pieces while she provides the expensive little items. I'm just finishing a job for her and I'll give you her numbers."

"Is this the clairvoyant?"

"Right. Ava Dillinger."

"I love that glass tower you built for her birds."

They sat in Ben & Jerry's ice cream parlor sipping at chocolate sodas. Corey felt that he stood atop the cockatoo tower and saw the whole of Malibu, its entire twenty-six-mile length, with all its complexity and interlocking parts.

"Of course I'll have to fly all over the world to find the right items," she mused. "I'll go buy those Maltese chairs if they haven't yet sold. They go all the way back to the Crusades. Here in California—even if I paid a big shipping and insurance cost—I could make one hell of a profit."

She took a deep pull on her straw, making that rude little sucking noise at the bottom of the glass.

⌁ Golf Alone

In the warm bowl of the Santa Monica mountains Corey played
golf alone at midmorning. As he followed his shots he considered
the game: close-cropped fairways, rolling and deceptive greens,
and the subtle traps of a nature that was almost tamed, yet not
quite.

For more control and accuracy this morning he drove with a
five wood, yet he hit all his irons badly, as usual, and struggled to
keep his concentration.

He played better alone, but what golfer didn't? With his buddies the stresses of the game increased: bad shots were witnessed,
tiny negative emotions swam in the bloodstream, and the social
distractions accumulated.

The same held true with houses. The craft itself was hard
enough: measuring correctly, squaring the angles and joints, all the
taxing physical details. But then came the human factors: a frantic
owner, a weak suggestion, an unreasonable demand, money and
emotion.

He hit a wedge near the green and walked toward the shot.

Ava had her glass tower and had become a business partner with
Crystal Tolson. Corey and Ava had become a moment in the past,
and her fascination with the mystic life, he decided, was fading
away, too. Laura McVey had a deal at the studio. The worrisome
center post in the game room was now gone—replaced with new
steel beams to steady the house because no one could ever figure
out the TV mechanics—but the game room had also been converted into Laura's new office and screening room. The stained-
glass window for Crystal and Ollie still hadn't arrived. The trailer
had been moved from Ava's vacant lot to the hills across from Paradise Cove where groundbreaking for the new palace had already
started.

He lined up a putt, took a deep breath, slowly went into the
backswing, pushed the ball toward the hole, and missed.

There were no time-outs, he told himself. He knew this.

Addressing the ball once more, he took his time. Nobody around. Concentration. He wanted to make this short putt coming back. He studied it, then made a smooth stroke, but missed again.

Stuntman

His agent calls to announce that the most famous special-effects man in the business has summoned the Stuntman to a new destiny.

"Do not consult your horoscope," the agent argues. "The pay's right. And remember, he's done work with everybody from Fairbanks to The Duke, everybody from Eisenstein to Frankenstein!"

"He lost two guys last year," the Stuntman answers, not meaning to be irreverent. "I read about both in the Association Bulletin."

"The film's in Spain!" the agent continues. "One of your lucky countries!"

"In two trips to Spain I broke my hip and shoulder."

"See, you survived twice already."

"What insurance company this time?"

"New Orleans Fire and Theft. And the pay's fifteen hundred per."

"Any chance I could get a line of dialogue?"

"Didn't ask, but, look, I'm working on getting you your own tent on location!"

"I'm looking up New Orleans Fire and Theft in my little green book," the Stuntman says. "And I don't find it."

"It's probably a subsidiary."

"Very bad if it's not even listed in the green book," the Stuntman remarks, still turning pages. He begins to suspect the worst again.

—

The Stuntman was once married, but Shirley wanted a stay-at-home.

Now he owns a Porsche with two dents, Lanvin shirts, assorted blue jeans, the old boxer dog, the usual sixteen items manufactured by the Sony corporation, and an etching of a saint full of arrows and dying which was evaluated on El Camino Boulevard in Beverly Hills at $1,000.

He eats no more goddamned wheat germ.

There are two steel pins in his limbs, a permanent plate in his skull, and one leg is shorter now. Of all the major injuries, it's the tailbone that bothers him most. He has to sit on the toilet at an angle.

—

On location in Spain, the Director and the Special Effects Man, both of whom are dedicated to the industry, explain to the Stuntman exactly what is required.

"Before the rough stuff," the Director says with soft assurance, "we want you to take the motorcycle around that curve down there at about forty," and he points to a narrow mountain road where the asphalt shimmers with heat. "Forty is perfectly fast enough," he explains, "because this is all illusion, you understand, and later we can speed up the film to get just the quality we want. We're employing the techniques of Godard and Renoir, you can be assured of that."

The Stuntman thinks of his femur, all healed at last.

"Now the truck will come around that bend and hit you—well, not exactly head-on," the famous Special Effects Man says.

"Try to give us some nice cartwheeling and bouncing along the pavement down there," the director puts in.

"Get your arms and legs flopping as you hit and bounce," the Special Effects Man goes on.

The Stuntman remembers how well his pelvis healed, how perfectly symmetrical it is again.

"We'll get some terrific slo mo," the Director divulges. "And we're using the zoom; don't worry we won't capture every nuance."

Fitting on his helmet and pads, the Stuntman considers his elbows—he loves each one—and his kneecaps.

The Special Effects Man steps aside now, his eyes adream. A

man of artistic qualifications, that's how he views himself, a man who studied with the famous Yakima Canutt.

—

In Munich, once, the Stuntman was in a science fiction film in which he wore rollerskates. He was never shown the script or figured out his probable part, and when the film was released later he was no place to be seen. It became like a dream, since he had survived the production with no broken bones, as if nothing at all had happened, and he could only remember walking alone at night through Schwabing, the student quarter, and talking to a couple of girls who sold leather bracelets in a kiosk on the Leopoldstrasse.

They were both intellectuals, and later in the Holiday Inn he let them count his scars.

"Do you feel that by risking your life you savor it to the fullest?" the short girl student asked him.

"Do you feel—as, say, Camus felt—that life has to be pursued to its final meaningless negations?" asked the tall one.

"And this scar here," he went on, keeping up his recitation, "I got in Vera Cruz; Burt Lancaster gave it to me personally."

—

The Special Effects Man offers the Stuntman a toothless grin. "Now for the good parts," he says.

He is over fifty now; the only trick he can handle himself is falling downstairs. He's pretty good at that, give him credit, the Stuntman decides, but he's old and morbid now, he mainly dreams up mayhem for others.

"We've developed a way to make flame come out your mouth, nose, and ears," the Special Effects Man drones. "An explosive disk to put you in orbit. And a new harness we call the Slingshot!"

The sternum, the tibia, the cranium, the good old coccyx.

Behind all creativity, the Stuntman decides, is cowardice.

—

The Annual Stuntmen's Association Banquet was always disgusting. Guys on crutches, old blindies being led up to the awards table, a few stumpies crawling up there to accept their trophies and to rasp their thanks.

The speeches honor Fellini, Lon Chaney, Burt Reynolds, Truffaut, Buster Crabbe, all such as those.

The Stuntman seconds the motion that hereafter all awards be sent by mail.

—

Now the Star has joined the Director and the Special Effects Man in sinister laughter behind the Panavision camera. The cinematography unit, the gaffers, the grip boys, the extras, and the whole fire brigade wait around. The Star combs his wavy hair as he laughs, the hair which has made him the hero of two Mafia movies and the TV series about the doctor in Tanganyika.

"The Star hears the heroine's cry and dashes into the flames to save her," the Director comes over and explains to the Stuntman. "Then we cut. Next, you run into the flames and jump on the disk."

"Be sure to hit the disk with both feet, or it'll blow you sideways when it explodes and you won't be in the shot," the Special Effects Man continues. "Hit it right so you'll sail straight up out of the flames. And give us something special when you fly up. Remember to break your fall coming down because you'll be up there twenty, maybe thirty feet; we're not exactly sure how much charge we've got under the disk according to body weight. What'd you weigh?"

"Without bones, one hundred even."

"Anyway, break your fall. But don't worry if you can't get up and run or if your asbestos underclothes get a rip, because our fire brigade will be right in there with extinguishers."

"I wish I had one line of dialogue somewhere," the Stuntman suggests.

"Tell you what," the Director says, strolling over. "Give us a nice long wail. If it doesn't sound right, we'll take it off the sound track. We're using montage here, you see, and what I call Sound Sequence Montage as well. It's a highly sophisticated filmic-audio technique known only in Europe until now."

—

The Stuntman falls in love with all his nurses and occasionally seduces them with technical discussions.

"Now you take harnesses," he told the one who wore so much Shalimar perfume. "You wear a harness too low, you get whiplash and maybe a broken neck. You wear one too high, you get a busted tailbone and have to sit toilets at an angle."

With his body, limbs, and head in a cast that time, nothing sticking out except one hand, one foot, and his nose, he followed her movements around his bedside by scent.

"Tell me more," she said, and he could feel her weakening.

"I wore a harness which was too long last time in Spain," he continued, lowering his voice and making it sexy. "My motorcycle went over the cliff okay, but I went out there with it too far. The harness snapped me back into the side of the cliff, splat, right into the rocks."

"Splat," she said, and settled herself against one of his exposed parts.

He lay there enveloped by her perfume.

"Up until now," she told him, "I wasn't sure you were really a stuntman."

—

Waiting for his cue, he watches the explosion, the mushroom of fire, flames gushing toward the sky, and fixes his mind on a precise spot inside the inferno. He is dedicated to the production, to the industry, to the history of this art, and he knows he must go in there head up, eyes open, running in a straight line and pouncing on that disk.

He longs for a single piece of dialogue, one small thing to say, but words aren't his, his talent is momentary pain, the instant of impact.

He dreams of perfect execution, that sudden arch, that split second in which he is revealed and known, and he wishes the camera could freeze the frame and capture it, the diver's jackknife twist, the dancer's pirouette.

On his toes now, he tips forward.

He runs at full speed.

The flames lick his breath away. The little hairs edging out from underneath his asbestos hairnet are singed off, he springs into the air, feet together, leaping, and pain is beauty, that is all you need to know on earth, even the worst audiences know that much.

His face is gone, his skin burns off, his bones splinter and crack, his entrails explode, and just as promised he feels the flame come from inside him like a blowtorch, he disintegrates, but he knows this is his craft and gift, it is all illusion and make-believe, they will do things to the film to correct any problems, they will edit and shape the world, they will run it all backward, if necessary, and put his bones and life back together again.

Pretty Girl and Fat Friend

We were in this dark airport bar watching the afternoon movie on a television set perched above the bottles and mirror. The two of them sat at a nearby table, their heads thrown back, the fat one laughing and talking all through the action, while I sat at the end of the bar sizing them up—and taking stock of my own waning powers to hit on younger women. The pretty one was this vision in a Fendi scarf, dark, with a kind of nighthawk cool about her. The fat friend wore two mismatched shades of green and drank down her gin like a pig, then dabbed at her dark lipstick with the back of her pudgy hand. Maybe the lipstick was green, too, but I couldn't quite tell in that shadowy room: blinds pulled against the dying sun, the bartender down at the far end washing last night's tumblers, the ceiling fan clacking out an uneven, oddly Latin beat.

When the movie ended I sent over a round of drinks. They raised their glasses in acknowledgment and I was allowed to join them.

"Jerry," I said, naming myself as I pulled up a chair.

The beautiful one—even better looking up close—was Callie, and the fat friend was, simply, Peach.

We talked about the movie, *Body Heat,* the one in which poor William Hurt gets screwed over by Kathleen Turner, and I explained that the plot and quite a bit of the dialogue came out of another movie, *Double Indemnity,* and Callie offered that, yeah, she knew that picture, too, but there was also another film, another one where the lovers teamed up to knock off the husband.

None of us could think of it.

"Barbara Stanwyck," Callie said, and we all agreed, but what was that other picture?

We started talking about how everything out of Hollywood

these days was a remake, and by this time I talked exclusively to the fat friend, turning my chair slightly toward her. An old trick: you ignore the one you really want to score with, then, somehow, the best possible thing happens. It was one of the things, like movies, I knew about.

I told them about Graham Greene's famous script for *The Third Man*. "It was a movie script, then a movie, then finally a novel," I explained.

"It's usually that way, isn't it?" Peach asked.

"Sometimes, but not usually," Callie added, and by this time she was forced to lean over my shoulder to get into the conversation.

"Bet you're in the movie business, right?" Peach wanted to know.

"No, but I'm a photographer and I live in LA."

"Whereabouts?" Peach's word, adorned with several additional syllables, came out in a thick southern drawl.

"Malibu," I lied. "Been there for years. I'll bet you've done some acting."

"Me? Why do you think so?"

"Oh, I don't know. You've got a quality."

"We do sports medicine," Peach informed me. "I'm a trainer, but Callie's a real doctor. We're here at this conference at the airport hotel."

"No kidding?" I said, grinning, and giving Peach my closest attention. When she drawled out her sentences, her mouth went wide, then sort of puckered up and kissed the air: a coy gesture, girlish, yet she remained woefully plain and stupid-looking doing it.

"We used to be on the same basketball team," Callie put in.

"Now Callie's in orthopedics," Peach said, just managing that last word. She seemed suddenly too southern and too drunk.

They wanted to know what sort of photography I did.

"Used to work for the production companies," I told them. "Did the still work. Now I own a photography lab in Santa Monica."

"What's still work?" Peach asked.

"When they were shooting a movie I'd go out and take photos

of the actors, the crew, and the director—you know, for publicity. Also for the studio archives. And, naturally, for the egos."

"Then you were in the movie business," Callie said, and I turned to her for the first time.

"It was just some freelance work."

"You must've done all right if you own a photo lab now."

"Financially? Sure, I guess so. And you're a doctor?"

She answered with her eyes: a lowering and raising of the lids, slowly.

When another round of drinks arrived I confirmed my success in life by flashing both my overstuffed wallet and the Rolex. Inventing myself: the old game, intoxicating, and I considered concocting a story about how these days I worked for the major travel magazines—taking assignments whenever I needed a holiday. But I resisted saying this. Too strong.

Eager to know more about Callie, I concentrated even more on Peach, asking her what sort of trainer she was.

"Women's volleyball," she confided. "At a small college in Kansas. This conference is all about knees and joints. You know, sports injuries." As she went on, I only half listened. Everything seemed to be working. My strategies in the past, after all, had scored a few women almost as beautiful as Callie, so why not again? Maybe I was still handsome enough, not altogether fatherly: I had a prosperous waistline, yes, but a good-looking nose and profile, and not many wrinkles beneath the suntan. As Peach drawled on, I wished I could see all of Callie, standing away from the table, say, in a more brightly lit room. A stunning face. Her basketball legs, I decided, probably went forever.

We talked about travel, the monorail here at the airport, and this strange labyrinth of hotels, bars, conference rooms, and terminals. The bar, we agreed, had a manufactured antiquity: old velvet, dark panels fabricated out of cheap facade, cut glass that didn't look right.

"Brand new antique," I remarked. "Like me."

No, not at all, they replied, and Peach nudged me with her plump little fingers as they laughed.

I ordered a last round and paid the tab.

"I am a Victorian," I insisted. "Not like you two."

"You're very hip to movies," Peach added, as if that mattered.

"My idea of romance is a candlelight dinner. Violins. Very good wine. We talk in low voices and at one point, say, our fingers brush together across the table."

"Who the hell doesn't want that?" Peach asked, laughing. "Besides, who's to say what comes later?"

"What comes later is this: we hold hands, I see her to the door, and we put our cheeks together. It's not even a kiss, not really, just—you know, a loving touch. And a great memory."

"I don't think you're all that nice," Callie said with a low, wicked, little laugh. Her hand was on my sleeve.

"I'm exactly like that. And I'll tell you what. Let's find the fanciest restaurant in this complex. There's probably at least one place around here with a real wine list. My treat. We'll keep this going."

"Why not?" Callie said, and she slid her fingers away from my sleeve and gave Peach a glance. "I'm for it."

"I've got the panel discussion," Peach told her, sighing.

"Blow it off. Let's have a nice dinner."

"Callie, I'm on the damned panel, remember?"

"You're too drunk anyway," Callie argued.

"When I'm drunk I'm especially articulate," Peach offered, botching those last words so badly that we all laughed. "You two go ahead without me. Really, fine with me. Sorry, Jerry, but maybe we can meet later for a nightcap, okay?"

I turned to Callie. "Just the two of us all right with you?"

"Perfectly all right with me," Callie answered, and her voice contained a happy, drunken expectancy.

We went out into the confusing corridors of the airport complex where the sounds of jet engines punctuated the early evening. Peach and Callie embraced, saying good-bye, and the thought arrived that they might be lesbians—lady jocks, after all—but then Callie turned and fixed her eyes in mine: an inebriated and wanton stare, unmistakable. A sense of wonderful good luck washed over me.

The best restaurant turned out to be a hotel dining room: fake Edwardian, bowls on the tables adorned with floating rose petals, yet somehow not much more than a decorative coffee shop. Asking directions, we started off again toward what an indifferent head waiter described as "a nice tavern, cozy" on Concourse C, but after walking another quarter of a mile Callie stopped.

"Let's have dinner in my suite," she suggested. "If you want to know the truth, my high heels are killing me. We can order up some steaks, all right?"

"I don't want to intrude," I argued weakly.

"Come on, why do all this walking?"

Tipsy, we made our way back to the hotel. In the elevator she leaned against me so I held her elbow to steady her. The touch of her, her perfume, and the soft luster of her skin brought back thoughts of previous conquests—damn fewer than one wanted—in a lifetime of pickup techniques, flatteries, lies, and what seemed at times endless efforts. I remembered the woman at the dog show in Denver: we went back to her suite at the Marriot, where I found two male Afghans roaming through her rooms. She was a beauty, too: the sleek lines of an aristocrat with small breasts, a hard backside, and an angelic face. Her husband, she told me, had been cheating on her. Meanwhile, those two dogs slipped silently across the rugs, coughing slightly, as if speaking to one another about what transpired in the bed, and later toward morning I sat up, cold, the covers around me, to watch one of the hounds with his paws on the wall above the toilet in the lighted bathroom as he urinated like a man into the bowl. Creepy. Or another time: a woman in Manhattan who claimed she was a spy and that somebody was out to get her, who clung to me as if I'd be the last person on earth to hold her. In casual sex, as they say, the neurotic woman is often preferred, but never the psychotic. Or yet another time: the aerobics instructor down at Del Mar who hurt my shoulder during some rough foreplay, then insisted on taking away the pain with acupuncture. Before our evening consummation—she had decided to give herself a little relief, too—we joined our needled bodies very carefully like two porcupines.

Memories of my long, tortured obsessions: as a teenager in the backseats of cars, as a student in dorm rooms, as the husband's guest, as a constant and clumsy player in the sexual follies. Now I was in my fifties, growing soft, wondering when the last ounces of testosterone might drain away so that I could enjoy the serenity of old age.

We arrived at Callie's modest suite. Pastels, a mini-bar, the oversize TV set, the bedroom over there, its king-size coverlet peeking at me through a door slightly ajar.

"Peach could only afford a single room," she was saying. "But I thought I might—well, entertain."

She excused herself to remove those high heels. Nervous, I strolled to the window, gazed across the way toward the monorail, and cracked my knuckles.

"That movie!" she called to me. "Jessica Lange!"

"What movie?"

"The one we couldn't think of! Same plot! Jack Nicholson and Jessica Lange!"

"Oh, *The Postman Always Rings Twice!*" I shouted back.

She came out nodding and smiling, pleased with herself for having remembered. She had also changed her clothes entirely and wore a pair of old blue jeans and a faded denim shirt with the top buttons undone. Work clothes, I said to myself. Not anything flimsy or accessible. Barefoot, she strolled around the room like a panther, letting me admire her movement and feel the heat.

We kept talking movies, our references getting more suggestive.

"Lana Turner was in the first version of *Postman*," I said. "You're probably too young to have seen it."

"No, I saw it on late-night television," Callie told me, and she removed two small airline bottles from the mini-bar and started stirring up additional drinks. "But the Jessica Lange version was best. Remember how Jack nailed her in the kitchen?"

"On the table. Wasn't there flour all over the table?"

"Flour, yeah, and he rolled her like a big cookie."

"You think movie sex is done well?" I ventured.

"Nah, not really. It's never right."

"What's not right? In your opinion, I mean."

"That scene with Jack and Jessica, it was good. But usually it's just too romantic and wrong. You know, slow movements and music."

"Soft porn," I suggested.

"Exactly. And not even good porn, How about another gin?"

She stirred up another. We touched glasses, gave each other a look, and sipped.

"There was a movie with Julie Christie and Donald Sutherland," I went on. "Nick Roeg was the director. I knew him a little. He used to be a cinemaphotographer. Anyway, he cleared the set on this movie and shot the sex scene by himself—just the three of them and the camera. Rumor was, Christie and Sutherland really did it."

"Screwed each other for real?"

"The scene sure as hell looks authentic. *Don't Look Now,* that's what the movie's called. It's about, hm, psychic stuff."

"You really do know movies."

"I know a little about a lot of things," I offered.

"Me, I've always been a specialist," she said. "Medicine. The human body. Are you looking into my shirt?"

"I guess I am," I admitted.

"You can unbutton more of it, if you want to."

"Love to," I said, and I closed the distance between us. She stood there balancing her drink, one hip jutted out while I made the move. Everything was as if a script had been written. Yet an uneasy knowledge tugged at me while my fingers found the metallic button: Callie was young and lovely, smart, and I was this sagging specimen on the erotic downside, a creature of strategies and lies, a guy who merely worked in a photo lab, who had been back home to visit his ailing sister, who wasn't even named Jerry.

"Can you think of a movie where they ever get the sex right?" I asked, staying with the topic while struggling with the button.

"They never get it right," she answered. "I mean, we pump like wild animals, don't we? We sweat. We come hard. It's never on cue with the cameras trying to make it look romantic, is it?"

That metal button, I decided, was maybe a snap. I couldn't get it. Then Peach was beside me, angry and frowning, sober, with a pistol leveled at my head.

Is this, I asked myself, the nightcap? I already knew better.

"Look here," Callie whispered, and she opened her shirt easily, giving me a brief glance, but also getting my attention so that my profile turned to the correct angle. Peach hit me with the butt of the pistol and my eyes filled with tears: a blinding pain as if the shattered bone in my nose had been driven up into my brain. My knees buckled and I started to fall, but Callie grabbed me by the collar and pulled me away.

"Not all over the rug," she told Peach, and it was a strange, fastidious concern, I thought, crazy, as they led me toward the bathroom. A dumb thought rose out of my pain: is this something kinky, do they both want me, do women rape men?

They pounded me with those high-heeled shoes as they stripped me. Great welts rose up on my head and body, little volcanoes of pain, and the bloody membrane from my nose soaked us as they pushed me into the bathtub.

"Don't kill me," I managed, losing consciousness, then reviving again. One called the other Louise and I thought, wait, Thelma and Louise? The spiked heel went into my eye and I knew, god, my sight's gone, they've blinded me, and they were both more agile and stronger, moving around me with athletic skill, finding openings in my defenses as I protected myself with my arms and elbows. I tried to draw myself into a fetal ball, but they straightened my legs with sharp blows to my knees, then jerked my pants off, getting at my wallet. Another blow entered the top of my skull, sending bright shock waves down my spine, and when I woke up again, instantly, they had the Rolex.

"Get the picture, movie man," Peach said, laughing, and she used the pistol butt again, cracking the side of my head with it, and I was going, then gone, adrift, fade to black. They were both laughing when I entered the netherworld.

After midnight I woke up, naked, sliding around in the gore at the bottom of the tub, then climbed out and made my way to the phone. Its cord had been cut. My own room key was missing, of course, so I couldn't go there. Wrapping myself in a sheet, I staggered down the hallway to the elevator. When I arrived in the lobby a bloody coil hung down from one nostril and I could only see out of one eye as I made my way to the concierge's desk. The young woman sitting there looked up from her magazine, smiled, and asked sweetly, "What can I do for you, sir?" It took her forever, it seemed, to actually look at me.

While the ambulance was on its way, a house detective opened my room to find my cameras, luggage, and clothing gone. He was a slovenly Asian, his shirttail dangling and cigarette ash decorating his paunch. Giving me the bad news, he also informed me that Callie's room was registered in the name of a Mr. J. J. Cutworth.

The next morning I learned that six pairs of tickets had been purchased on my credit cards to destinations that included London, Boston, and Rio. The morning detective, a member of the local police force, looked like an elderly Steve McQueen.

"Tell me the story again," he suggested wearily.

"You look like you've been up all night," I said. "Have you?"

"I never sleep," he replied, scratching himself and giving me a wisecrack grin, almost a smirk, definitely Steve McQueen.

"Two guys," I began again, embarrassed. "Said they were at this sports conference. We had some drinks together at this tavern on some concourse. Tall guy said he was a doctor. Little guy was some sort of trainer or coach. We talked movies. We went up to their suite before dinner and they pistol-whipped me."

"So that's where you got all these god-awful bumps?"

"The nurses won't give me a mirror," I protested. "But, damn, these places all over my body feel gigantic."

"I think they beat you with a high-heeled shoe," the detective said.

"The butt and barrel of a pistol," I assured him. "I don't know what caliber."

"Maybe," he agreed, shrugging, but he knew. "What place were the three of you drinking?"

"This tavern. Cozy place. I can't remember."

"Go over their descriptions again."

My sister came to see me before I left the hospital. She brought new clothes and a fruit basket, but I couldn't chew anything except the bananas. On a TV set mounted high above my bed I watched Gary Cooper in two AMC movies.

On the flight back to Los Angeles I sat in first class—thanks to my boss, who paid for the upgrade. A pretty stewardess asked how I came to be so beat up.

"Hotel robbery," I told her. "Pistol-whipped."

She sat on the arm of my aisle seat, concerned. The lack of hotel security—even in the top hotels—frightened her. She told me how a friend of hers, another stewardess, once woke up with a man crawling around her bed. "He took the wristwatch off her bedside table," she said. "Then crawled around the room until he found her purse. Then he crawled to the door, opened it, and crawled away."

"Terrible," I answered.

She kept sitting beside me, not tending to the other passengers, and I learned that her name was Myra and that she had gone through nursing school before joining the airline. Her hair was cut in the pageboy style: silky and full, blonde. She had a soft prettiness, not really beautiful, sort of like Jodie Foster: a girl next door, caring, a girl to fall in love with, and I found myself playing on her sympathies—the oldest move of all. After helping with the beverage service she came back and sat on the armrest again.

"I'm a photographer working for several of the big travel magazines," I lied, unable to resist her. "I only take assignments these days when I want to go someplace exotic. You know, Kenya or New Zealand or Machu Picchu. Of course I'm going to need an assistant when I travel now. Until the skull fracture heals up. I get these dizzy spells."

Our bodies were close. Her perfume was White Diamonds.

Was I over the top with this? Would I say that I lived in Malibu? Would serenity and peace never come to me?

The Big Bang Theory of Love

Letti, the astrologer, met Paco Whelan in her chart room—part of
her beach house out in Malibu—and gave him the usual reading
for a new client: general good fortune, the position of Saturn not
all that favorable, but good health, new love, and prosperity all assured. She took notes on the few things she learned about him:
unmarried, forty, a Scorpio, somehow connected to the movie
business. Nothing much personal passed between them, but then,
two weeks later, he phoned and asked if he could take her to
dinner.

When she asked if he wanted some additional interpretation,
he said no.

"What you told me reading my chart made me a fair amount of
money," he informed her. "But that's not it, exactly. It's you. I
can't stop thinking about you. How about Giorgio's?"

"I suppose so," she answered, flattered, and she could only recall that he wasn't especially handsome, that he was slightly bald-
ing, and that he had a gold tooth that revealed itself in his smile.

She fretted over what to wear. He wouldn't wear a suit, she decided, but something casual and expensive. Didn't he wear a big
Rolex with a blue face? Didn't he have some sort of accent? And,
Paco Whelan, what kind of name was that? She went out and
bought a black dress with spaghetti straps and a new pair of knock-
out pumps.

At Giorgio's they sat just left of the doorway at a candlelit table
for two. The odors were roses and garlic. Paco was all eyebrows
and a toothy smile: bushy dark brows that rose and fell with emotion and wide teeth that featured an occasional flash of gold.

"Don't object to this," he insisted, and he counted out a number of crisp one-hundred-dollar bills on the linen tablecloth.

"There. Five thousand dollars. Cash. You won't have to pay taxes on it. It's for the tip you gave me when you read my chart."

"But I said nothing about your business, not really."

"Saturn, you said. Watch out for Saturn. You said the position of Saturn wouldn't be all that favorable, so I sold short on the market. Saturn, the conglomerate. I'm giving you 10 percent of what I cleared. Tax free."

"I can't take that," she told him, laughing.

"I want you to have it. And I want other readings. And always be as specific as you can. Good news or bad news, whatever, I'll handle it. See, Letti, I think you've got the gift. You really understand the stars."

"I'm not taking this money," she said firmly, her eyes fixed on the stack of bills.

The wine steward came around to refill their glasses. Paco sighed, folded his hands, and leaned forward. His eyebrows became hoods over his deep frown. "I guess money's an insult," he said. "I've been too crude. Maybe I was trying to bribe you."

"I'm not insulted," she insisted. "I just didn't really earn this. And how could it be a bribe?"

"I wanted to impress you. So I could get close to you."

"How do you mean, close?"

"Personal. Intimate."

"But we don't know each other."

"From the moment you looked at my chart, you knew me. I could feel it. You're gifted, Letti, and intuitive, and I don't think any woman has ever seen me for who I am. Not ever. And to me you're as dazzling as the night sky. And mysterious. You're deep space. The mystic infinity. And I'm going to rocket right into your life."

It was an extraordinary seduction speech that turned Letti's thoughts to herself. She was well over forty—though she knew she certainly didn't look it—and he was years younger, but also more handsome than she had first noticed, flamboyant, and wildly poetic.

Besides, her own romantic house hadn't been in order for a long time. She had come from Texas to California a dozen years ago with a drunken husband who soon lost his construction business. For a time she consulted the zodiac as a solace, leaving her tears on the pages of cheap astrology magazines as she divorced and tried to sort out a new destiny. She waited tables at the Crocodile Café in Santa Monica, then rented a trailer near Paradise Cove out in Malibu where she drove a delivery van for a florist. In Malibu she witnessed up close the anthropology of the rich while filling their rooms with floral arrangements: the sadness in their success, their forlorn children, their restless marriages. She started reading charts for some of them in her little trailer. As she became known, she found that the more she charged the more business arrived. Word of mouth made her reputation, so that she bought the trailer, sold it, fixed up a clapboard beach house at the shabby end of Zuma Beach, sold it, went upscale, then up again. An affair with a guy who owned a surfboard shop—no hint of it appeared on her own chart—ended in disaster, and love became a word reserved only for her clients.

But that evening at Giorgio's her fingers entwined with Paco's across the table. They neglected the veal and the lovely flounder, gazing at each other until he took her home to claim her fantasies and her bed as if he owned them.

The next morning, satisfied and giddy, she watched him dress his hairy body and listened to his promises.

"I'll phone you all day. Every day. We're probing into another galaxy, you know, Letti. Into a magical zone. We need to live together. Consider it, really. And chart our course. I'm a believer, completely, and I want the stars and planets lined up for us. This is fate, a thing written in the cosmic dust."

Yet later that day—he had phoned twice—she found herself doubting her craft. More than once in the past—especially in terms of her own loneliness—the signs and prophecies had betrayed her. She sometimes wondered if she could be just a hopeful fake and if the rhythms of the great whirling constellations had little to do with her terrible isolation on this minor planet at a faraway corner of the universe. Paco wanted the stars to guide them, but would his infatuation burn out? Would that big Rolex continue to rest on her bedside table, its luminous digits staring out from the darkness at her. Was that five-thousand-dollar offer genuine? Should she have taken it?

Hoping for the best, she went on a strict diet and roasted herself on the sundeck, tanning every inch of her body. During a week of nine appointments—including two with the actress who slept with her Dobermans—she saw Paco every evening. Flowers, dinner at Ivy's, a kiss in the hidden cove of that obscure state beach, his tireless athletic skills in bed: he pursued her by phone, by fax, by the oils and secretions of his body until she became dizzy with his attentions.

Ten days after meeting him she prepared a barbecue on her deck, and while they drank a light Chablis and waited for the chicken on the Weber cooker she asked him exactly where he lived.

"At the Bel Air," he answered, shrugging. "The only house I actually own is out in Van Nuys and I can't say I live there, can I?"

"Because you have to impress people?"

"Letti, yes, my love, correct. It's all glitter, superficiality, and pain. That's why I need guidance and counsel. Somebody like you who's in touch with the greater forces."

"Paco, I want to be candid with you. I'm not sure I'm in touch," she admitted. "A lot of my business is guesswork."

"Jesus, Letti, mine too! Look, you have an informed intuition. That's genius. In the movie business, especially. Wait, lemme tell you. I've got this partner. We're in this deal together, hoping to make a movie. We've put up money for the script, all that. I'd love it—this would be a real favor—if you could read his chart. I'm not sure I trust him completely. Like, is he going to bring all the money he says he'll put on the table? If you could just meet him."

"Sure, I'll be glad to read his chart."

"Maybe you could figure out if this deal is going to happen. If not that, maybe you could just tell me about him. I mean, something that seems insignificant might be really important. Like when you mentioned Saturn and I sold short. His name's Tom. He's from Iowa. So can I trust a guy like that?"

"I'll help in any way I can."

The cooker sent up a cloud of smoke; beyond, great clots of brown seaweed undulated atop the turquoise ocean.

"Letti, what a woman you are," he told her. "Pure vision. Beautiful."

—

Doubts about the world of astrology weren't new to Letti.

Months ago she had bought the famous little blue book by the theoretical physicist Stephen Hawking, but *A Brief History of Time,* supposedly written as a popular work aimed at amateurs, baffled her. She placed it on a coffee table so that her clients could see it and be impressed, but there it sat, unfathomed, to mock her ignorance with concepts such as quantum mechanics, antimatter, and the exotic mysteries of the expanding universe. (Expanding, she wondered, into exactly what?) She sort of understood the big bang theory: matter, densely compressed, had exploded, sending everything into the void of space, every object moving away from everything else. Sad, she felt, that all the galaxies and tiny particles zoomed away from each other at the speed of light. So sad. It stuck in her mind as a wistful metaphor for love: poor men, poor women, forever moving out of reach.

One day after Paco's arrival in her life she stopped at the discount bookstore after a lunch at Bambu's sushi bar. There, to her amazement, she found a comic book on the life and work of Stephen Hawking, an introduction with cartoon drawings that made sense of the densities of the little blue book. After reading it—and returning to the author's own work with renewed understanding—the real universe seemed both awesome and real, while astrology felt oddly insubstantial. Trying to recover her faith in the zodiac, she repeated parts of its language like an incantation: causal relationships, ascendants, glyphs, ruling planets, the tables. Words and concepts, yet she felt like a priestess suspicious of her idols. Yet why? Because, although she was a professional, the signs had never worked for her personally. And Paco was a magnetic field, a bright sun, a destiny she craved.

One morning after a night in her bed he produced a Frisbee with a centerpiece of rhinestones, and after breakfast they went down to the beach to sail it with and against the breeze. He was all energy: the hairy chest and thick arms, the dancing eyebrows, the golden tooth glinting in sunlight.

They talked about the movie he wanted to make, a story about the old buffalo hunters. Yeah, kind of a cowboy story, he explained, but not exactly cowboys. His partner, Tom, liked it a lot.

"If this deal doesn't make, I'm sunk," Paco lamented.

"I thought I was going to meet this guy," she offered again.

"I need your help in this, but I don't want to pull you into my business affairs," Paco said, and his eyebrows slanted up and down with worry.

"I advise a lot of people on business," she assured him. "If this is important for you, set up an appointment."

"Okay, but one thing. Don't talk about me. Please."

"I won't mention you," she promised.

"See, I need to find out if I can trust this guy. You'll see through him. It'll be right there in the stars and you'll, like, know. But you'll keep our confidence, won't you?"

"Of course I will," she said, and at this she made her best throw: a long curving toss that carried the Frisbee on the rising breeze so that it sailed above the surf, then swooped back onto the beach.

—

Tom Barlow, the partner, had a shuffling, candid, midwestern charm: a Henry Fonda type, long legged, hands and elbows moving at restless odd angles, a drawling voice. He sat at Letti's large black marble table admiring the room's decor and occasionally glancing at the ocean beyond. Finally he just watched her as she studied his chart.

"First off," she began, smiling at him, "you're a very special Libra. I'd say you had a stable childhood and loved your parents. You're intensely loyal. You, ah, enjoy beautiful surroundings. And you're drawn to the arts and creative people. And you have a talent yourself. From what I see here, I'd say, oh, drawing or painting."

"Photography," he added quietly, and he grinned and fixed his gaze on her. Before she could begin again, he said, "Paco wanted me to meet you. He said you have a kind of magic. You do."

"You've had a loss," she said, tracing her fingers along the lines of the chart again. "And a change. And you're impulsive. Not exactly decisive, but impulsive. And I see here that you're optimistic—often to a fault."

"Make that gullible," he said, amending her. "But, really, this is uncanny. How do you see these things?"

"I'm being accurate?"

"My father had a big farm east of Des Moines. He and my mother both died within a year of each other, so I sold the place and came out here hoping to find something in the movie business. I met Paco. How well do you know him?"

"I just read his chart," she replied, being evasive.

"Well, go on. What else do you see in all those geometric lines on the page?" A short laugh came out of him, a laugh that Letti considered skeptical.

"You don't believe in any of this, do you?" she asked.

"No, but I think I believe in you. You're Paco's best suggestion so far."

"How do you mean?"

"He thinks I ought to meet somebody and fall in love."

"Does he? So that's why he wanted us to meet?"

"Oh, I reckon he wants me to feel secure about our deal. You gave him confidence in it, he told me, but, yeah, I think he just wanted us to meet. Maybe he was matchmaking. Paco's got lots of secrets and hidden agendas for all of us."

"He's the classic Scorpio," Letti agreed.

"I wish I trusted him more."

"He makes you uneasy?"

"Well, I put up all the money in our deal. Optioned a book and paid for a script to be written. He seemed to have a few contacts at the studios. But then his expenses piled up. Last week he needed a rental car, a Lincoln, blue. He already has a car, but he needs this blue Lincoln. Am I too suspicious? Or gullible? What does my chart say about it?"

"According to your charts, you and Paco seem compatible."

By way of avoiding further discussion of Paco, Letti returned to the conjunctions on Tom's birth chart. She noted that he probably suffered from occasional headaches and that he might be a sloppy housekeeper, and he nodded, confirming these things, then interrupted.

"Maybe we could take a short walk on the beach," he suggested.

"You don't want to finish this?"

"Maybe we could take off our shoes and walk barefoot. Is that too corny for you?"

"Not at all," she told him, and they went out on the deck then down her circular stairway to the sand. She wore her white flowing caftan, one of those she always wore when she gave personal readings, and she gathered it up as she walked beside him. His feet were large and white. They made smalltalk for a while, then he spoke both to her and to the afternoon whitecaps beyond the surf.

"Don't you think we all live in the future too much?" he began. "I mean, everybody out here in California seems to live in the future. When my ship comes in, everybody says. When my movie is greenlighted. When I become famous. Maybe it's an American affliction and maybe my own dad was that way. He worried about next year's weather. Or feed prices. The farm and future possibilities. And, well, look at the two of us: I come out west looking to make a movie—and don't know much about it or where to start. And you make a living talking about what the fates have in store. So it's always something. If the deal makes. If Paco delivers. Letti, don't you think the future is—well, sort of our crazy religion?"

She had to admit he was right. In fact, he had the serenity of a gentle hick philosopher as he said all this, and she believed every word. She wanted to cry. She trusted him in a strange, light-headed sort of way.

"And if we live in the future, we miss the moment," he went on. "Not that I'm into Zen, but that's the idea. You and I meet, for instance, but we're locked in the future, so we don't really see each other. Or we walk along the beach and don't really feel the wet sand between our toes. We don't feel how great we are together. And we are. You know it and I know it."

Hearing him say it, she did know it. She felt an odd rapture.

"Paco wanted me to meet you, but I resisted. Lately, to tell the truth, Paco's ideas haven't been so good. But I agreed and drove out here. And met you. And you're beautiful. Can we have dinner tomorrow night?"

"I guess so," she managed. She felt barely able to get the words out, dizzy and transfixed. Having gone so long without a man's attentions, she felt confused and bombarded: first Paco, now Tom.

"My exact hour of birth and the conjunctions of the planets I don't care about," he continued. "But you're different. When I saw you I thought: wait, here's somebody I'd like to sit with in the mornings and have coffee with. Read the papers and not say anything. Wake up next to. I know you think I'm impulsive—that it's in my character—but I've never married, Letti, and I've waited a long time for, well, the moment. Don't say anything negative. Don't stop me just yet."

She had no intention of stopping him. Half a mile down the beach she got a grain of sand in her eye, though, and they touched for the first time as he removed it. He kept talking about plans and projects: how insane they make us. His deal with Paco, he said, probably wouldn't happen, but now, strangely enough, he didn't care all that much. The whole adventure had led him to Letti.

She wanted him to take her in his arms, but he removed the grain of sand skillfully, scarcely touching her, and remained a country gentleman, sweet yet formal, and she thought, damn, he's fallen in love with me, maybe I love him too, we're in the moment, Paco's a fake, the future is shit, this is real.

They walked back toward her place and he went on talking, yet his voice was slow and reflective, no hint of a hustle in it, so that she felt compelled by it. Too soon they were at her front door saying good-bye, reminding each other about dinner the following evening.

"Let's go for fish," he suggested. "Never got enough in Iowa. That's all I eat when I'm here on the coast."

She wanted to grab him and offer her lips. If Paco was flashy, Tom was true bedrock, the sort of man to get pregnant by, genuine, so that even his shuffling awkwardness at the door endeared him to her. Aching for just a kiss on the cheek, she watched him stroll out to his car. A Chevrolet. As soon as he pulled into the traffic on the Pacific Coast Highway she hurried to the telephone to see if Paco Whelan was actually registered at the Bel Air Hotel.

He was.

—

She spent the next day reading Stephen Hawking, deciding that astrology was truly simplistic and dumb. The unified field theory, Hawking said modestly, was probably a mirage: there was no great single theory of the physical laws, like God, but a lot of interacting laws, variations and exceptions, all very complicated, that constituted what we know. The famous theorist also argued that we might never predict anything with complete accuracy or certainty or even see the tiniest particles—smaller than the electrons and quarks which we currently regarded as the smallest pieces of known matter—much less the vast clouds and galaxies of distant space.

As an Aquarian, Letti enjoyed real science—things measured and fixed—yet she felt more than ever like a fraud. How could she presume to advise clients on love and business? Not even physicists are certain. And since time isn't even a real concept—speaking cosmos-wise—why should the astrologer worry about one's exact second of birth? Carl Sagan argues that false science is everywhere. Einstein asserts that space is curved. The future, Tom says, is bad religion.

That night Tom stopped at Gladstone's to buy lobster, oysters, crab claws, and prawns, arriving at Letti's to announce he would cook dinner at home, so she went to her bedroom, shook off the new black dress, and put on tight jeans to match his. While he boiled water and sliced up vegetables, she returned a phone call to her mother in Houston, answering all complaints by saying, never mind, Pluto is entering your tenth house and that means money and fun for a month. As soon as she hung up, the phone rang again. But when she saw Paco's name on caller ID she decided not to pick up.

"When I told Paco we were having dinner tonight, he didn't seem too happy about it," Tom divulged as they ate dinner.

"He's getting dependent," Letti answered.

"You know what I think? He said he paid this kid writer a hundred thousand to write our script, but now I can't find the guy. He's listed in the Guild handbook, but he never answers his phone."

"Maybe he went to Europe to write."

"No," Tom drawled, "I think the guy whose phone doesn't answer isn't the same kid I met."

"How do you mean?"

"Paco pays this kid with screen credits one hundred thousand.

I meet the kid and he gives us the script. You know, the buffalo hunt."

"Is the script a good one?"

"It's exactly like the book with a different format. I could've written it myself, but Paco says, no, we need a credited screen-writer on this, someone hot. To impress the studios."

"But what? You meet somebody who isn't really this writer?"

"Somebody, I think, who just impersonated the writer with credits. That's what I suspect. Tell me I'm wrong and that a Libra never gets paranoid."

"You're really upset. Here, have more wine."

"I wanted to make love tonight, but I ate too much. Sorry, Letti, I feel awful."

"Who said we were going to bed so soon?"

"I wanted to," he said, grinning shyly. "I was going to make my best move." Again, he was so honest and charming that she didn't care if the evening was lost to indulgence and flatulence. Also, all his emotions focused on Paco.

They went out on the deck, sat in a glider, held hands, and listened to the surf. They saw a shooting star.

"If I'm right, see, Paco didn't pay anybody to write a script," Tom continued. "He pays a young actor fifty bucks to impersonate a famous screenwriter, then Paco writes a script himself and pockets the money."

Tom got up suddenly and went to the bathroom for half an hour. When he emerged his drawl had altered into a whine.

"Paco has this one major contact," he went on. "Lou Levin. One of the giants. Maybe you've heard of him. I met him at Jerry's over on Ventura, the deli where all the deals are being made these days. So I have it confirmed that Paco knows Lou. The morning we had breakfast together Paco buttered Lou's bagel for him, but I didn't mind."

"Lou Levin," Letti repeated, trying to follow.

"Lou can make a movie happen. But he won't speak to me in private or return my phone calls. And now he doesn't return Paco's calls—though all of us had bagels and eggs together. God, sorry, I have terrible gas since dinner."

Clearly, the future had recaptured Tom's mind. Letti tried to say something helpful, sounding like a mother unable to console a child.

"My stomach is in knots," Tom groaned. "Got any Tums or Rolaids?"

"No, but maybe I can give your neck a massage."

"It's my gut," he reminded her, getting snappish.

"Maybe you should drive home while you can make it."

"That's probably a good idea. If I stay around here I'll throw up or something. Anyway, I hope you enjoyed my cooking."

"It was delicious," she told him.

—

The next day Paco arrived with a fruit basket wrapped in bright pink cellophane. He paced between the oversize Egyptian vase in the living room and the glider on the deck.

"My deadbeat partner," he said, fuming. "I hope you didn't fall for his particular line of hick crap."

"Nothing's going on," Letti assured him. She was glad to see Paco again, hopeful, and convinced—especially in the glare of the noonday sun—that Tom Barlow was something less than a potential lover and a midwestern philosopher.

"He's ruining my contacts," Paco complained. "Somehow he got Lou Levin's private number. He's also bothering the screenwriter. And now he won't transfer money into our account when the Bel Air wants me to pay up."

"Paco, are you living off Tom's money?" Letti asked outright, sounding, she realized, wildly naive.

"I'm living off the project," Paco explained, pacing. "Tom drives into town in his dumb Chevrolet and tries to set up a meeting with Lou. Nobody just walks up to Lou in the deli. He's got, like, bodyguards. Anyway, eventually Lou turns Tom over to me."

"So you're what? A lieutenant?"

"Lou and I go way back, maybe four years. See, Letti, guys from all over the world with story ideas and big dreams try to get to Lou. They pay to get inside. Like Tom, who has no imagination, just money, and who at the moment won't let go of the money. And, like, who am I to disturb somebody's fantasy? Sure, Lou throws some business my way from time to time. I develop projects for him. Listen, Letti, I need sex. How about it?"

"Not today."

"I didn't think so. How about some horoscope, then?"

"Pluto is making a transit. Beware."

"I love it when you talk that way. Pluto, like in Disney?"

"Pluto the planet that rules Scorpio."

"The Disney Company will be perfect for this buffalo movie," Paco said, quietly ignoring her. "Lou knows somebody there, too."

She was suddenly tired of Paco. Even his misguided enthusiasm for astrological tips annoyed her. She decided to tell him this, but he was quickly on the phone—calling Lou Levin. She went off to the kitchen to brew a pot of tea.

After a few minutes, though, he bounced in, wringing his hairy hands with excitement. "Lou wants you to do his birth chart," Paco announced, pleased with himself. "I know what he'll see, too: a Scorpio, me, as an important part of his whole aspect. Help him see that, okay, Letti?"

"I'm not taking anyone else in the business."

"Why not? What's that supposed to mean?"

"For starters, you're all such fakes—though I suppose you can't help it."

"Faking, that's the whole business! Same as yours! Can I have a cup of that tea?"

"Even your Rolex is a fake. C'mon, Paco, you think I don't see things?"

"You've taught me a lot about myself, Letti, honest," he said, letting his free hand slip across the wristwatch, hiding its luminous blue face from view. "Even though I lied to you about that Saturn deal, I did it to impress you. Because you were so gorgeous in that white caftan. Because you're the moon and the stars and you dazzle me."

"Paco, you don't know me and you never will. Know why? Because you'll never even ask about me. You're project oriented. Selfish. Constantly thinking about what comes next. Oversexed. A little creative, maybe, but a hustler. You use people. You're getting every cent you can out of Tom Barlow—who probably deserves to get skinned—and you used me to try and keep him hooked on the deal."

Paco sighed heavily, as if he had been found out and as if he had gone through this moment previously with other girlfriends or wives.

"Three sugars and lots of cream," he mumbled, waving his fingers at the teapot.

"Let me tell you about myself," Letti went on, pouring. "I came from Texas years ago with a drunken husband who almost convinced me to swear off men. My mother and I don't get along. I play the flute. I'm a pseudoscientist, but I'm growing, so lately I'm into real astronomy and it's awesome. You listening?"

Paco nodded as he sipped the hot tea, then blew into the cup.

"Since I'm an Aquarius," Letti went on, "I'm good at helping people, but usually I don't get too involved with them. When they have too many problems, I always back off. I'm objective and practical that way. Anybody who's too demanding, I just treat them as a client. Yet I'm a spiritual person. I want to walk around barefoot in the silence of my own house, thinking my own thoughts. Maybe reading. Being alone. I love my solitude."

"But, Letti, wait, you're also great in the sack," Paco argued.

"Maybe so, but I hold back even there. I mean, you were all hairy and sweaty and making noises."

"Noises? What kind?" he asked, and he laughed over his teacup.

"Whooshing noises," she said, and the word made her smile. "At times it got so funny that I felt like a spectator, somebody just listening to the comedy."

"Whooshing?" he repeated, spilling tea into his saucer. They had a laugh together, and when he recovered himself he said, "So the two of us are finished, are we? Then how about a little consulting? Like you do my weekly horoscope on the phone?"

"My rate for that is twenty dollars for five minutes."

"Done, no problem. And we're never having dinner together again?"

"Not anytime soon. Paco, please, you're wearing me out. Do your deals. And, by the way, if you were lying to me about the Saturn business you weren't actually going to give me five thousand dollars, were you?"

"I figured you'd say no. It was a bluff."

"You take a lot of chances. I almost accepted it."

"It's in my stars to gamble," he said, shrugging. "It's who I am in the universe," and with that he gave her a short, coughing laugh and drank off his tea.

And exactly who are we in the universe?

Sitting alone on her deck that evening, alone with the exquisite silence of a starry night overhead and with the restless torture of the surf below, waves hammering ashore one after another, she floated in uncertainty and the tiny beginnings of knowledge. Nothing was ever truly known or understood, she realized. And no other person. But also this: the arcane observations of a minor astrologer might possibly help somebody in his brief journey— perhaps as much as some proved and scientific fact or the wisdom of some genius physicist. We are so alone and moving away from one another, lost matter in the sea of the big bang, solitary, dying planets, yet oddly aware, some of us, and content—if not fully happy—in our comprehension of how sad it all is. If Stephen Hawking is right, she decided, and if the universe is expanding to-ward entropy and possible death, then maybe others in their time held tiny pieces of theoretical knowledge, too. Even the legendary astrologers who knew so little: Ptolemy, Bacon, Kepler, and the others.

At any rate, she felt strangely reconciled to herself. Without Paco or Tom she also felt wonderfully relieved. In the upcoming week she had six appointments, so she was making a good living. And she'd soon buy a telescope for this deck, she decided: one of those big fat ones, one that allowed her to see as far as possible.

Africa and Anarchy

The Magician of Soweto

First I swiped this peach and ate it, then I took a package of almonds and ate those while I shopped for my main course.

This was a supermarket on Wanderers Street—great name— right in the middle of Johannesburg, and the clerks were busy, my movements were unhurried, I was taking my time.

Then this little guy starts following me around the aisles. He pretended to read the labels on things, but there he was, always behind me. What did I care? He was just another piece of dark background: a scrawny black guy who would get in trouble himself if he told anybody what I was doing.

There was this barbecued chicken on a rotisserie, just like in some big supermarket back home, so I took that, then picked up some cheese, a carrot, milk, and candy bars. Everything went into my backpack, and this little guy was watching talent, trying to see what the hands were doing, but I was too quick.

After I finished, though, he was waiting for me outside. He had lots to say, but I was moving on down the sidewalk.

It was a cool, breezy morning with a slight odor of cyanide in the air: the residue off those big mounds around town. In the old days they used cyanide to leach the gold away from other minerals out at the mines, so now the wind blew it in the air, everyone getting his nose and eyes burned, everybody here sort of waiting around in the poison for things to get worse.

This little guy fell into step with me, saying, "Work for me, see, and we make ourselves rich?" I paid him no attention, but he kept on. "You're American, aren't you? You look American and my name is Moses Kawanda? I operate this stall in Soweto? But I plan to open a shop here in the city?"

He talked in questions. As we made our way toward the railway station, the stores got cheaper. After Woolworth's came the used clothing outlets.

"The new law?" he went on. "It says a black man can open his own business in town? So the shop owners don't have to be white or Indian now? And why should the rest of us work out of open stalls in the townships?"

I ate a barbecued drumstick, pulling it out of nowhere just to impress him. We sat on this patch of grass near the station, the little guy kneeling beside me while I ate.

"I know you've been sleeping outdoors because of how your jeans look? But the nights are getting cold, I know that, too? So I have this room in back of my shop? I signed a lease? And there's a bed, nothing fancy, so you can stay there while we get items to sell?"

His voice rose with every sentence and he had this crushed-down face, as if somebody had stepped on him and mashed his brow, nose, eyes, and mouth all together. He also wore a mismatched suit: brown pinstripes, but not the same coat and pants.

"African artifacts, that's all I need? The easiest things in the city to shoplift, you see? Beads and bracelets? A little ivory? Or if you find something really valuable, we can sell it? But for your room rent and salary—a very small salary—you can just bring me cheap rings, ebony trinkets, all those things they put in open bins, see? It is such an easy matter for you, correct?"

"You're a crook," I told him.

"Who can do things honest here?" he asked, turning his palms toward the sky as he would do when he talked politics. "This land came from cheating and killing, didn't it? And is governed by lies? No, think about it, who can play fair?"

Traffic honked around us. As the midday clouds built up, the air became chilly with the scent of rain: the month of June and the coming of winter in South Africa.

"Well, okay, show me the room," I said.

I followed him back toward Wanderers Street. I didn't even need the room or money all that much, but it was something to do.

—

For two weeks I worked the suburban shops in Sandton, Hillbrow, and Melville, then I worked the western part of the city, then shaved my stubble, bought a change of clothes, and doubled back to some of the easiest places. Moses Kawanda's shop picked up quite a bit of merchandise, and in the evenings he arranged for me to have girls from Charmaine's Escorts. I had the room, food and drink, ladies, and worked only a couple of hours a day doing what I enjoyed: strolling around, sitting in outdoor cafés, going into shops and letting my fingers trail across the goods. I was having a good time.

"These, look, what did you do?" he asked one day.

"When there are big crowds at the Carlton Centre, I can pick up anything," I told him. "These are gold. That, I think, may be a real ruby."

"Don't you know we will have to sell these tonight?"

"What I'm thinking, Moses, is that we should have one case of nice stuff."

"Dangerous and crazy? Is that what you want?"

"Half the shops don't even know they have pieces missing."

"Tommy, we should stick to cheap items, please, like I told you?"

"No pain, no gain," I said. "See, we could put our class merchandise in this case right here."

I had my pride. A talent can only swipe so many elephant-hair bracelets and plastic Zulu masks.

We were arguing all this when Mr. Rashi, the Indian rug dealer in the shop next door, stepped into our place. He wore his silk Nehru suit and folded his hands across his belly as if he might soon break into prayer. We got a little nod hello, then he sniffed around through the goods. Moses wanted to stay cool, but failed. Mr. Rashi was big time: a blue sapphire on his finger and a blue Mercedes to match.

"I was going to expand," he said to the walls and ceiling. "I meant to lease this place myself."

He had a way of addressing blue space.

"This is Tommy, my partner?" Moses managed, and he bowed and smiled as if he expected a blow from Mr. Rashi in return.

Mr. Rashi just tilted his head back and talked. He was used to being listened to, so Moses paid attention while I sorted through the day's take, spreading everything out on a piece of old velvet. Mr. Rashi discussed his daughters, the falling value of the rand, and how the Transvaal winters seemed so long. When he spotted a ring he liked, his eyebrows went up.

"See, gold, you see?" Moses prompted him.

"Nice design," Mr. Rashi admitted.

"Take it, will you? A present? From your new neighbor?"

The ring was two serpents entwined, their mouths and fangs locked. Mr. Rashi liked it a lot, though it looked puny next to that big sapphire of his.

"I could give a rug in exchange," he said to the ceiling. "Something small. To wipe the feet on."

"Hell of a deal," I said with a smirk, but Mr. Rashi just held the ring up, admired it, and paid me no attention.

Worried that Moses might give away the ruby as well, I wrapped up the rest of the stuff and tucked it away.

Mr. Rashi, gazing over our heads, described the rug he had in mind. Moses countered by bragging that we would have ivory, fine jade, gold, semiprecious stones, and the usual Africana. They talked about security: alarm systems and guard dogs. As I watched Moses move up in class, I calculated that I'd eventually have to knock off the Kimberley mines to compete with this snob next door.

Before Mr. Rashi left, he and Moses talked about Soweto, where they both lived. I tried to figure Mr. Rashi and his Mercedes out in the ghetto, and after he was gone I asked Moses about it.

"You know Lenasia?" Moses asked. "Where all the Indian merchants live?"

"No, can't say that I do."

"Big houses with swimming pools and black servants? You don't know Lenasia?"

"That's part of Soweto?"

"You come to my house?" he said, turning his palms up. "We can eat soup?"

"Sure, okay," I agreed.

Both of us looked around the shop as we talked. Through the

doorway with its thin curtain of beads we could see my unmade bed in the back. Everything needed fixing up.

—

Moses disapproved of all the girls from Charmaine's and hated paying the bill, but got local prices.

"Don't get emotional," I told him. "Those girls are like fast food. And what else am I going to do?"

"Do you think I'm proud? Having a partner with low habits?"

"Look, so what? You cheat in business and I buy my romance."

Only a couple of things got me high, never girls, I told him: one was good surf and the other, lucky for him, was shoplifting. It was a buzz swiping things, it was like the top of a good wave. He could understand sport, but he got upset when I told him about Cape Town, how I went there for the surf and hung around Sea Point making out with the high-school girls.

He asked didn't I realize he was a Methodist?

I did get soup, as promised, that first time in Soweto. Mrs. Kawanda, who was twice his size with that same mashed-down face, spooned it out for me and maybe ten kids. I never got it straight how many of those kids were theirs.

They lived in this two-bedroom frame house, and if you stood on some of the junk in their backyard you could see these same houses all the way to the horizon in every direction. Soweto—which I thought was some shantytown ghetto—turns out to be fifteen miles long and six miles wide and filled with these little government bungalows. There are also neighborhoods of three-bedroom brick houses with wide lawns. And Lenasia: the biggest houses of all and a mosque with a gold dome. And, of course, White City: a pretty punked-out neighborhood. And floating over everything was this coal dust and soot pouring out of the Orlando Power Plant, lots of smoke in the air, including more cyanide, and hundreds of buses hauling everybody to jobs in the city and back again.

At supper we talked about the rent boycott.

"Half the people here don't pay rent?" Moses carried on. "Good idea, right? Who wants to pay the government for this? But I say, let somebody else get evicted at first, let me see if the boycott works, then I'll stop paying, too?"

The big kid at the table, a sixteen-year-old with some hair on his chin, wanted to burn down the schools.

"There's no leader for them to arrest, is there?" Moses went on. "They've got all our leaders in detention, don't they? So nobody pays rent and nobody thought of the idea? It just happened, didn't it?"

Everybody ate bean soup while Moses, palms up, talked politics. Then, afterward, I did magic tricks for the kids, except for the sixteen-year-old, who went outside and stood in the cyanide. I pulled cards out of the girls' ears and made coins disappear until Moses got concerned about how his daughters sat too close to me on the couch. He suggested that we go to Klipstown to see his stall at the market.

Under some drooping eucalyptus trees at this big flea market, Moses had five wobbly tables piled with clothing, hardware, plastic kitchen utensils, and secondhand plumbing fixtures: corroded faucets and coils of dirty copper tubing. A rooster pecked around on top of all this.

"A dump," I told him.

"My daughters are damned young?" he said in defense. "You kept touching their ears with that trick, didn't you?"

"Up yours, you crook," I said, not giving him the edge.

As we bickered the Klipstown market depressed us even more, so we went to a makeshift bar constructed out of old oil drums and corrugated tin where we drank glasses of warm lager that almost gagged me.

"Do you know I'll make more off those old plumbing fixtures than I'll ever make on Wanderers Street?" Moses asked, gripping his beer in both hands.

"So why open a shop in the city?"

"Years ago all those fixtures were stolen? Families moved into a new housing development here and their toilets weren't attached to any pipes? And eventually I had it and everybody in Soweto knew it, so they bought from me? But a shop in Wanderers Street, Tommy, ho me, think about it, why do I want that? When the law finally changed, who was the first Kaffir to lease himself a shop? Moses Kawanda!"

Soon I ought to move on, I was thinking. Maybe I would go see a lion in Kruger Park before going home. I'm halfway around the world, I decided, working as a necessary evil for a little black crook's upward mobility.

—

In the big shopping mall out in Sandton suburb I waited until all the jewelry stores were filled with Saturday shoppers, then I asked to see the trays of rings. While the clerk bent over the trays with me, I picked up four, five, six rings at a time, looked at them, then said no, thanks anyway, these aren't for me. They never figured it out. Once I got this nice silver bracelet because the salesgirl worried about another bracelet with diamonds. Another time this guy just walked away, leaving me under the rotating eye of this camera on the wall. Just me against the camera, I liked that a lot.

Mr. Rashi now came into Moses's shop every day to see what we had. He folded his hands on his belly, cocked his head, and looked at the ceiling as if to say, great holy krishna, I know exactly where you're swiping this stuff.

I gave him my blank stare, showing him nothing.

The shop looked good by this time, and Mr. Rashi told Moses he'd help with the opening, which made the little crook giddy with pride. Mr. Rashi also suggested that Moses might want to sit in on a weekly poker game out in Lenasia.

"Card playing? At your house? But, see, I don't play cards, do I?" Moses said, his voice getting squeaky with excitement.

"I play some," I offered, butting in.

"Then you should both come," Mr. Rashi told us. "You can be our American cardshark. Cash only. Table stakes. Do you know table stakes, Tommy, my friend?"

"You can explain it," I said.

Mr. Rashi looked at the silver bracelet, shaking his head slowly from side to side as if he recognized an old friend.

—

To pay back the Kawandas for the meal at their house, I took them to the Carlton Hotel—not the coffee shop, not the lousy café with the Spanish motif, but the main dining room with the heavy silver and all the candlelight. We were thirteen at the table and we were noisy. The big sixteen-year-old looked around like this had to be a trap. Moses and his wife got small and quiet. I did a fork trick for the girls.

We had soup, two starters each, the lobster, a cheese course, two desserts, and three kinds of Cape wines. By the time I ordered cognacs for Moses and me, he was getting worried.

"How will you pay for all this?" he wanted to know.

"Oh, we don't pay," I said. "We walk out of here one by one. Women and children first."

"Tommy, how can we do that?"

"Then loan me some money."

"Tommy, don't fool me," he said, sinking lower in his chair.

"Look, Moses, what are we? We're gangsters, right? Gangsters don't pay."

Across the room these two businessmen and their dates got up to leave. One of the girls was from Charmaine's, a Maylasian named Kiwi, and she gave me a tiny wave of the hand as they went out.

Moses talked with his wife about how we might have to escape. I was about to tell him I was just joking when the waiter appeared and gave the kids a sneer of a look.

"To whom do I give the check?" he asked in this crappy British accent. Because of the way he said it, I went on with the joke.

"We can't pay, but we're willing to leave one of the kids," I told him.

He took a deep breath and tugged at the lapels of his dinner jacket. "We obviously have a liberal policy here," he said, viewing the Kawandas with a smirk. "But we must all pay, musn't we?"

I popped my American Express card at his nose.

"Write yourself a 1 percent tip," I said. "And hurry up with our cognacs."

Moses wanted to leave right away, but we sat there as the kids got squirmy. As he finished his cognac, he asked to see the American Express card and he studied it and rubbed its letters and numbers. Mrs. Kawanda said, no, she didn't want to touch it.

"My dad allows me three hundred a month on it," I admitted. "You guys just ate up my July allowance."

My confession was translated around the table, each kid looking at me as it became clear how rich I was.

It was so late when we went outside that the buses had stopped running. We found two black taxi drivers, but had to argue with them about fares to Soweto and about overloading their vehicles. Moses made a deal with one of them, something about used pipe from his stall, I didn't hear all of it. The taxis cost him plenty, but he shook my hand and told me that he never thought he'd eat lobster or have a friend with an American Express card. The big kid gave me a good-bye nod, raising his hairy chin maybe an inch.

—

Mr. Rashi's house had lots of marble and was padded with rugs, pillows, and fat women. His daughters, aunts, cousins, and a grandmother carried trays of food from one room to another.

The victim that night was supposed to be this Afrikaner salesman with a roll of hundred-rand notes. The game room had old movie posters on the walls—Bogart and everybody—and the poker table had a green hooded light over it. Mr. Rashi took off his Nehru coat and underneath was more silk, silk all the way to the bone, I supposed, and I knew I had to win early in order to stay around.

Moses gawked at everything, being too polite, and ate chocolates off some fat woman's tray.

When the Afrikaner pumped my hand, I told him I loved his beautiful country and that I was here scouting business investments. There was Mr. Rashi, the Afrikaner, me, and these four Indian geeks who smelled like talcum powder. One of the fat daughters ate this fruit and gave me a slow wink. Moses sat on a high stool so he could see the table, and he was getting wasted on chocolates and the fear that I would lose our operating capital, but I was happy when I saw the deck Mr. Rashi put into play: those standard blue Bicycle playing cards.

I won six of the first nine hands, staying alive in little pots. Mr. Rashi observed—not without sarcasm—that I paid very close attention.

"Because I'm a beginner," I told him, and actually I was counting aces when he interrupted me.

"You're a strong boy," the Afrikaner said, slapping down his cards as I won again. One of the geeks took up whiskey drinking.

We played for an hour, nobody talking much, and I sat out three big hands that Mr. Rashi won. Playing with their money, I tried to look interested and hide. I dropped out of another hand when the geeks and Mr. Rashi started all their signals. They took the salesman pretty good, everything rehearsed, and my host wouldn't look at me as they did it.

After another hour, I decided to have a little run. I pulled stray cards into my hand at every opportunity. One of the geeks went head-to-head with the Afrikaner, neither of them paying me much attention, and I turned four deuces for the biggest pot so far.

Then we took a break. The fat women pushed sandwiches while everybody tried to smile and act social. Moses was sweating too hard to make much conversation, but Mr. Rashi, speaking to me and yet to the whole room, asked, "Tommy, do you agree with the philosopher who said that in an immoral society only the criminal is moral?"

"That's a good one, Mr. Rashi. I don't know."

"One could offer that this also defines the terrorist or the revolutionary in any evil regime," he went on, gazing at a slow ceiling fan above us. "Or it could perfectly describe a simple thief. Thieves have their own small way of correcting inequities in corrupt social systems, wouldn't you say?"

"You're over my head," I told him.

The Afrikaner added his genius to the topic by declaring that thieves were no good in any situation.

Mr. Rashi chewed a chicken sandwich and peered into the darkness above that hooded light. "Evil against evil can become a good," he went on. "And I suppose the lines between the two are thinly drawn."

"These are certainly bad times," the Afrikaner stated, turning his gaze on me. "But I say they'll pass away."

"Quite so," Mr. Rashi answered. "But where, Tommy, did you learn to play cards?"

"On the beach in California," I lied. "We used to play slapjack on top of our surfboards."

The fat daughter who had winked at me led me toward the toilet down this long hallway. There was a lighted statue of two naked lovers with snakes in this alcove, but I didn't want to stop there with her.

Now that I knew where everyone sat at the table, I fixed two decks—allowing that one geek might soon quit the party. This ought to be enough evil against evil, I decided. I flushed the john and tried to clear my head. I did have this one twinge of doubt, wondering if I'd spill cards everywhere since I hadn't practiced this, but by the time I got back to the table I felt like pure talent.

Moses asked if we shouldn't quit, but I explained, no, hold on, so he went back to his perch.

The Afrikaner won a nice hand that put him in a good mood. He started giving me glances like, okay, we're the white guys here and we should stick together.

Then it was my deal. I took a sandwich off a passing tray, got a beer and some napkins, and stacked all this and my chips in front of me: lots of props. I shuffled and shuffled, then switched decks and dealt real slow, giving everybody a good hand with special service to Mr. Rashi, one of the geeks, and the salesman.

Somebody kicked my leg.

"I'll just play these," Mr. Rashi announced.

"So will I," said his geek friend who only had a flush.

As I planned it, everyone else dropped out and I took one card, the same as the Afrikaner. When everybody raised, I got another little kick. Mr. Rashi wanted to bet his shop, sapphire, Mercedes, and marble house. I could hear Moses sweating over all our money.

"Get out, kid," the Afrikaner salesman said, giving me another friendly kick. "You can't beat me." He thought we were in this conspiracy together, but I hurt his feelings by raising with all the money I had. When the cards were down he was second best: four nines against my four queens.

It got pretty uneasy after this.

"Tommy, I believe you are a magician," Mr. Rashi told me.

"You haven't seen his tricks?" Moses put in, helpfully. "He entertains my children? You didn't know?"

Mr. Rashi paid this information little attention because the Afrikaner was leaving. The other losers began putting on their jackets, and the host accompanied them to the door. I drank my beer, moved my chips and cash around, and managed to get rid of that extra deck of cards.

"You play too good," one of the geeks complained, looking over his shoulder in my direction.

"Up yours," I said. "You give out signals."

Mr. Rashi came back to the table during this exchange.

"Moses," he offered, "allow me to give you and your partner a ride home."

—

The Mercedes crossed Soweto Highway and turned toward White City. The driver was this untouchable who wore a chauffeur's uniform that looked like it was padded with muscles and weapons.

Mr. Rashi spoke in a reasonable tone. He wanted ten thousand rand—his estimate of our night's take—and he wanted me to never show my face on Wanderers Street again. He also wanted Moses to sign over the lease to his shop and move out.

"No way," I said, braving it out.

"Please," he said with a long sigh. "I'm taking you into White City, don't you see that? Do I have to threaten you?"

Moses and I agreed to pay up. With a certain amount of protest. I fumbled in my pockets for the cash.

"You and your buddies signaled back and forth all night," I told him. "You took mine and I took yours. You should let us keep our stake."

"You thieves cheated me in my own house," he argued. "You gave me a stolen ring. You took money from my Afrikaner."

Moses was pleading with the driver. "See, this is the wrong place? Don't you want to be back on the highway?"

The driver gave him a grunt in reply.

"Make a fuss about paying and we'll put you out here," Mr.

Rashi said calmly. "Try explaining what you're doing in White City after midnight: a white boy and a little black man from the wrong tribe!"

"Here, that's everything," I said, dumping a handful of crumpled banknotes in his lap.

"He's paying you, isn't he?" Moses pointed out. "So don't we want to turn around?"

Mr. Rashi counted the cash as the Mercedes turned a corner and slowed for a roadblock. Two dozen black figures danced behind a barricade while a bonfire spewed ash and gobs of flaming paper into the dark sky.

The untouchable grunted again, hit the brakes, and attempted to shove the car into reverse, but too late. A kid beat on the window beside Mr. Rashi's face with what looked like a piece of Moses's secondhand pipe. Then the door on the driver's side flew open and the untouchable was among the enemy. As he reached inside his uniform, he was dropped: struck from behind with a cricket bat.

Then Moses was outside the car, too, his palms upturned, talking politics with the rabble. A missile flew by his head, but he kept jabbering. Mr. Rashi attempted to lock his door, but two kids pulled him out. As his shiny silk suit caught the reflection of the bonfire, I thought, get ready, it's evil against evil for sure, think fast, it's the revolution.

"Who doesn't hate the landlords?" Moses said, addressing the crowd in his usual interrogative. "Do you think I'd pay rent? I haven't paid for weeks, have I?"

The kids around the bonfire looked maybe fourteen years old.

I came out of the car with my hands high. At the top of my reach, at the very tips of my fingers, I produced an ace of diamonds and sailed it off into the darkness. Eyes widened. But to make sure they caught my act, I did it again and again: my queens, my deuces, another ace. Mr. Rashi's tormentors stopped to watch.

Next, a cigarette lighter with flame aglow—swiped from Charmaine's. I pitched it toward the kid with the cricket bat, and he caught it. The whole crowd had gathered around me now, so I tossed out the money—picked up in the car after Mr. Rashi had been dragged away. I heaved a handful in the air, putting it up there with the floating cinders and glowing ash. With the last handful, I yelled at Moses, "Let's get out of here!"

As we started running, a security force arrived. They came out of the darkness, jumping out of lorries without headlights: big, uniformed men with nightsticks and long quirts. But rand notes filled the air along with burning debris, so nobody knew exactly what to do. This fat soldier arrested me, then ordered me to help find money. When I found some, he stuffed it in his pockets.

Mr. Rashi kept telling the security men that he lived in Lenasia. "What riot?" Moses asked his soldier. "You think this is a riot? Don't you know a riot?"

—

At the station I was placed in this lounge with purple walls, a television set, and a coffeemaker. The police sergeant explained that I was the first American ever "involved in an incident of unrest." They phoned my embassy, so someone could take me away.

I wandered the hallway, drinking coffee and looking for something to swipe, some little souvenir, but there were only police manuals.

They had arrested nine kids, Mr. Rashi, and Moses, but nobody knew anything about the big driver. Breakfast was this hard biscuit and more coffee, then I saw the sixteen-year-old, Moses's kid, and when I asked him about his father he didn't seem to speak English.

Toward noon this embassy representative in coat and tie arrived. He asked me if I wanted to leave the country.

"What do you mean?"

"In these circumstances," he said, "it might be less delicate for you to leave. We can advance you plane fare."

"Sure, I'll take the ticket. But can I see Moses Kawanda first?"

He wrote the name in a small leather notebook.

Then there was a long conversation in the hallway with the security officials until, eventually, Moses appeared. Somebody had hit him in the stomach and he was feeling sick, but they had allowed him out of his cell to sit with me on this bench.

"Yeah, I'm flying home," I told him.

"But what about our shop?"

"You've got plenty of stuff. You don't need me anymore."

"And what about Mr. Rashi? Won't he report all the stolen jewelry?"

"Nah, he won't bother you."

"How do you know this?"

"Because he's crooked like everybody else."

"I don't feel too good?"

"You'll get better." I patted his knee, but he looked bad.

"And we lost our money? And I'm in jail? And my son is here, so I'm embarrassed because he'll never believe me?"

"I'm sorry, Moses, I really am, but you'll be out soon."

"And look at you: you're a thief and you go free?" he said. "You go free and here I am?"

"Moses," I said, "it's the way of the world." I gave his bony knee a last slap, then got to my feet. "And I'm doing my disappearing act," I said, and I did.

The Warrior

When I served in the American army my trick was crawling by a
sentry in the dark of night. No one was ever better at it: inching
along, scarcely breathing, rippling a muscle here or shoving off
gently there so that my body sometimes passed at an enemy's very
feet in the good strong shadows of a moonless watch. I've passed a
man so close that he could have turned and stepped on me, in
which case, of course, he would never have taken another step.
This was my specialty, getting by a man this way, and I did it in
Korea and later when I wasn't an American anymore—just one
of the world's mercenaries as I am now—in Algiers, the Congo,
Biafra, and so on.

Africa, lovely restless continent, is just out that way across the
water. This is my home now, this little port, Javea, and if you look
out from our hill you can see the beach, Cabo de San Antonio,
with the lighthouse, the city, and the mountain beyond it. Being
just across from Africa this way pleases me, and lately I've considered going back over with El Fatah, say, or even the Israelis if
they'd give me a good platoon, which they probably wouldn't.
Spain is fine, but it reeks of peace now; not that I don't enjoy it
with my family here, but before too long I always start contacting
old friends in the business or reading the classified sections again,
seeing who wants a warrior this season. One job of mine came
right out of the London *Telegraph* and another I got out of *France
Soir.* Always in Africa: that old dark continent over there where a
good savage is always appreciated.

This is my villa, all paid for, my pool, over there the vineyard
and terraced olive grove. We sit here in the *naya* in the evenings,
my wife, Val, and I, and drink these good local wines and repeat

the old stories; I'm not one of those who can't talk about battles or the things that go on during a good fight. My daughters, Jenny and Kip, sleep just above us in their own rooms. You've seen the antiques in the house, the gardens, the Porsche and Rover, my motorbikes: you know we have a good life here. This is a nice place, better in climate than southern California, say, where I've lived, or the Riviera—which gets too cold for me in the winter. It's just that I get restless, as I say, and of course it was much better here on the Costa Blanca a few years back before the tourists found us, before the entrepreneurs—there's this queer film festival down on the beach right now—and before the big contractors moved in and started building these cut-rate villas. This part of the hillside twenty years ago was all fruit trees, lovely; that was when I came here, when I was in my twenties just after Korea and hard as an oak and just a mean kid.

Val sits there in the cool afternoon breeze reading about the film festival in the provincial newspaper. She told me they're having one Fellini, one Mike Nichols, and the rest of the movies are by Frenchmen: Christ, some show. The kids and tourists have been in town for days, sprawling out on the sand down there eating paella at our beach restaurants. Look at my wife: quiet, that good Spanish profile, still with me. My heart's blood. We have a generation of naked little flower girls now, not a woman among them like my Val.

This is the arsenal, yes, and everything's about ready. A solid room: these old tiles make a fine echo when you walk on them. The sound—I've thought about this some—lends a little importance to every movement made in here. These are the automatic weapons, here are the mortars and a few heavier pieces, over there the explosives—some of which, I admit, I confiscated from the local *Guardia Civil.* I sat at this table and filled all these cartridges myself. Everything is sorted out and inspected, and I've confiscated a boat, too—I'll tell you about all this later—and I have a motorbike and car waiting in strategic spots. No one suspects a thing. I'm still a man who can slip by in the darkness.

Sit here on the *naya.*

Get us some drinks, okay, Val, baby?

We should have a long talk and I should explain a lot of myself to you, but of course there isn't time for much of that. This domestic life—let me say this much—is great when I come back from assignments. We water-ski, skin-dive along the reef, go over to the club for tennis in the late afternoons. But after a few weeks shadows start coming over me, and let's lace it: there isn't anything here that measures up to crawling by a guard in the darkness or running headlong into an attack. Not that we should get too philosophical, but paradise is a moody place. I get into the glooms, then, and start sitting around my table in the arsenal drinking and reading. Oh sure you saw all the books inside the house: I'm no brute.

What will really come after nationalism—have you thought about it? As I see it this tribalism will eventually go away, and no, not because of the United Nations, noble though the effort is. The UN is just a referee among the nations, after all, and so basically approves of the spirit of nationalism. No, big business will take over the masses. Men's loyalties in the next century or two, in my view, will shift from France and Pakistan and Brazil to Olivetti, Westinghouse, and Shell Oil. The big corporations are already cutting across borders. And government—think how obvious this is—will become a kind of regulation agency which will determine when the big corporations are cheating and when they're not. Clandestine business—war of sorts, yes—will go on. But men won't finally be as emotional about products and companies—especially if they can change jobs easily after all—as they are about their homeland. Things will settle down and my sort should eventually become obsolete.

But make no mistake about it, eh: we're not obsolete yet, are we? And war is still a great education in reality—the way things really are. The kids on the beach need to learn that lesson; they nourish a lot of vague hopes unawares.

Ah, thanks, Val. Sit here with us.

Civilization has been a long breeding process, true, but we aren't all bred and civilized yet, so there's the gap between our hope for ourselves and what really is. The warrior is out of favor nowadays, for instance, because so many people imagine that it's surely time for him to be finished. But that's hardly realistic with new nations still emerging, guerrilla wars, protest movements flaring up. The old warrior should be given his due. Ah, let me tell you, I dream now and then, you know, and shadows come over my sleep, names and faces swimming up inside me: Marathon, Alexandria, Hastings, Lyons. Does any of this make sense? Some times I feel that I just got back from, say, Dunkirk—or Okinawa. I've had strange dreams for months, and when I wake up—the really curious part is this—I'll know how to work a crossbow or I'll remember a particular coat of mail I've worn with blue ringlets. And I forget my rank—have I just been a captain, a foot soldier?—and once I turned to Val and said, hey, remember how we walked out of the trees at Shiloh and found that road and made it up toward the next town with our wounded, and she gave me this odd look. Val indulges me; we've been together a long time and naturally she knows the humor I've been in lately.

You came here wanting to know what I'm going to do, I realize, and I'm going to tell you. Perform my art: that's all. It's partially for the old shell-shocked ego and self-satisfaction, sure, and you can invent your own explanations—such as, oh well, he never had any sons and this is part of his masculine anxiety and that sort of thing. Whatever, I'm going to show some of my repertoire of moves; the old ballet master will rise up and dance—while you stay up here, naturally, with Val. But it won't be *just* to demonstrate my skills. My attack will be a lesson in history. If everything goes right—and it will—I'll kill a thousand of the unwary this evening; I'll be identified, of course, and someone reading tomorrow morning's news will decipher some of the meaning of it all.

Some ice? No, my limit's one this afternoon.

Listen to me, where is history? My notion is that the philosophers can never tell us—not the artists or anyone else. They can only record things static and gone while the world nowadays powers along at an overwhelming speed. Only speed and power themselves are listened to: things that zoom and explode beyond our immediate comprehension like comets so that we stop and ask, "Hey, what was that?" All lessons now must be actions: scars that wound the world's face so that it can never quite forget. And there's an irony here you ought to consider: it turns out that I'm one of the great humanitarian instructors saying, Wake up, see that you're still in a twilight of barbarism, be ready! It's a tough truth to take, but valuable—far better for mankind than so much idle wishing about its nature.

Well, you should know. This evening I'll attack the film festival. All those passive onlookers down there on the beach. They're down there pondering their various apocalyptic films, conning themselves with art and sand, imagining they're seeing something important flicker in front of their eyes. They're zombies, those hip children passing love messages around. It's not that I hate them— I have no particular intolerance for one lifestyle or another—it's just that, oh, I don't flatter myself here either, I'm their instructor. I hope you can glimpse what I mean: time is against them, they don't know where they are, their fantasy is a dream of death.

Look at this view. A few sails out there on the bay this afternoon. I'll hate leaving here, but Val will join me, naturally, and there'll be many more days like this. We may live in Istanbul—I was there once years ago, I forget exactly when.

You'll want to know exactly how it will be. All right, I'll come down from the rocks so that I can sweep the whole beach before me. There should be about a thousand bathers, another thousand gathering inside the canopy to watch that stupid promoter—he calls himself an impresario—unwind his dull films. Weighted down with ammo, I won't move fast—I won't have to. When I open fire, I'll just get some astonished looks. You odd little soldier, they'll be thinking before they die, you're all baggy with packs and weapons and you rattle when you walk and look silly. Their eyes will fill up with hurt, then, and I'll just move through them; strangely enough, it will take several minutes before they even start running ahead of my fire. A big Scandinavian girl will be blown right out of her bikini, and if you had the right mind about it the sight would strike you as funny: zap, she's undressed, flying off in a little slow-motioned erotica. One brave idiot will come at me with a rubber float after he's wounded; oh, please, don't hit me with that, and I'll cut him in two. A group of rowdies, their motorcycles there beside them in the sand, boys in their marbled T-shirts and girls lying on towels with their halters loosened: I'll empty on them at very close range because they're too cool to move. Almost casually, now, I sweep down the beach, walking near the surf where the sand is packed underfoot, spraying my fire into the wall of bodies just ahead. They start to fall over each other now as I step into a sand castle and advance. No time to finish the wounded, but surprisingly there aren't many of those. Under the canopy just ahead the crowd begins to stir, but by this time I stop, set up my mortar, and lob a few shells—first just beyond them and then into the tent itself. Human parts everywhere: our beach runs a little red now. As they race toward me in confusion and away from those first volleys, I let go with the remainder of my .50-caliber material. This turns them back again, and now I have the crowd on the run. Heavy ammo mostly gone, I leave weapons and empty cartridge belts and become more mobile. I carry the mortar only a few more quick meters toward the flaming canopy, let fly a few more lobs in the direction of the beach restaurants— a skillet, a Fanta sign, a Cinzano bottle high in the air—then leave the mortar, too. Our impresario steps out on stage in front of a camera, and I give him the first voice of the burp gun; he and his camera dissolve, film cascading out into a strange and shiny black flower among the ruins. In a hurry, I move out again, calculating my minutes. The local police force—seven white cheerful uniforms, three pistols, four whistles strong—should be arriving in the next five minutes, so I dash toward my screaming crowd once more. Two grenades: they turn like wild horses, stampeding over each other, some of them diving off into the canal where the boats for the hotel are at dock. I burp a few volleys into them, they turn again. With my .45 in hand and the burp gun strung on my shoulder, I start my last run. A Spanish kid with his spearfishing gun advances on me and with my .45 I amputate his right leg. Spare the brave in heart. Reaching my motorbike with one twilight hour left and work to do, I start up the main road toward the village, cut across a field, join another smaller country road, and hurry toward the charges I've planted. By this time the *Guardia Civil* scurries around, each man inside the armory searching for his rifle, shouting orders at the next man; the captain talks to the police commissioner on the telephone. Great confusion: they speculate on how many men attacked the beach and port and whether or not this is a communist or loyalist uprising. Meanwhile, I set the fuse on the armory, pausing there at the rear of the building, my motorbike leaning against the white stucco wall. An old man passes on his mule-drawn cart, nodding at me and smiling. Then I move on, two blocks away to the school—which is empty, naturally, but which will occupy the citizens when it, too, goes up. Here I drop the motorbike—some crafty policeman probably spotted me on it as I headed away from the beach—and in an MG which I recently confiscated in Alicante I start driving back to my carnage. Keeping my grenades, the burp gun, and my .45 I shuck off the recognizable fatigues that I wore during the beach extravaganza. As I drive slowly along, the concussion of my plastic explosives thuds throughout the valley and mushrooms of gray smoke dot the village. At the port everyone still runs amok. Mothers are crying out names, and one of my enemies, a white-frocked policeman with a silver whistle, directs traffic from his usual position beside the fountain in the square. Coasting through the congestion, I honk. Spaniards and tourists move courteously aside. I muse about the town, my Javea: the village up there on the hill was built first away from the sea so that pirates would be discouraged from attacking. Later, in our century when such precaution wasn't necessary, the town grew down toward the harbor. Incredible. At the port, I pull back the rayon coverlet on my waiting cabin cruiser. All is ready: food, the radio and radar set, enough armament to take on anything at sea. I work leisurely, starting the engines, as off in the distance columns of smoke rise up evenly from the village. Four or five shots ring out and one wonders what they're firing at or who is left to shoot? For a moment, then, my dreams overtake me and I'm somewhere else; voices of hundreds rise off a plain, the cry of a long charge, and I'm there, yet not. Revving up, I cast off and smoothly set forth into the canal. A final gesture now: I deposit my last grenades in the docked cruisers as I pass. One goes up in a ball of pleasant fire, then another, another, and I roar into the bay without one parting shot to protest my exit. From the hillside, secure, Val—and you—can see my departure. Everything goes as planned, and I am adream; names flutter in my thoughts, many names of comrades and victims, and I see a castle on a distant promontory flying a single black flag, the body of a friend—dressed as a legionnaire—swollen in the desert, a smiling Asian boy armed only with a sharp stick.

All this will happen.

Africa, gleaming under starlight now, awaits us. In Cairo later, at the Ding Dong Bazaar, Val will join me and we'll have a drink at a sidewalk table, hold hands, and talk about you and others. I'll eventually be at work again inching by a man as he sleeps on his rifle at an outpost, scouting a jungle camp, sighting an enemy in my scope, instructing the innocents.

On Location

On the raging floodtide of the mighty Congo River he arranges canoes: this one for the camera crew, one for the second unit director, another for the hero—an overpaid leading actor—and this one for the savages in pursuit. The shot and setup are discussed. There are references to Joseph Conrad. Everyone agrees this will be a terrific sequence: the rapids, arrows and spears, gunfire, the set of the hero's jaw. A Panavision camera is secured in the stern of the canoe. Instructions come through the megaphone.

The sun breaks out of the clouds, everything is ready, roll it!

No one understands that the great Congo's rapids flow from this point for one hundred miles, a torrent which sweeps everything before it: primeval trees and ferns, all the creatures who wander too close to its banks, all life and decay in its reach.

Neither the crew, the second unit director, nor the overpaid actor are ever seen again.

The technical adviser cables his answering service at the Norfolk Hotel, Nairobi, indicating his availability for another production.

When movies are made in Africa—animal documentaries, Arab epics, low-budget jungle specials—he is paid top dollar.

—

A thorn *boma* is constructed according to the technical adviser's instructions.

Inside that thatched enclosure a camera is made ready. Outside, a helpless gazelle is tied to the thatch, so when a leopard comes to kill and eat the murderous skills can be recorded in bloody close-ups. A fine plan. Everybody congratulates everybody else—which is what movie people do—and the night of anxious waiting begins.

The director of this movie is a serious young Californian. He believes he can capture the essence of Africa. He wears a Colpro safari suit exactly like the tanned, distinguished-looking technical adviser.

The director also wants, if possible, to get this flick in the can and get down to Mombasa for some surfing in those renowned and wonderful breakers rolling in from the Indian Ocean.

The young director settles down for the night inside the *boma* with his cameraman. Around midnight a leopard arrives and kills the poor gazelle with a single blow.

"Did you hear something?" the young director whispers sleepily, but the cameraman, who is wide awake, can't speak.

The leopard begins to gnaw at the thatch of the *boma*. Twigs crack, green limbs squeal in the darkness, thorns snap as the leopard begins to eat its way inside toward the men.

Because his cameraman is paralyzed with fear, the young director begins to record this awful phenomenon. Yellow eyes gleam, teeth flash, and the hideous rosettes of the leopard's skin move into view.

The young director peers through the lens viewer, the leopard appears with a snarling sigh of breath, the cameraman passes out.

All the *watu*—the production boys—yell at the leopard from their hiding places, but the creature seems determined. The technical adviser searches in vain through his Gucci safari luggage for a firearm.

Keeping the camera between himself and the beast, the young director gets a great shot: the leopard clamps its jaws on the unconscious cameraman and begins to drag him back through the hole in the *boma*. Since the cameraman doesn't really fit the narrow opening this process is slow and messy, but every nuance is captured on film.

For more than an hour after the marauding leopard has gone, everyone waits silently in the darkness.

"Cut!" the young director finally calls out.

In the course of his career the technical adviser has witnessed many changes. Some years ago he watched naked natives on the streets of Nairobi eating locusts at little fires banked up from the stones from the curbsides, but now Kimathi Street is aflame with neon. Malaria, he recalls, claimed a good friend. A rhino's curiously accurate charge took another. Wives, lovers, clients, cronies all moved or passed on. Few originals are left—and nature has spared some, like himself, who aren't especially talented at survival.

The technical adviser sits in the Thorn Tree Café considering such mysteries.

Before he got on with the movie people he had been reduced to running one-day safaris out to the local game reserves. Retired schoolteachers and hippie campers always wanted to view that rag-tag zoo.

He remembers all this and wonders if a new start will ever come again, if some producer might discover him, if someday, maybe, he might have his own TV series.

Beyond the café—he's the last patron of the night—and beyond the far reaches of such speculation the capricious darkness sings to itself.

A rickety Convair flies him into the International Airport near Moshi, where he meets the starlet Andrea.

That afternoon they shoot a sequence with Kilimanjaro as a backdrop, but clouds obscure the peak so they retire for an early cocktail hour.

When Andrea talks she cups her sizable breasts with her palms and makes lisping noises. Her basic theme is that Africa is a wild setting, everyone should go naked, animal instincts should prevail.

That night the technical adviser goes dutifully to her room, where she has adorned herself with Masai war paint, a Halston nightie, and a pint of Revlon scent.

Technically, the adviser's performance is satisfactory, but the next day a helicopter is chartered to fly the starlet to safety.

She has broken out with boils and jungle rot and the whole sequence is canceled.

—

The most famous director of African spectaculars confers with the technical adviser in the South Sudan. Together, they devise a shot. Worried that their elephant might go bonkers and trample the expensive equipment, they place a camera inside a zebra-striped VW that follows the beast. This results in what the famous director describes as "low-angle rear-end compositions."

"Absolutely original," the technical adviser admits.

The elephant is an old cow named Princess who was years ago in a Jeff Chandler movie.

Walkie-talkies keep the director and the zebra-striped unit in touch. "Now zoom it!" he barks into his walkie-talkie. "Pan left! Stay in close! Dolly right! Zoom in!" The famous director knows all the terms.

But Princess the Elephant sits down on the VW, crushing it.

Everyone goes into Juba, the only real town for several thousand miles of desert and scrub. Efforts to find a blowtorch fail.

"Did you get the shot?" the famous director keeps asking the men trapped inside. "Was the take okay?"

The men groan inside the twisted metal. Meanwhile, they receive straws—carefully fitted through tiny spaces—through which they are fed quantities of chicken soup and beer.

—

On location in Zanzibar.

The island is an exotic, perfect setting for an action-and-intrigue thriller. Twenty stuntmen are on hand to perform the greatest dockside brawl in the history of cinema.

The Tanzanian government, left-wing, but helpful in such traditional capitalist enterprises, provides free Red Chinese rice wine, which the technical adviser distributes to the crew and players.

There follows widespread and profound diarrhea.

—

The world's finest actor joins the crew of a new production in Cairo. Everything is ready to roll, but written into the contract of the actor is a clause that allows him two weeks in the Valley of the Kings so he can meditate. His melancholy is well documented, going back to his Shakespearean days before he turned to chronic marriage and constant infidelity as a means of dealing with life.

The technical adviser admires the fine actor more than any

mortal, so gives him a pet—a tame civet cat—as a gesture of sympathetic comfort.

"You'll make another comeback," the technical adviser assures him like a loyal fan. "I know you will."

The animal, though, is infected with some obscure and morbid disease. The actor's skin turns yellow, his old melancholy grows into extreme nervousness, then depression, then hysteria. He shuts himself up in his suite at the Nile Hilton, the great sphinx waiting out there in the moonlight, and cries all night long.

—

The technical adviser sits alone in a tent outside the great Hausa city of Kano at the edge of the Sahara. He fondles that automatic firearm which finally turned up in his luggage. A handkerchief covers his mouth as he tries to breathe, but a fine dust blows off the desert covering everything and blurring the air and his senses. In the screaming wind all the cameras, booms, and sound consoles have lost their shape and reality.

To the south the Nigerian jungle offers its maze of river systems; waterways become swamps and deltas of crisscrossed streams, men and animals blend, and millions of insects send up a wild descant and form swirling clouds of noise. Then, further on, the raw savannas: unending grasslands, distant hills changing their shapes, valleys of bone and time where mirage tricks the eye. The sandy wind blows over all this, too, covering every trail and trace.

The technical adviser ponders this, but knows that out there—and in his own loose wiring—there are those clumsy, hideous, accidental rhythms. Sitting there holding the pistol, he tries to gather his thoughts. Suddenly, though, the firearm discharges.

The safety was off.

There is a small, silly hole in the top of his tent as the wind howls on.

Sun City

As a singer Denna Wilson was pretty rather than talented. She had done only a few gigs: one at her college, another at a place called the Afterthought in Little Rock, then a benefit in New Orleans where she met an agent who offered her a ticket to South Africa. She worried about the politics there, but took the ticket and went.

Sun City is a small oasis out in some scrubby desert beyond Pretoria. Every hour busloads of tourists arrive to gamble at the government casino, but in a year's time not many real highrollers come around. There are two hotels, both similar, with lots of stained glass and oversize swimming pools. The tone of the place, which advertises itself as the Las Vegas of Africa, is one of strained good times. The stand-up comics, head waiters, chorus girls, and shills are all insistent: everyone should smile and do it now. The mainliners at the floorshows are usually Chinese acrobats, actors with failed careers, or young kids like Denna just starting out.

Her renditions were standard, never awful, and yet at times she and the skinny black horn player in the backup trio achieved some intimate sounds. Toppy was in love with his lead singer. He had a way of showing it onstage, leaning his trumpet against her bare shoulder and aiming those muted notes right at her as she got her breath for a few bars, smiled at the audience, and bit her lower lip in her most seductive manner.

Offstage, she paid him little attention—or at least until she heard that he had spent the previous year in jail for some minor offense. When she learned from the other musicians that he had been tortured while in detention, a strange new interest rose up in her. She asked him to stop backstage for a sandwich one evening after their show, and after that little meal together Toppy started turning up at the pool where she sunbathed every day.

"You are the most beautiful thing," he blurted out one day, admiring the stretch of her brown legs on the white towel.

"Toppy, you're sweet. But aren't you hot out here? Why don't you take off your shirt?"

"No, I'm fine, I am."

"Tell me. And this is embarrassing to ask, but, well, do black people get sunburned?"

"Oh, this is not a matter of sunburn," he said. "It's my scars. They don't look so good out here in public."

"Scars you got in prison?"

"Sorry, yes. I'm afraid they put their mark on me."

"Oh, Toppy, god."

"I'll show you sometime," he said, and they exchanged the sad smiles that are so well understood in this part of the world.

She touched his hand, a frown creasing her face. "But about my question," she went on. "If you don't mind."

"Black skin?" he asked, taking no offense and laughing. "Oh, sure, it's sensitive. We get burned by the sun, too."

He gazed at Denna as if she were a vision of the new world, a continent of dreams: the naked peninsulas, the slopes, the islands of desire.

But the man who would become Denna's lover was Becker, a reporter for the big American newsmagazine in Johannesburg who came up to Sun City in a taxi with his two buddies one weekend. They all got drunk, including the taxi driver, who miscounted his passengers and returned to JoBurg without Becker, leaving him in the hotel suite half clothed and reeking.

In his morning haze, Becker decided to summon Denna. He had forgotten almost everything about the night before, but he remembered her blonde hair, so he sent her his impressive business card: the name of the magazine in large engraved lettering with the scribbled message that he hoped to write a short notice about her career.

Denna was more ambitious than apprehensive, so on her way to the pool that day she dropped by his suite. When Becker opened the door, he found her dressed in an open caftan with a black bikini underneath. She saw, in turn, a disheveled man with a mean, intelligent look in his eyes—not at all like any of the boys she had known in Arkansas.

They stood on the balcony overlooking the tennis courts as he told her he needed to get to know her better, how she deserved more than the short notice his editor had originally planned for her, and how she should have a full interview. As they sipped their drinks, he put an arm through the open caftan and around her waist.

"What's going on here?" he asked with all the assurance of a man who knew exactly.

Denna started going down to Johannesburg after her shows to be with Becker. They often slept late in his apartment, then had lunch in Melville or Hillbrow, walking through the boutiques or bookshops or going to movie matinees. They began to talk about what they wanted for themselves. She wanted to be more serious, she said, and not just a shallow showbiz type. He wanted to be a great reporter who won prizes, and at the moment, he confided, that meant writing a story that would get him expelled from the country.

"The government won't let us write about the unrest. No real facts or figures. None of the cruelty and none of the truth. So we defy them—and that's all right, but I want to cut deeper. I really want to make them bleed."

They sat at the tables of sidewalk cafés and she held his arm tightly when he talked like this.

"You're wonderful. I've never met anyone like you," she said, and in truth she hadn't. He was forty years old with hard views about life, especially about women. Two weeks after their affair started, he was finding ways to avoid that long drive up to Sun City, saying he was busy with deadlines. She rented cars and came to him. Love was a tough assignment for Becker, and he knew that he preferred to live it headline by headline rather than in depth.

The affair might have soon ended, but Denna and the trio got a contract in the jazz club of the Athos Hotel right there in Johannesburg, so the commuting ended. She also told Becker something that very much interested him: Toppy's descriptions of how, even in detention, black prisoners got worse treatment and poorer food than whites.

"That sounds like my story," Becker said. "I wonder if you could give me a little help with it?"

The invitation appealed to Denna in lots of ways, so she quickly agreed. She hoped to get closer to the real world, she told him: a lot closer than just standing in a smoky spotlight singing "My Funny Valentine."

The next night during the break she stopped Toppy backstage, holding his hand and surrounding him with her perfume.

"I talked to this friend of mine about what happened to you in prison," she said.

"Your reporter boyfriend?"

"Yes, and I want you to tell him your stories. He wants to fight apartheid, Toppy, he really does, he hates it. And he's got this powerful magazine behind him. This way, we can all get into the fight."

"I got me enough fighting," Toppy said, giving her more of a smirk than he intended. "Look, I got stopped by this policeman when I was walking home around midnight after a gig. I explained I was a musician. But he put his dog on me anyway. When I kicked the dog off, that got me five months in detention even before my trial came up. At the trial I was fined for breaking curfew and resisting arrest. When I paid my fine, they waited another two months before they let me out."

"I know it was awful, god, I do, Toppy," she said, squeezing his fingers. The pressure of her hand on his made him hear a soft inner wail of music.

After this, Toppy thought of Denna night and day, watching her leave the club after their shows, counting the times she was with her reporter, asking around, suffering every minute. He thought, no, there's no damn hope, I'm scrawny, I'm black and miserable looking, and why would she ever consider me? He began to hate all the perverse attention he gave himself.

"I'll talk to him," Toppy agreed. "But he can't use my name, so make that clear." He consented to this much, he knew, just to be near her.

The three of them met for late supper.

"I think I might manage to get into one of the prisons," Becker told them. "If so, I'd like to contrast what the government says is going on inside with the real facts. But I do need you in this, Toppy, and I need you to be very specific."

The supper lasted only an hour, then Toppy didn't see either Denna or the reporter for several days. When he got time off, he visited the Mamelodi Township where his mother lived in a flat above a small grocery store she had owned for years. His old boyhood room was still there and intact: yellowed sheet music and a scuffed football. Years ago he had wanted a bicycle, but his mother took an old trumpet in trade for somebody's overdue grocery bill and he learned to play it. By age fourteen he had become a horn player and nothing else. He wanted to be another Louis Armstrong, an ambassador of jazz in a wonderful crossover world where everyone blent in the same rhythms. He wanted to travel to New York, to buy a car for his mother, to marry white. Curious wishes: an old grocery-store dreamworld where sex, status, freedom, and the blues got all mixed up.

When Becker went on assignment in Cape Town, a buddy of his, one of those who had accompanied him on that drunken weekend with the taxi driver, a photographer, managed to take the first actual photos in Soweto of a necklacing: an informer being killed by a mob who draped the victim with burning tires. The photo made the front pages in the States and the photographer became famous. Becker felt nothing except raw envy.

"I'm getting permission to visit the big state prison near Paarl," Becker told Denna by phone. "So talk to your horn player and start getting his stories for me. I intend to use everything of his."

"Do I take notes?" she asked.

"Sure, notes. And get the grisly stuff. Doesn't matter if everything happened to him personally or not. Stories he knows or heard about in prison. And we want to put this story together fast."

"I love you and want to see you," she put in.

"Love you, too. And, again, what's this guy's name? I've got so much here that I can't remember."

"Toppy. And my name's Denna."

"Denna, hey, that's right. I'd forgotten everything except the curve of your butt."

She laughed and wanted to talk on the phone for hours, but he had to go.

That evening she invited Toppy over to her hotel suite. While she opened a bottle of beer for him, he strolled around touching the furniture and pillows in the room. He could also see into her bedroom beyond: an open closet door, her caftan spread on a chair, and the golden coverlet of the bed itself.

He showed her his fingers.

"They put these in a desk drawer on the night they arrested me," he explained. "A policeman leaned against the drawer and it hurt, but not so bad that I couldn't stand it. Besides, it was my left hand and I kept thinking, all right, I press the keys of my horn with my right hand, no problem. Then the policeman stepped back and I thought he was going to walk away, but he turned and kicked the drawer and broke these fingers right here."

"Oh, Toppy, no," she said, and she wrote all this down in a little yellow tablet.

He took off his shirt.

"They put a belt of barbed wire around me," he went on. "Here, touch the holes."

She did, then recoiled to make more notes.

"I decided to keep still, so the belt would make only these single holes where the barbs went in. I tried to think that way when they questioned me. I was always telling myself how much torture I could take. I talked to myself like crazy."

"Did they want you to confess something?"

"They wanted me to be a communist or a pervert or anything. They just picked on me. I asked the other prisoners why the wardens paid me so much attention, but nobody knew."

He took off his pants. His legs were two thin pipes extending from his blue boxer shorts to his oversize shoes and socks.

"They mostly worked on my legs," he told her. "Maybe because I'm so skinny they could get right to the bone."

"What about the white prisoners?" Denna remembered to ask, curling herself into a defensive ball on the couch and not wanting to look at Toppy's gnarled legs.

"Sometimes the white prisoners ate curry with rice, but we always got mealie. I had bread nine times in six months and I got soup maybe a dozen times, but mostly mealie. When they interrogated white prisoners they sometimes beat them, but they saved their specialties for us."

His legs were ribboned with welts and scars and looked as if they had somehow been turned inside out.

"They worked on this leg with a broken bottle," he said. "And on this one with a cigarette lighter. I didn't see how they did it, but I could smell the flesh burning and I couldn't hear anything except my own loud cries."

"Bastards," Denna said.

He knelt beside the couch, taking her hand.

"I want you to touch and feel me," he said, and his tone disturbed her. She attempted to make another note. "I want you to know me as a man."

"I do," she swore, and she gave his hand a squeeze in return.

"I went to the prison doctor because of my legs," he continued. "He said I was lying about what the wardens did. He said that burns like these were caused by a petrol bomb. He said I was probably a communist whose petrol bomb blew up."

He removed his shoes and socks, then stood up to take off his boxer shorts.

"I'm a complete man," he said. "See, they didn't ruin me. Because here I am, all of me. And I want you to touch me and know me."

It was a repulsive seduction speech, yet she didn't know what to do. "Body and soul," he was saying. His genitals were dark and heavy, so she could only give that yellow tablet elaborate attention. He was talking about some grocery store. In spite of herself, she was no longer listening. His first horn. A bicycle. Some place called Mamelodi. "I loved you since the first day I saw you," he went on. "You respond to me, too. We have counterpoint. Onstage and off, you know this!"

She tried to withdraw, but couldn't. "Put your clothes on, Toppy, please," she asked.

He was on the couch with her, still talking. She felt sorry for him and she wasn't at all afraid, but she wanted him off.

"They made us stand in water," he told her. "Our feet in water, then they turned on this electric shock. I don't know how they did it, but we could feel a charge running up our legs and going out the tops of our heads! Smoke came out of this prisoner's ears and you know what we did? We laughed! It was so horrible that we laughed, and then they did it some more."

"Get off me, Toppy, please, I'm asking you," she said.

"You wanted to see. You wanted to hear all this," he reminded her. "Here I am and these are my stories."

He attempted to press his mouth on hers, but in turning away she threw him to the floor. Burying her face in a pillow, she felt her own drool wetting her cheek.

Then he stopped and stood up. Slowly, he fumbled into his clothes. For a moment, feeling like one of his torturers, she watched him.

"Give the man your notes. What the hell do I care?"

"If this story gets written, Toppy, maybe we can make them pay a little for what they did to you," she said. "If we can tell the world what goes on here, don't you see the good in that?" She looked away as he finished dressing, trying to act as if nothing improper had occurred.

"Do what you want, it doesn't matter."

"I care for you, Toppy, god, you know I do."

"Tell my story. And let me say this to you: I'd do it all over again if I could somehow do it for you."

"I don't think you mean that," she said calmly.

"You don't know," he told her, and he picked up his shoes and socks and walked out of the suite barefoot.

Becker wrote his story, and the magazine used it as the cover piece for its next issue with Toppy quoted at length on the horrors of detention. When Becker was flown to New York to receive the personal praise of his publisher, the South African government canceled his visa, so he couldn't return. He was elated. As a reward, he got his choice of assignments and took London. After a few weeks he wrote to Denna, asking her to come visit, but she went to a gig in Atlanta instead.

She sang for a short time at the Hilton and let time pass. Then she phoned Becker at his flat in Hampstead, suggesting that they could get together again. She had never been to London, she said, and maybe he could show her around.

"How's your career?" he asked her.

"Maybe I'm giving it up. I can't get a record contract—although I did meet this lawyer who tried to arrange things for me."

"Well, if you ever get a gig over here, I certainly do want to see you."

"What exactly does that mean?"

"To tell the truth, Denna, I've got this live-in girl right now. It probably won't last forever, but that's it for now."

"I see," she said, and they listened to the heavy static in their phone conversation.

"I suppose you heard about Toppy?" he asked.

"I wrote to him, but he didn't write back," she replied.

"He was arrested again. They kept him in detention for three months, then his trial finally came up."

"Oh, no," she whispered.

"They gave him seven years," Becker said. "I feel like hell about it. Maybe I shouldn't have used his name as a source in that story. He got seven years for making treasonable statements to the detriment of the state."

"Oh, no, oh my god," she told the noisy static. "Oh, Toppy, no, oh please, that's awful, it's horrible, oh no," and she remembered how he rested his trumpet against her bare shoulder, how it happened so long ago now, so far away, and how it happened so badly.

The Future and Forever

Roller Ball Murder

The game, the game: here we go again. All glory to it, all things I am and own because of Roller Ball Murder.

Our team stands in a row, twenty of us in salute as the corporation hymn is played by the band. We view the hardwood oval track which offers us the bumps and rewards of mayhem: fifty yards long, thirty yards across the ends, high banked, and at the top of the walls the cannons which fire those frenzied twenty-pound balls—similar to bowling balls made of ebonite—at velocities more than three hundred miles an hour. The balls career around the track eventually slowing and falling with diminishing centrifugal force, and as they go to ground or strike a player another volley fires. Here we are, our team: ten roller skaters, five motorbike riders, five runners (or clubbers). As the hymn plays, we stand erect and tough; eighty thousand sit watching in the stands and another two billion viewers around the world inspect the set of our jaws on multivision.

The runners, those bastards, slip into their heavy leather gloves and shoulder their lacrosselike paddles—with which they either catch the whizzing balls or bash the rest of us. The bikers ride high on the walls (beware mates, that's where the cannon shots are too hot to handle) and swoop down to help the runners at opportune times. The skaters, those of us with the juice for it, protest: we clog the way, try to keep the runners from passing us and scoring points, and become the fodder in the brawl. So two teams of us, forty in all, go skating and running and biking around the track while the big balls are fired in the same direction as we move—always coming up behind us to scatter and maim us—and the object of the game, fans, as if you didn't know, is for the runners to pass all skaters on the opposing team, field a ball, and pass it to a biker for one point. Those bikers, by the way, may give the runners a lift—in which case those of us on skates have our hands full overturning 175 cc motorbikes.

No rest periods, no substitute players. If you lose a man your team plays short.

Today I turn my best side to the cameras. I'm Jonathan E, none other, and nobody passes me on the track. I'm the core of the Houston team and for the two hours of play—no rules, no penalties once the first cannon fires—I'll level any bastard runner who raises a paddle at me.

We move: immediately there are pileups of bikes, skaters, referees, and runners, all tangled and punching and scrambling when one of the balls zooms around the corner and belts us. I pick up momentum and heave an opposing skater into the infield at center ring; I'm brute speed today, driving, pushing, up on the track dodging a ball, hurtling downward beyond those bastard runners. Two runners do hand-to-hand combat, and one gets his helmet knocked off in a blow that tears away half his face; the victor stands there too long admiring his work and gets wiped out by a biker who swoops down and flattens him. The crowd screams and I know the cameramen have it on an isolated shot and that viewers in Melbourne, Berlin, Rio, and LA are heaving with excitement in their easy chairs.

When an hour is gone I'm still wheeling along, naturally, though we have four team members out with broken parts, one rookie maybe dead, two bikes demolished. The other team, good old London, is worse off.

One of their motorbikes roars out of control, takes a hit from one of the balls, and bursts into flame. Wild cheering.

Cruising up next to their famous Jackie Magee, I time my punch. He turns in my direction, exposes the ugly snarl inside his helmet, and I take him out of action. In that tiniest instant I feel his teeth and bone give way and the crowd screams approval. We have them now, we really have them, we do, and the score ends 7–2.

—

The years pass and the rules alter—always in favor of a greater crowd-pleasing carnage. I've been at this more than fifteen years, amazing, with only broken arms and collarbones to slow me down, and I'm not as spry as ever, but meaner—and no rookie, no matter how much in shape, can learn this slaughter unless he comes out and takes me on in the real thing.

But the rules. I hear of games in Manila, now, or in Barcelona with no time limits, men hashing each other until there are no more runners left, no way of scoring points. That's the coming thing. I hear of Roller Ball Murder played with mixed teams, men and women, wearing tear-away jerseys which add a little tit and vulnerable exposure to the action. Everything will happen. They'll change the rules until we skate on a slick of blood, we all know that.

—

Before this century began, before the Great Asian war, before the corporations replaced nationalism and the corporate police forces supplanted the world's armies, in the last days of American football and the World Cup in Europe, I was a tough young rookie who knew all the rewards of this game. Women: I had them all— even, pity, a good marriage once. I had so much money after my first trophies that I could buy houses and land and lakes beyond the huge cities where only the executive class was allowed. My photo, then, as now, was on the covers of magazines, so that my name and the name of the sport were one, and I was Jonathan E, no other, a survivor and much more in the bloodiest sport.

At the beginning I played for Oil Conglomerates, then those corporations became known as ENERGY; I've always played for the team here in Houston, they've given me everything.

"How're you feeling?" Mr. Bartholemew asks me. He's taking the head of ENERGY, one of the most powerful men in the world, and he talks to me like I'm his son.

"Feeling mean," I answer, so that he smiles.

He tells me they want to do a special on multivision about my career, lots of shots on the side screens showing my greatest plays, and the story of my life, how ENERGY takes in such orphans, gives them work and protection, and makes careers possible.

"Really feel mean, eh?" Mr. Bartholemew asks again, and I answer the same, not telling him all that's inside me because he would possibly misunderstand; not telling him that I'm tired of the long season, that I'm lonely and miss my wife, that I yearn for high, lost, important thoughts, and that maybe, just maybe, I've got a deep rupture in the soul.

—

An old buddy, Jim Cletus, comes by the ranch for the weekend. Mackie, my present girl, takes our dinners out of the freezer and turns the rays on them; not so domestic that Mackie, but she has enormous breasts and a waist smaller than my thigh.

Cletus works as a judge now. At every game there are two referees—clowns, whose job it is to see nothing amiss—and the judge who records the points scored. Cletus is also on the International Rules Committee and tells me they are still considering several changes.

"A penalty for being lapped by your own team, for one thing," he tells us. "A damned simple penalty, too: they'll take off your helmet."

Mackie, bless her bosom, makes an O with her lips.

Cletus, once a runner for Toronto, fills up my oversize furniture and rests his hands on his bad knees.

"What else?" I ask him. "Or can you tell me?"

"Oh, just financial things. More bonuses for superior attacks. Bigger bonuses for being named World All-Star—which ought to be good news for you again. And, yeah, talk of reducing the two-month off-season. The viewers want more."

After dinner Cletus walks around the ranch with me. We trudge up the path of a hillside, and the Texas countryside stretches before us. Pavilions of clouds.

"Did you ever think about death in your playing days?" I ask, knowing I'm a bit too pensive for old Clete.

"Never in the game itself," he answers proudly. "Off the track—yeah, sometimes I never thought about anything else."

We pause and take a good long look at the horizon.

"There's another thing going in the Rules Committee," he finally admits. "They're considering dropping the time limit—at least, god help us, Johnny, the suggestion has come up officially."

I like a place with rolling hills. Another of my houses is near Lyons in France, the hills similar to these although more lush, and

I take my evening strolls there over an ancient battleground. The cities are too much, so large and uninhabitable that one has to have a business passport to enter such immensities as New York.

"Naturally I'm holding out for the time limit," Cletus goes on. "I've played, so I know a man's limits. Sometimes in that committee, Johnny, I feel like I'm the last moral man on earth sitting there and insisting that there should be a few rules."

—

The statistical nuances of Roller Ball Murder entertain the multitudes as much as any other aspect of the game. The greatest number of points scored in a single game: 81. The highest velocity of a ball when actually caught by a runner: 176 mph. Highest number of players put out of action in a single game by a single skater: 13—world's record by yours truly. Most deaths in a single contest: 9—Rome vs. Chicago, December 4, 2012.

The giant lighted boards circling above the track monitor our pace, record each separate fact of the slaughter, and we have millions of fans—strange it always seemed to me—who never look directly at the action, but just study those statistics.

A multivision survey established this.

—

Before going to the stadium in Paris for our evening game I stroll under the archways and along the Seine.

Some of the French fans call to me, waving and talking to my bodyguards as well, so I become oddly conscious of myself, conscious of my size and clothes and the way I walk. A curious moment.

I'm six foot three inches and weigh 255 pounds. My neck is eighteen and a half inches. Fingers like a pianist. I wear my conservative pinstriped jumpsuit and the famous flat Spanish hat. I am thirty-four years old now, and when I grow old, I think, I'll look a lot like the poet Robert Graves.

—

The most powerful men in the world are the executives. They run the major corporations which fix prices, wages, and the general economy, and we all know they're crooked, that they have almost unlimited power and money, but I have considerable power and money myself and I'm still anxious. What can I possibly want, I ask myself, except, possibly, more knowledge?

I consider recent history—which is virtually all anyone remembers—and how the corporate wars ended so that we settled into the Six Majors: ENERGY, TRANSPORT, FOOD, HOUSING, SERVICES, and LUXURY. Sometimes I forget who runs what—for instance, now that the universities are operated by the Majors (and provide the farm system for Roller Ball Murder) which Major runs them? SERVICES or LUXURY? Music is one of our biggest industries, but I can't remember who administers it. Narcotic research is now under FOOD, I know, though it used to be under LUXURY.

Anyway I think I'll ask Mr. Bartholemew about knowledge. He's a man with a big view of the world, with values, with memory. My team flings itself into the void while his team harnesses the sun, taps the sea, finds new alloys, and is clearly just a hell of a lot more serious.

—

The Mexico City game has a new wrinkle: they've changed the shape of the ball on us.

Cletus didn't even warn me—perhaps he couldn't—but here we are playing with a ball not quite round, its center of gravity altered so that it rumbles around the track in irregular patterns.

This particular game is bad enough because the bikers down here are getting wise to me; for years, since my reputation was established, bikers have always tried to take me out of a game early. But early in the game I'm wary and strong and I'll always gladly take on a biker—even since they put shields on the motorbikes so that we can't grab the handlebars. Now, though, these bastards know I'm getting older—still mean, but slowing down, as the sports pages say about me—so they let me bash it out with the skaters and runners for as long as possible before sending the bikers after me. Knock out Jonathan E, they say, and you've beaten Houston; and that's right enough, but they haven't done it yet.

The fans down here, all low-class FOOD workers mostly, boil over as I manage to keep my cool—and the oblong ball, zigzagging around at lurching speeds, hopping two feet off the track at times, knocks out virtually their whole team. Finally some of us catch their last runner/clubber and beat him to a pulp, so that's it: no runners, no points. Those dumb FOOD workers file out of the stadium while we show off and score a few fancy and uncontested points. The score, 37–4. I feel wonderful, like pure brute speed.

—

Mackie is gone—her mouth no longer makes an O around my villa or ranch—and in her place is the new one, Daphne. My Daphne is tall and English and likes photos—always wants to pose for me. Sometimes we get out our boxes of old pictures (mine as a player, mostly, and hers as a model) and look at ourselves and it occurs to me that the photos spread out on the rug are the real us, our public and performing true selves, and the two of us here in the sitting room, Gaelic gray winter outside our window, aren't too real at all.

"Look at the muscles in your back!" Daphne says in amazement as she studies a shot of me at the California beach—and it's as though she never before noticed.

After the photos, I stroll out beyond the garden. The brown waving grass of the fields reminds me of Ella, my only wife, and of her soft long hair, which made a tent over my face when we kissed.

—

I lecture to the ENERGY-sponsored rookie camp and tell them they can't possibly comprehend anything until they're out on the track getting belted.

My talk tonight concerns how to stop a biker who wants to run you down. "You can throw a shoulder right into the shield," I begin. "And that way it's you or him."

The rookies look at me as though I'm crazy.

"Or you can hit the deck, cover yourself, tense up, and let the bastard flip over your body," I go on, counting on my fingers for them and doing my best not to laugh. "Or you can feint, sidestep uphill, and kick him off the track—which takes some practice and timing."

None of them knows what to say. We're sitting in the infield grass, the track lighted, the stands empty, and their faces are filled with stupid awe. "Or if a biker comes at you with good speed and balance," I continue, "then naturally let the bastard by—even if he carries a runner. That runner, remember, has to dismount and field one of the new odd-shaped balls, which isn't easy—and you can usually catch up."

The rookies begin to get a smug look on their faces when a biker bears down on me in the demonstration period.

Brute speed. I jump to one side, dodge the shield, grab the bastard's arm, and separate him from his machine in one movement. The bike skids away. The poor biker's shoulder is out of socket.

"Oh yeah," I say, getting back to my feet. "I forgot about that move."

—

Toward midseason when I see Mr. Bartholemew again he has been deposed as the chief executive at ENERGY. He is still very important but lacks some of the old certainty; his mood is reflective, so that I decide to take this opportunity to talk about what's bothering me.

We lunch in Houston Tower, viewing an expanse of city. A nice beef Wellington and Burgundy. Daphne sits there like a stone, probably imagining that she's in a movie.

"Knowledge, ah, I see," Mr. Bartholemew replies in response to my topic. "What're you interested in, Jonathan? History? The arts?"

"Can I be personal with you?"

This makes him slightly uncomfortable. "Sure, naturally," he answers easily, and although Mr. Bartholemew isn't especially one to inspire confession I decide to blunder along.

"I began in the university" I remind him. "That was—let's see— more than seventeen years ago. In those days we still had books and I read some, quite a few, because I thought I might make an executive."

"Jonathan, believe me, I can guess what you're going to say," Mr. Bartholemew sighs, sipping the Burgundy and glancing at

Daphne. "I'm one of the few with real regrets about what happened to the books. Everything is still on tapes, but it just isn't the same, is it? Nowadays only the computer specialists read the tapes, and we're right back in the Middle Ages when only the monks could read the Latin script."

"Exactly," I answer, letting my beef go cold.

"Would you like me to assign you a specialist?"

"No, that's not exactly it."

"We have the great film libraries: you could get a permit to see anything you want. The Renaissance. Greek philosophers. I saw a nice summary film on the life and thought of Plato once."

"All I know," I say with hesitation, "is Roller Ball Murder."

"You don't want out of the game?" he asks warily.

"No, not at all. It's just that I want—god, Mr. Bartholemew, I don't know how to say it: I want *more*."

He offers a blank look.

"But not things in the world," I add. "More for *me*."

He heaves a great sigh, leans back, and allows the steward to refill his glass. Curiously, I know that he understands; he is a man of sixty, enormously wealthy, powerful in our most powerful executive class, and behind his eyes is the deep, weary, undeniable comprehension of the life he has lived.

"Knowledge," he tells me, "either converts to power or it converts to melancholy. Which would you possibly want, Jonathan? You *have* power. You have status and skill and the whole masculine dream many of us would like to have. And in Roller Ball Murder there's no room for melancholy, is there? In the game the mind exists for the body to make a harmony of havoc, right? Do you want to change that? Do you want the mind to exist for itself alone? I don't think you actually want that, do you?"

"I really don't know," I admit.

"I'll get you some permits, Jonathan. You can see video films, learn something about reading tapes, if you want."

"I don't think I really *have* any power," I say, still groping.

"Oh, come on. What do *you* say about that?" he asks, turning to Daphne.

"He definitely has power," she answers with a wan smile.

Somehow the conversation drifts away from me; Daphne, on cue, like the good spy for the corporation she probably is, begins feeding Mr. Bartholemew lines, and soon, oddly enough, we're discussing my upcoming game with Stockholm.

A hollow space begins to grow inside me, as though fire is eating out a hole. The conversation concerns the end of the season, the All-Star Game, records being set this year, but my disappointment—in what exactly I don't even know—begins to sicken me.

Mr. Bartholemew eventually asks what's wrong.

"The food," I answer. "Usually I have great digestion but maybe not today."

—

In the locker room the dreary late-season pall takes us. We hardly speak among ourselves, now, and like soldiers or gladiators sensing what lies ahead, we move around in these sickening surgical odors of the locker room.

Our last training and instruction this year concern the delivery of deathblows to opposing players; no time now for the tolerant shoving and bumping of yesteryear. I consider that I possess two good weapons: because of my unusually good balance on skates I can often shatter my opponent's knee with a kick; also, I have a good backhand blow to the ribs and heart, if wheeling along side by side with some bastard he raises an arm against me. If the new rules change removes a player's helmet, of course, that's death; as it is right now (there are rumors, rumors every day about what new version of RBM we'll have next) you go for the windpipe, the ribs or heart, the diaphragm, or anyplace you don't break your hand.

Our instructors are a pair of giddy Oriental gentlemen who have all sorts of anatomical solutions for us and show drawings of the human figure with nerve centers painted in pink.

"What you do is this," says Moonpie, in parody of these two. Moonpie is a fine skater in his fourth season and fancies himself an old-fashioned drawling Texan. "What you do is hit 'em on the jawbone and drive it up into their ganglia."

"Their *what?*" I ask, giving Moonpie a grin.

"Their goddamned *ganglia.* Bunch of nerves right here underneath the ear. Drive their jawbones into that mess of nerves and it'll ring their bells sure."

—

Daphne is gone now, too, and in this interim before another companion arrives courtesy of all my friends and employers at EN-ERGY, Ella floats back into my dreams and daylight fantasies.

I was a corporation child, some executive's bastard boy, I always preferred to think, brought up in the Galveston section of the city. A big kid, naturally, athletic and strong—and this, according to my theory, gave me healthy mental genes, too, because I take it now that strong in body is strong in mind: a man with brute speed surely also has the capacity to mull over his life. Anyway, I married at age fifteen while I worked on the docks for Oil Conglomerates. Ella was a secretary, slim with long brown hair, and we managed to get permits to both marry and enter the university together. Her fellowship was in General Electronics—she was clever, give her that—and mine was in Roller Ball Murder. She fed me well that first year, so I put on thirty hard pounds, and at night she soothed my bruises (was she a spy, too, I've sometimes wondered, whose job it was to prime the bull for the charge?) and perhaps it was because she was my first woman ever, eighteen years old, lovely, that I've never properly forgotten.

She left me for an executive, just packed up and went to Europe with him. Six years ago I saw them at a sports banquet where I was presented an award: there they were, smiling and being nice, and I asked them only one question, just one, "You two ever had children?" It gave me odd satisfaction that they had applied for a permit but had been denied.

Ella, love: one does consider: did you beef me up and break my heart in some great design of corporate society?

There I was, whatever, angry and hurt. Beyond repair, I thought at the time. And the hand that stroked Ella soon dropped all the foes of Houston.

I take sad stock of myself in this quiet period before another woman arrives; I'm smart enough, I know that: I had to be to survive. Yet I seem to know nothing—and can feel the hollow spaces in my own heart. Like one of those computer specialists, I have my own brutal technical know-how; I know what today means, what tomorrow likely holds, but maybe it's because the books are gone—Mr. Bartholemew was right, it's a shame they're transformed—that I feel so vacant. If I didn't remember my Ella—this I realize—I wouldn't even *want* to remember because it's love I'm recollecting as well as those old university days.

Recollect, sure: I read quite a few books that year with Ella, and afterward, too, before turning professional in the game. Apart from all the volumes about how to get along in business, I read the history of the kings of England, that pillars of wisdom book by T. E. Lawrence, all the forlorn novels, some Rousseau, a bio of Thomas Jefferson, and other odd bits. On tapes now, all that, whirring away in a cool basement someplace.

—

The rules crumble once more.

At the Tokyo game, we discover that there will be three oblong balls in play at all times.

Some of our most experienced players are afraid to go out on the track. Then, after they're coaxed and threatened and finally consent to join the flow, they fake injury whenever they can and sprawl in the infield like rabbits. As for me, I play with greater abandon than ever and give the crowd its money's worth. The Tokyo skaters are either peering over their shoulders looking for approaching balls when I smash them or, poor devils, they're looking for me when a ball takes them out of action.

One little bastard with a broken back flaps around for a moment like a fish then shudders and dies.

Balls jump at us as though they have brains.

But fate carries me, as I somehow know it will; I'm a force field, a destroyer. I kick a biker into the path of a ball going at least two hundred miles an hour. I swerve around a pileup of bikes and skaters, ride high on the track, zoom down, and find a runner/clubber who panics and misses with a roundhouse swing of his paddle; without much ado, I belt him out of play with the almost certain knowledge—I've felt it before—that he's dead before he hits the infield.

One ball flips out of play soon after being fired from the cannon, jumps the railing, sails high, and plows into the spectators. Beautiful.

I take a hit from a ball, one of the three or four times I've ever been belted. The ball is riding low on the track when it catches me, and I sprawl like a baby. One bastard runner comes after me, but one of our bikers chases him off. Then one of their skaters glides by and takes a shot at me, but I dig him in the groin and discourage him, too.

Down and hurting, I see Moonpie killed. They take off his helmet, working slowly—it's like slow motion and I'm writhing and cursing and unable to help—and open his mouth on the toe of some bastard skater's boot. Then they kick the back of his head and knock out all his teeth—which rattle downhill on the track. Then kick again and stomp: his brains this time. He drawls a last groaning good-bye while the cameras record it.

And later I'm up, pushing along once more, feeling bad, but knowing everyone else feels the same; I have that last surge of energy, the one I always get when I'm going good, and near the closing gun I manage a nice move: grabbing one of their runners with a headlock, I skate him off to limbo, bashing his face with my free fist, picking up speed until he drags behind like a dropped flag, and disposing of him in front of a ball which carries him off in a comic flop. Oh, god, god.

—

Before the All-Star Game, Cletus comes to me with the news I expect: this one will be a no-time-limit extravaganza in New York, every multivision set in the world tuned in. The bikes will be more high-powered, four oblong balls will be in play simultaneously, and the referees will blow the whistle on any sluggish player and remove his helmet as a penalty.

Cletus is apologetic.

"With those rules, no worry," I tell him. "It'll go no more than an hour and we'll all be dead."

We're at the Houston ranch on a Saturday afternoon, riding around in my electrocart viewing the Santa Gertrudis stock. This is probably the ultimate spectacle of my wealth: my own beef cattle in a day when only a few special members of the executive class have any meat to eat with the exception of mass-produced fish. Cletus is so impressed with my cattle that he keeps going on this afternoon and seems so pathetic to me, a judge who doesn't judge, the pawn of a committee, another feeble hulk of an old RBM player.

"You owe me a favor, Clete," I tell him.

"Anything," he answers, not looking me in the eyes.

I turn the cart up a lane beside my rustic rail fence, an archway of oak trees overhead and the early spring bluebonnets and daffodils sending up fragrances from the nearby fields. Far back in my thoughts is the awareness that I can't possibly last and that I'd like to be buried out here—burial is seldom allowed anymore, everyone just incinerated and scattered—to become the mulch of flowers.

"I want you to bring Ella to me," I tell him. "After all these years, yeah: that's what I want. You arrange it and don't give me any excuses, okay?"

—

We meet at this villa near Lyons in early June, only a week before the All-Star Game in New York, and I think she immediately reads something in my eyes which helps her to love me again. Of course I love her: I realize, seeing her, that I have only a vague recollection of being alive at all, and that was a long time ago, in another century of the heart when I had no identity except my name, when I was a simple dockworker, before I ever saw all the world's places or moved in the rumbling nightmares of Roller Ball Murder.

She kisses my fingers. "Oh," she says softly, and her face is filled with true wonder, "what's happened to you, Johnny?"

A few soft days. When our bodies aren't entwined in lovemaking, we try to remember and tell each other everything: the way we used to hold hands, how we fretted about receiving a marriage permit, how the books looked on our shelves in the old apartment in River Oaks. We strain, at times, trying to recollect the impossible; it's true that history is really gone, that we have no families or touchstones, that our short personal lives alone judge us, and I want to hear about her husband, the places they've lived, the furniture in her house, anything. I tell her, in turn, about all the women, about Mr. Bartholemew and Jim Cletus, about the ranch in the hills outside Houston.

Come to me, Ella. If I can remember us, I can recollect meaning and time.

It would be nice, I think, once, to imagine that she was taken away from me by some malevolent force in this awful age, but I know the truth of that: she went away, simply, because I wasn't enough back then, because those were the days before I yearned for anything, when I was beginning to live to play the game. But no matter. For a few days she sits on my bed and I touch her skin like a blind man groping back over the years.

On our last morning together she comes out in her traveling suit with her hair pulled up underneath a fur cap. The softness has faded from her voice and she smiles with efficiency, as if she has just come back to the practical world; I recall, briefly, this scene played out a thousand years ago when she explained that she was going away with her executive.

She plays like a biker, I decide; she rides up there high above the turmoil, decides when to swoop down, and makes a clean kill.

"Good-bye, Ella," I say, and she turns her head slightly away from my kiss so that I touch her fur cap with my lips.

"I'm glad I came," she says politely. "Good luck, Johnny."

—

New York is frenzied with what is about to happen.

The crowds throng into Energy Plaza, swarm the ticket offices at the stadium, and wherever I go people are reaching for my hands, pushing my bodyguards away, trying to touch my sleeve as though I'm some ancient religious figure, a seer or prophet.

Before the game begins I stand with my team as the corporation hymns are played. I'm brute speed today, I tell myself, trying to rev myself up; yet, adream in my thoughts, I'm a bit unconvinced.

A chorus of voices joins the band now as the music swells.

The game, the game, all glory to it, the music rings, and I can feel my lips move with the words, singing.

The Arsons of Desire

One begins in familiar ways: a civil service test, a training school, and later the excitement of one's first fires and the fancy of wearing the uniform and helmet. I began this way, becoming a fireman, setting out to serve the citizens while serving myself some needed solitude, but lately I'm ambushed with dreams and visions. This sort: I'm in the company of a beautiful girl in a room filling with smoke. We exchange a love glance, her fingers brush my face, we start to embrace, then, disconcerted by the smoke, we look for a way out. She takes my hand as I lead her around the walls searching for a door; she wears a translucent gown, flowing like flame itself, and her dark hair spills over her shoulders. Then, the room stifling, we grope and panic; somewhere in the next few moments, terrified, our hands lose grip, and when I finally kick through the thin wall with my heavy rubber boot she fails to escape with me and I lose her.

Visions of a high blaze now and lovely lost women: I believe, lately, that I'm carrying disaster with me; my mind is catching fire.

This is the station house. In the old days bachelor firemen usually lived at the stations, but now I'm one of the few in all Chicago who continue. Others here have families, work in three shifts— twenty-four hours on, forty-eight off—but I stay near the alarms, I must, and attend every call. My bed in the dorm upstairs is in a homey corner: books, clock radio, my boots, and britches stacked and ready. Downstairs are the big Seagrave trucks: the two quads, the ladder truck, the new snorkel, the new pump truck with its shiny deck gun, and the Cadillac rescue unit. Over here is the classroom, the kitchen, and the rec hall with Ping-Pong and television. The office and alarm systems are near the front door, and in the rear are repair shops, storage rooms, and the garage where we keep the boats and drags. Sometimes our station is involved in dragging Lake Michigan or the river, but I've traded for other duties—I do considerable cleaning and mopping up around here—so that I can stay near the alarms. A dragging operation isn't a fire, after all; one gets a sore back, a head cold or sunburn, a soggy corpse, at best, and never peers into those bright and mystic flames.

Here we go: a two-alarm, the Lake Shore station and us.

Hanging on to number-one truck with Captain Max, I curse the traffic as we whip into Lincoln Avenue. The siren begins to rev me up; I pull my suspenders tight, fasten my chin strap, and wonder who awaits me. In recent weeks it has been old Aunt Betty, the old family barber, a former high-school buddy of mine from up in Skokie, a girl I used to try to pick up in a bar on Gross Point Road. Strange, all strange: I can hardly wait.

Max is something: not a particularly good captain by the book and usually in trouble with the fire marshals because he's a real buster. We hit a building and he's off the truck, yelling, coupling hoses, and going in. I stomp in behind him, naturally, pulling the hose, my ax waving like his. But he's not one to stay outside and direct the proceedings, not our Max; he's a rowdy, likes his work and leads the way. I say he's a lovely old bastard. He keeps us trained and sharp and any man on our team can handle any task, so he never has to stand around with the crowd getting us organized and looking official. The two of us usually bust right in and go to work, then, each careful to watch out for the other. He's sixty years old, fearless, and thinks I ought to be the next captain—though, of course, that's politics, as even he knows, and some dreamer like me who wants to live right in the fire station doesn't have much chance.

This alarm is another dilly: an empty apartment on the second floor of a new four-floor complex has smoldered for days with its occupants gone. It has finally erupted and the entire floor crawls with flame. We attack its fringes with water as I begin to bust doors looking for occupants. My eyes are wide with excitement because I expect anyone behind the very next door: some relative, a clerk from the grocery store where I trade, perhaps a forgotten acquaintance. Everyone I ever knew is burning up, I tell you, and my throat is tight with every new room and corridor. "Here! Over here Coker baby!" the captain booms, and we follow the smoke looking for its source. Fire is a tricky viper: it runs in the walls, gets in the conduits and vents, strikes at unexpected moments. I charge through a room, send an end table flying, jerk a closet open. Nothing. The snorkel passes the window, Charlie Wickers peering inside like an idiot. He never knows where he's going. We cross the hall and quickly batter through another door; these new apartment houses are like kindling, but the doors are easy to bust. As Max turns the hose on the ceiling of the hallway, I hear a cry. The walls all around us are hot and scorched, but we press on; somewhere behind all this smoke is a fist of fire we have to find— and probably a tenant or two, for I think I hear the cry again.

Rafferty arrives with another hose and coupling, so that Max directs him to retrace our steps and gather what we've trailed behind us. This keeps him busy and out of our way. We run through another series of rooms, smashing windows as we go, for the smoke thickens. A dead pussycat, choked and gone. Water cascades helplessly against the outside of the building now, so that Max turns to me with a smirk, once, and says, "Jesus, they need to get in here where the fun is, right?" At about this point we meet a wall of heat: a kitchen, the source. Max lays down a steady stream from the hose while I quickly circle back into the hall to look for another entrance.

An old man wanders the hallway. Coughing and gagging, he grabs my arms as I hold him, and we recognize each other. In the smoke he manages to speak my name, then gasps, "My daughter in there!" And I point him on his way, assuring him there's no trouble in that direction, while I go in further search. My mother's former pastor, I knew him well: Rooker, his name was. The steepled Congregational church in Evanston. But now a variation of the dream: she is a lanky, naked girl, screaming her head off, and I can't be sure if its because of the fire or because her closet filled with clothes writhes with flames; I try to wrestle her to the window, but she fights me as if I wanted to throw her out. Reasoning with her, I see her try to cover her parts; she runs here, there, like a dazed antelope. "Quit it, please," I address her, trying to sound logical. "Just stop this and follow me out!" We wrestle again, fall, and her eyes open with even wider terror at my minor disfig-urement. "Look, miss," I plead, "never mind your state. Take a blanket off the bed. Here, take it." But she claws at me, tussles free, and locks herself inside the bathroom before I can catch her again. By now the wallpaper is a sagging black curl. She screams and screams from behind that door and I pause, ax ready, and call to her. "Don't resist me, lady, come on! Wrap yourself in a towel because we don't have much time!" Her scream, then, alters into a baleful moan. Too late I dislodge the door with a single stroke. The room has caved in, and she is gone to the lapping heat; the in-tensity turns me away, so that I find myself in the hallway, Max's voice nearby. He has discovered the old pastor, who took a wrong turn immediately after leaving me, burned into a crisp pudding. Left for a moment to hold the hose and direct the stream of water, I recall the brief sensation of that girl's breasts on me; my thoughts flare and my whole life dances in the smoke and surging orange before me.

—

At the station Max and I take each other's Polaroid snapshot. He poses beside one of the pump trucks, the words *American LaFrance* beside his jutting jaw. I pose in his office beneath the only wall decoration in the station, an engraving of one of the old rigs with six plump firehorses, the good side of my face turned to-ward the camera.

Max knows a bit of what goes on with me, but doesn't ask much.

"You have to keep your pleasure to yourself in this business," he tells me solemnly, so I suspect he has a glimmer of what is hap-pening. And of course he knows my bad luck these last weeks, all those near rescues and disasters, but he considers that I'm one of the bravest firemen he has ever known, someone who will match him step by step into the center of a blaze, and figures that all the victims were doomed anyway.

Perhaps he feels something more: that all the unusual number and kinds of alarms in our district have to do with me. But he keeps this to himself, for he's a man who likes to do battle.

We've been close, a team, telling each other our lives. He at-tended DePaul University long ago on a voice scholarship; now he is married, has a grown son, and doesn't go home when he can stay on call. He'll get up from the breakfast table or out of bed late at night and rush to help us, and he says it's for the extra money, but I know him too well. In his heart is nothing except a fire-fighter. Meanwhile, I share a few vignettes of myself with him. Not a very happy childhood, but okay now. This birthmark on my left side covers my ear, my cheek, my neck, and encircles my eye, and it looks something like a burn—even the skin wrinkles a bit on that side like an ill-fitting mask—and my dumb mother said this was God's kiss. My less theological schoolmates turned their eyes away, pretty girls of my dreams like popular Alice Durning of the ninth grade fretted when I came near, and even now those who give me a few necessary services—waitresses, the butcher—learn to do so without looking at me. Otherwise, until lately, I'm terribly normal; I like steak and potatoes, the Cubs, movies, and girlie magazines. Last year I read mostly the *Tribune* and *Newsweek*. I weigh 180 and have a few dental problems.

This is one of my sleepless nights again, so I go down to the re-frigerator to cut a slice of my new cheddar and there is Max watching the late show. Glad to see him, I sit down and catch Brian Donlevy and Preston Foster in World War II. Then we talk. He's sleeping at the station because his wife's sister has arrived to occupy his bedroom. We discuss the woes of marriage, Leo Durocher, Ron Santo, slumps, bad seasons, hard luck, and getting tickets from mean cops in about that order. Max, pointing a fin-ger, says, "Policemen need guys to break the goddamn laws, you see, just like teachers need stupid students, doctors need the sick and dying, and soldiers need victims. It's all the same."

We ponder this together and talk on.

"You know this Rooker girl?" he finally asks me.

"Knew her father," I sigh. "Or rather my mother knew him. Maybe I knew the daughter, too, a long time ago when she was just a little girl."

Max doesn't press further. He is in the presence of mystery, knows it, and prefers to let well enough alone; also, he's thinking that if the alarms go tonight he'll get in on the action.

"These girls," I muse. "We're having more and more contact,

but I still don't get them out. I got scratches wrestling with this last one."

"I know, kid, I know," he comforts me. "Take it easy on yourself."

A routine day passes: two grass fires, a smoking trash dump, an auto blaze, a call for us to come wash gasoline off an intersection after an accident. Nervous, I stay at the station and don't attend these minor calls. I varnish a ladder, check couplings, show two kids around, and work a crossword puzzle. Max appears for regular duty in the afternoon and brings me a milk shake.

On the following noon we have another big one: the furnace at Parkside High School explodes and the old firetrap is a sudden maze of smoke and flame. We're the first there, Max leading the way, but the noise of every unit in The Loop is just behind us. I'm pulling on my jacket, barking at Rafferty to set up the rescue unit because the lawn is already strewn with kids crying with burns; some old biddy in a charred dress wanders among us giving off a descant of hysteria, and Wickers, the idiot, tries to ask directions of her; Max and I decide to hit the basement, where the flames are a steady roar. As we head down the concrete stairs with the hose, students trapped on the second floor call for us. "Hold on," Max promises. "Others coming!" And ladders and nets are unloaded from arriving engines as we head down toward the boiler room.

No secret where the blaze is centered this time: the boiler-room heat is impossible. Max stations himself outside the door and, shielded by a thin hot wall, aims the hose around the corner at the flames; I try to assist, but I'm useless. "Check that far door!" he yells, so I dash by the flaming door and follow a narrow hall to a door, mostly wired glass, which I demolish. Inside, protected from the boiler room by a thick fire wall, I find no trouble, so decide to circle behind the fire. Dangerous—because Max is occupied and out of sight—but there may be someone trapped there. Anyway, I figure that the fire has spiraled upward through the hollowed-out ceiling and except for the furnace area the basement is possibly safe, so I bust another bolted door.

I run headlong into the locker room of the girl's gymnasium.

Madhouse: twenty or thirty girls running amok shrieking, flitting near the flames on the side of the room where I enter, then retreating like moths. The broken door lets in a swish of oxygen and the flames suck toward it, cutting off the way I've come in as a possible exit, but I have my ax and don't panic. I go to the opposite wall, scramble over benches, climb a locker, and smash two paneled windows. "Here! Girls!" I shout, but all movement blurs into a strange slow motion now, the room igniting in a soft and frenzied dance; the girl in white panties is Midge Prinz, I remember her well, and she glides near and brushes me. Seconds, mere seconds, I tell myself, and we're all lost, but the reel of my senses rattles and slows, everything awhirl, and here are my teachers and all the darlings of my twelfth school year—ones who refused me at the prom, others who, casting down their eyes, knew me only as a voice. The typing instructor I adored: Miss Cates. A glistening nakedness now in the scorching heat of the room, her breasts rise in a high bounce as she floats by; the same silvered fingernails, the same mouth, and she hasn't aged in all these years. (She sat cross-legged on the desk beating time on her pretty white palm with a ruler: our lovely metronome.) And I'm calling, "Get out, Miss Cates, get out everyone," and my coat is off as I help one mount the locker; she slips—my gloves are gone, too—and her body wets my hands, and she grabs my neck as we fall. Midge jumps on me and rides me, her eyes rolled back, mouth agape, and pleads to hide in my arms; the far wall begins to cave in. My suspenders off my shoulders, shirt open, I toss them toward the window, but they're like dry leaves floating in the room's hot pressure; they settle against me, delirious, and a scalding kiss finds my neck. Another burns my stomach. A willowy coed circles the room with my ax, then expires; here is Miss Donnelly, too, my old homeroom teacher who taught me verses I was never allowed to recite before the class, her cotton undies in her withered grip. One girl is out, perhaps two, but the window clogs with a soft and undulating mass. Reaching up, I try to pull some of them back, but their bodies are slick with perspiration and blood where they've nicked themselves on the uneven broken glass, and down we go, swooning and falling, three or four of us, and I see that my coveralls are mostly burned away, black and shredded on me, though I feel no pain. "Here!" I call again, pointing the way, but Miss Cates tackles me and over we go, my head thumping against a bench.

Then, I'm outside on the cool grass. Max is there, his hands burned from holding the hose around the boiler-room door too long, and we receive treatment from two attendants. "Good work, Coke, baby," he tells me. "Just great. How you ever got out of there I'll never know."

—

The fire marshal visits the station, commends Max and me, but mostly talks about the increased alarms in our district. He mentions possible arson, and even before he's finished his speech we're out on another call—sure enough, some joker who tries to torch his own apartment.

Back at the station later I rub salve on my neck and stomach burns and read newspaper accounts of the high-school blaze; I have to find out if I dreamed it, but here it is: two janitors dead in the initial explosion, sixteen girls and two instructors in the fateful locker room, another teacher upstairs, twenty-two on the critical list in the hospital. And here: Miss Cates and Miss Donnelly and Midge Prinz, the names just right. A fever of puzzlement comes over me.

The next morning Max arrives at the station for breakfast and we linger at coffee, whispering to each other.

"These girls," he says. "All the ones you say you recall."

"What about them?"

"Maybe they're after you, trying to keep you inside until you get burned up." His face is drawn and serious and he places a bandaged hand across my arm.

"I've thought of everything," I whisper. "You ever heard of poltergeists? People who make things fly through the air or who move objects with their thoughts?"

"Could be," he answers, his jaw set. Good old Max.

"I've wondered if some corner of my brain is setting fire to things. But there's more I don't understand. Miss Cates, for example. God, how could she be in that school?"

"I know this," Max adds. "We've never had such a season for alarms. And one of the nation's biggest, too, right here in our district."

"Someone could be playing a joke on me, but I know that isn't it," I muse, my coffee going cold in my hands. "And it isn't a dream either—I know that much because of the newspapers."

Max pats my arm again and gives me a look of wonder and sympathy.

"Let's not worry about it," he concludes. "We both know something big is coming, another alarm. We feel it, right?"

"You too, eh?"

"Oh, sure, Coker, god, you think I don't feel it? My knees get weak. I know something else is coming."

Waiting, now, Max keeps me at the station during all small alarms. I set all the equipment in order: the asbestos suits, the Pyrene foam, the new soap machine, the "wet water" and other smothering agents. I dream of sophisticated disasters—all sorts of mean chemical fires and special catastrophes.

I speculate, also, on my peculiar malady; is it part of what's happening in the city, I wonder, and the whole crazy world? Is it anarchy breaking loose? The overthrow of reason by dark forces? Such involved speculations annoy me. I'm a simple case, I assure myself: a regular guy, somewhat marred, but on balance; I had some rough adolescent moments, sure, but shook them off. I wish none of these victims ill will, never did; I do my duty, think baseball and hamburgers, take pride in being Max's partner.

Why, though, why?

Somewhere, I know, a match has fallen into a chair to smolder; rags are seething into combustion in some stuffy closet; a cigarette has fallen away from someone's sleeping fingers, and my answer is out there.

On the day I begin to understand, I'm busy repairing the spring on a hose reel. Max and I have exchanged glances all morning and the afternoon has worn away into twilight. The reel is a bitch to fix, but I'm grateful for the preoccupation, and my tools are spread out in the office so that I can monitor the phones and the flashboard that lights when one of the sprinkler systems in our district is set off by heat.

The bell, when it finally comes, causes me to drop a wrench. Even before I finish taking information on the call, Max comes down the pole, bandages and all, and starts up the number-one truck.

Another explosion: this time in the lab of the big clinic over near Seward Park.

Seconds now: our rhythms are quick, practiced, and no squad in the city is better. We're halfway there in sixty seconds, and I think of the job, a lab explosion: chemical, perhaps, after all, so I strap on a portable extinguisher filled with foam.

Outside the building, a large rambling affair of only two floors, Max neatly dispatches the troops; the problem is clearly to save lives and evacuate the hospital wing. We confer in an instant with a young doctor who shouts information about the floor plan, then off we go. Always helter-skelter in spite of briefings, we move into infernos never really knowing where things are. Just another job hazard.

Most of our men head toward the wards to aid the patients, but Max, an edge on his voice, calls for me to join him down near the blaze, where someone may be trapped. So we start down another hallway toward what seems a holocaust, though there isn't much smoke because great holes have been blown in the sides of the lab; the flame boils, then, and the heat turns us inside a room.

We stand in there panting, Max saying, "That hallway is hell. Let's check out the rooms down here real quick and not get caught out there." I nod, reach back, touch my foam gun to make sure.

Then we rush out, each of us taking one side of the hallway. My first room, an office, yields no one, so I move to the second. A small examination room, nothing again, though it has a door that leads into the next. The windows are gone, I notice, and medicines and instruments are scattered: all signs of a whopping blast. And what happens next takes only seconds, another instant frozen in that old slow motion as I perceive it—for all our work is such, a science played against the clock and one's personal daring. As I pass through the door another explosion buckles the walls and I feel the hot gush of fire at my back; hurled forward into the room, everything yellow and searing, I see a woman, a nurse, as we're enveloped. Death has its hot instant, but I have some reflexes left; we're together in the far corner beside a metal table, crouched low, fire spewing through the broken walls as I open my foam gun to fight the flames head-on. The heat drives the substance back around us and suddenly we are in a cocoon of foam, a soft sponge of protection, and my eyes close, and I'm away, dream-like, letting go.

A floating bed of airy whiteness: in its liquid folds her limbs entwine me and her body opens. We heave and settle together in the old slow dance, cushioned in rapture, and the flames are distant things, painless, as she receives me. The gun empties, my finger relaxes on the trigger, and I'm gone, my senses incandescent. Lips and legs and a glowing thrust of skin: she bakes with me, melts, while the foam holds and caresses us. Then we lie still as the room subsides.

It is Rafferty, brave soul, who comes and plucks me out.

Strange, how suddenly doom and deliverance occur; we rush in, spurt water and bust doors in what seems a comic dream, take our consequences. Fate is a moment, a mere puff.

I insist, later, on leaving the rescue unit where they've bedded me down; stepping down from the van into the street, my legs wobbly, I view the carnage. Half the building is collapsed, thousands of gallons of water are still being pumped, and the pavement is lined with stretchers. I stroll among them, doped slightly from something they've given me, checking myself; I'm a mess—second-degree burns on my back and forehead. Shouts and sirens punctuate the scene, but I don't pay attention.

They show me poor Max, who really isn't there anymore. Then I go over and look at the nurse; the attendant pulls back the sheet and there she is, calm, the little black nameplate intact on her white uniform: ALICE DURNING. I lift my eyes back to the tower of smoke which moves across the early night.

What's happening to me, what?

I wander for another hour before someone leads me back to shelter.

On the way to the hospital, I have a curious surge of elation; I think, well, I'm alive, I made it again, and I'll be patched up soon enough and back listening for alarms. It's going to be exciting—and they might give me a chance at captain, so I'll always go in first. I'll be a lot like Max in that way. Then, moments later, depression sets in; my obsession waylays me again, and I think, what's wrong with me? I'm kissed by a strange and awful God; my dread and my desire are one.

Down the Blue Hole

This mystic arcadian village is called Poplar Bluff, Missouri, and, sure, you've heard of it, but you probably never knew that every day we have dozens of séances, prophecies by seers and visionaries, and the assorted practice of witches, astrologers, magicians, and even, perhaps, one ghoul.

This is the little town where I live, though I've thought of moving away because of all the competition. The pressure to exceed one's best effort is so awful here that I've considered moving up to St. Louis and losing myself in the mercenary and nonpsychic life.

For instance, the other night I had sixteen snickering tourists at my table, sitting in a circle with their hands extended and palms upright, lights out, and the thunder cracked and everybody jumped and screamed, their index fingers pricked so that a single drop of blood blossomed on each one. When I switched on the lights there they were, astounded—they all admitted it. And I blotted each finger with a Kleenex and put all the bloody tissues into my big glass cookie jar and told them wild stories about how I would mingle their blood and put them under a spell. They gasped and laughed and loved it. One of them asked how I ever did such a trick. Then they started talking about old Auntie Sybil, one of my competitors, and the whole effect dissolved.

Someone else wanted to know if I served refreshments.

My biggest act is my disappearing act where I just vanish. I go off into the Blue Hole, don't ask me how.

I've done this trick six times now: sit cross-legged under my velvet cloth, concentrate, melt my bones and my whole petty life into nothing, while the audience watches that cloth sag and empty

itself. It's a great act because it's no act at all; off in the limbo of
the Blue Hole I'm frightened, naturally, but I come back every
time. Once I did this at the annual Rotary Banquet, vanishing
under my velvet cloth at the rear of the hall, then coming up underneath the tablecloth beside the main speaker, rattling spoons
and spilling ham loaf onto the floor, rising like Vesuvius forty feet
from the spot where I disappeared. They were so pleased that they
gave me an extra twenty-five dollars and asked me back next year.

This is such a forlorn life for a great talent.

—

Funk and Wagnall's Encyclopedia describes our part of the
state as flat and alluvial. Sort of dull, right: this is an agricultural
stop, a market town for cotton and soybeans, a town with only a
few important ranchers and a nice high school.

True, Mrs. Marybush, the town matron and benefactor, dresses
like one of the key figures from the Tarot deck. Also, we have
some housewives who give the evil eye to the butchers and the
boys at the checkout counters at Kroger's—where one can sometimes detect a slight levitation in the vegetable scale.

How this place happened I don't know. When I came here
years ago there were just a few spiritualists and a couple of horoscope addicts. I was just a country boy from over in Stoddard
County, town of Zeta, and Poplar Bluff, I felt, had a ready audience for what I already reckoned was my considerable talent. Yet
this town has become a kind of curse: tourists pour in all year,
strangers all, there are loonies and charlatans everywhere, and the
pressure, as I said, on one's craft is enormous.

Tourists are so unappreciative, too. One night I was making ex-
cellent contact with the dead at my table, summoning up a clear
apparition, and this farmer recognizes the face and drawls, "Uncle
Pardue, hey! This here is Bobby Wayne! Where'd you put that
gold watch and fob you promised you'd leave me? We can't find
that baby nowhere!"

Just as Las Vegas has its slot machines in the supermarkets, so
our town exposes its soul in public; we have tea-leaf readers in
every dumpy café, newsstands with astrological charts and no

news, and one famous washerwoman—Auntie Sybil, yes—who advertises bona fide trances while she does up your clothes. In truth, Auntie Sybil's act is pretty good; she lives in a simple clapboard house on the edge of town, so a customer can drive out there with his bundle of wash and hear all the dire and wonderful predictions for his future while Auntie Sybil works. She's an old bag, about ninety, and very authentic. There with the Borax, her ironing board set up in her steamy kitchen, running your underwear through her old Maytag ringer, she communicates with the cosmos in your behalf. Also, voices from the past come straight out of her throat while she's in a trance—you pay five dollars extra for this. She does a terrific Caesar Augustus and a good Mahatma Gandhi.

—

My name is Homer Bogardus, though after I left Stoddard County I dropped the first name altogether and my sign out front now reads Mr. Mystic and, in smaller letters underneath, The Great Bogardus. This house of turrets, broad eaves, and Gothic hallways is my castle and dismay—a pox, dammit, on the plumbing.

My memory of my early real world is dim and colorless, and, as I say about that, good riddance. Women, money, plumbing, friends: every reality I ever met addled and confounded me. The town of Zeta, symbolic in its very name of last things, almost ended me, true enough, and I used to contemplate mutilation and suicide in that cupboard of an upstairs room in Daddy's farmhouse. I might have been an idiot child chained to an iron bedstead and thrown crusts of bread, for it was that bad: I felt my adolescence like a disease, I pined, I bit my knuckles with anguish. One day— this was after hearing about Poplar Bluff and the lure of its underground—I fell into concentration and poured myself a glass of water from the pewter pitcher on the bureau although I sat twenty feet across my room in the window seat where I gazed out over Daddy's fields. I extended my physical powers across space and moved the pitcher and floated a brimming glass of water into my hands. Ninety magic days later I packed my bag and came in search of destiny.

Life before that, in all its lousy reality, was a wound. A strapping neighbor girl, Helen Rae, invited me into her barn, once, then successfully fought me off, breaking my collarbone in the fracas. My best buddy, Elroy, sabotaged my 4-H project for no reason at all. And Daddy died, to spite me for being different, I thought at the time—though in a séance, since, he materialized and denied it. And we were helplessly poor: cardboard innersoles in my dismal brogans.

So I left everything and hitchhiked to Poplar Bluff and the closets of my head.

What's so good about reality anyway? My bills are still mostly unpaid, my colleagues consider me odd in a town of oddities, my plumbing groans, my love life is asunder. Some days, like today, I dream beyond my powers—what if I *can* do almost anything?—to the Blue Hole where it might not be so bad to live forever.

—

"Produce a girl for me, a true love," I beg Auntie Sybil.

We're sitting in her famous kitchen while she makes lye soap. A Hollywood game show screams from her portable.

"You're unlucky in love," she offers.

"Don't give me that old line. I need what I need."

She fixes me with those depthless eyes; all mystery is behind those black slits, all knowledge, the dream of dreams. "All right, for fifty dollars cold cash I'll give it one hell of a try," she says.

"Conjure hard," I plead, peeling off the bills. "And for this price, please, I ought to get some fast action."

"You shouldn't even dally with the flesh, Bogardus," she tells me, putting my money under the radio. "You possess a great talent, enough for anyone to live for. If you had any talent for promotion, you could get on television."

That night a miracle enters my house. Sally Ritchie is a local girl back home from college, a strange, lovely spirit—incidentally thin of waist and ample of bosom—who has come, she says, in search of my netherworld. Her heart, she adds, has been broken by an athlete.

"Give me some sign," she breathes.

"I certainly will," I tell her, and I show her my collection of Ori-

ental bells with no clappers. Then we sit holding hands in my parlor while I make them vibrate and ring.

"My god," Sally Ritchie breathes more heavily. "You are *good!*"

—

Though I'm trying to be in love and loved again, the town goes
on as usual. In the church the minister begins his sermon and
then begins to cry, as if possessed, a Black Mass.

Our postman, Mr. Denbo, refuses to deliver any more packages
to the Cabal Institute because, he says, there are live things inside.

At the annual cakewalk some hippie warlocks and vampiresses
appear, but Mayor Watson strolls across the gymnasium to reason
with them.

"We don't want your kind here," he explains.

One of the kids gets sassy and gives the mayor some vulgar lip.
"Decay," he says to the mayor. "Palsy. Extreme. Burp. Bloat. Pimple. Gronk. Kidney. Suck. Waddle."

—

Sally Ritchie contends that she adores me, but clearly she craves
only the sensation of my powers; ever since I told her that I'm capable of complete dematerialization she has pleaded and insisted.

"Love me, not my talent," I ask of her, but she claims this is psy-
chologically impossible. Her college boyfriend, the one who jilted
her, played guard on the basketball team, she points out, and she
adored his dribble.

She attends my nightly gatherings, applauding each wonder.

Tonight a dozen tourists receive a superior set of hallucina-
tions: my old reptile-and-animal special. Encircling my table,
hands touching, they sit and witness the ghostly albino Great
Dane who moves through the room, passes into walls, emerges
again. We detect his panting breath as he haunts us. This beast, I
explain, and I tell them the absolute truth, has been a resident of
this house for years, long before I came here; he is terribly restless.
Harmless pet, no problem, I assure everyone, and they tilt first
one way and then another—feel the pull of my fingers, Sally?—to
glimpse him padding around.

Then the snakes: I move them into the room and have them

slither across our shoes beneath the table. Hands tighten. Audible gasps. But this is just the frightening beginning; soon the serpents are coiling up and over us, a net of white underbellies over our arms and shoulders, and only my soothing voice prevents absolute hysteria.

The table is a writhing pit: black and green snakes everywhere. And now a thick furry adder: it rises among them like a sentinel, one large eye in the middle of its head, and I say, "Look at that eye, ladies and gentlemen, each one of you look into that eye!"

The one-eyed adder stops before each participant and stares him down. Meanwhile, the other serpents curl away and vanish— and the big one is gone, too, and the evening is a triumph.

"I could do my giant spider now," I tentatively offer.

"Oh, no, no, don't bother," everyone assures me.

"Wonderful," Sally Ritchie breathes. "And it was your eye in there, wasn't it, Mr. Bogardus? It was your eye inside that big snake, right?"

—

Deep in the Blue Hole.

I am here because Sally Ritchie wants a thrill.

The hole is like a cave, an indigo cavern, a gigantic drain that spirals down into the basements of the earth. Not so awful in here, really, after a time, so I sit here deciding exactly where I should now emerge. Should it be there in the parlor where I disappeared from Sally's side? No, I decide to make Sally suffer. I shall arise in the garden, calling and beckoning her outdoors so that she will find me bursting through the ground like a weird pod among all the dying autumnal stalks. A splendid gesture, true, so that's exactly how I do it: clods falling off my shoulders as I rise up, a primordial flower sprouting before her very eyes.

It occurs to me as I emerge that I'm trying to earn adoration.

"Forty minutes!" she breathes. "You were gone forty minutes! And look at you! Coming up through the dirt!"

"A new record," I observe. "Forty minutes in the Blue Hole."

—

The town ghoul, whose name is Ralph, is generally popular, but I find him morbid. He throws parties after which he tries to get Sally and her girlfriends to stay late and go skipping around graveyards, but thank goodness they don't go for that sort of thing. I like Ralph well enough personally, but his art and mine are at odds; he tends to press reality home while I just want to divert and delight. Oh, I throw a few harmless scares into the tourists, sure, but why face them with war, pestilence, and man's cruel heart?

Ralph, like most people, can be somewhat deciphered by his rooms. I slip away from one of his cocktail parties at the Christmas season and tour his house, finding on the tables of his den and bedrooms stuffed hawks, daggers, a dusty crystal ball, and ashtrays made of old manacles. His bedroom is a gray, dim dungeon of a place.

A few days later, still thinking about rooms, I decide to indulge in a little astral flight and visit my Sally's bedroom. She has the upstairs of her parents' big Georgian over on Maple Avenue.

I watch her sleeping, a brown shower of her lovely hair across the pillow.

Soon, I learn she is returning to school.

Do you want subtleties from me? The difference between my astral travels and complete dematerialization? All my mind-over-matter conquests explained? Do you want me to tell you why I'm so frivolous, why I don't use my powers to cure sickness, or, like that flashy French clairvoyant, fight crime and evil? Why should I compound my despair with endless explanation? What do you need except moments of profound awe?

—

Sally Ritchie writes that she is flunking biology.

It is darkest January and the Ozarks are blanketed in snow; at my window I can hear the world creaking beneath its ice, swaying and moaning in the winter thrall. The plumbing in my house answers noises.

I read my own palm and what do I see there? A private landscape as bleak as Poplar Bluff: a powerful life that can do all things, but is leaking away.

Accepting Ralph's invitation, I go over and catch the Super Bowl game on his crystal ball—nice reception, few ghosts, no commercials. We sit close at the table in his den, sipping cognacs, and staring into that small glass dream. Ralph, who is becoming morosely drunk, twitches his mustache and leers at me occasionally, but I don't mind.

"Thanks for asking me over," I tell him, and mean it.

—

In February I consider the Mardi Gras in New Orleans, the Acropolis, Kaanapali Beach in Hawaii, Marbella: all those vacation spots where I could go in an instant, where I could amaze the jet sets, charge supernatural fees, and forget Sally Ritchie and all the wretched consequences of my talents.

Instead, on the icy street outside the drugstore—valentine in hand, yes, ready for mailing—I draw my cape around me and tip my hat to Mrs. Marybush, who, today, is dressed like the Hanged Man. She smiles at my courtesy and informs me that she is sending friends from Kansas City to my table—skeptics, all, who need a good lesson.

"I'm not interested in the conversion of the masses," I snap at poor Mrs. Marybush. "Nor in offering proofs. Nor in metaphysical debate. I'm not going to call the lightning from the skies for another roomful of hicks. In fact, I'm retiring."

"No need to get huffy, Mr. Bogardus," she answers, and turns with her nose high and walks away.

—

In the spring there are county fairs, two of them, at Poplar Bluff and at Cape Girardeau more than fifty miles away, and I contract to perform my supreme act at them both—simultaneously.

The fair at Cape Girardeau is one of cheap tinsel and wheezing merry-go-rounds with all the splendor and illusion of a ghetto, yet the fairgrounds border the mighty Mississippi River, swollen with our winter rains, majestic, the elms and poplars on its banks rattling with extraordinary music.

All the people of my life mill around in the sunlit crowd: Daddy, Mr. Denbo, Auntie Sybil, Elroy, Mayor Watson, Helen Rae, Ralph,

Mrs. Marybush, Sally Ritchie, and hundreds I haven't told you about.

Odors of mustard and cotton candy assail us. The television crew hurries around, and the director, a sallow young man with a gold tooth, regards me with doubt—although the president of the Poplar Bluff Rotary Club has given assurances that this will absolutely come off as guaranteed. I eat a candied apple and gaze into the sky. A chilly day in April.

The cirrus clouds streak overhead, the pulse of the river is in us all, beating in our blood beneath the hurdy-gurdy sounds of the carnival. Today I will melt away under my velvet canopy; I will enter the endless cavern of the Blue Hole and rise again in Poplar Bluff, miles away, while two sets of cameras record the miracle.

A reporter from the *Post-Dispatch* interviews my colleagues, all of whom are here to bask in the fallout of publicity. There is Auntie Sybil, true to her down-home image, peddling a basket of lye soap and preserves among the crowd. That simple country crone. As Mrs. Marybush and the mayor sign up tourist business for the forthcoming séances, Ralph tells a reporter that "Poplar Bluff is the mysterious metaphor of America"—a phrase the reporter scribbles in a small spiral notebook.

"You'll meet someone else," Sally Ritchie tells me as we lurk by a sideshow tent. "You have a lot to give."

Faced with Sally's clichés, I'm tempted to ask her to join me, to disappear with me this afternoon under the velvet—she's such a fool for all the hoopla and drumroll.

She wears an oversize letter sweater, oxfords, a ribbon in her hair. "I'll be proud," she goes on, "to say that I once knew you, Mr. Bogardus." She squeezes my hand, the only way she has ever touched me.

As I mount the stage, cameras whirring, the river glistening beyond the trees, a chilly breeze billowing up under my cape, I think of my house. Not too far away, there it stands: all boarded up at last, my sign removed, the furniture draped and covered in each room, chairs turned upside down on the great table where my powers ruled. I can visualize inevitable details: my kitchen faucet still dripping.

Will the Great Dane remain there, I wonder, to haunt the dust of those rooms? Will my absence be interpreted as failure or as just a mighty one-way effort into the unknown? Will this negate all the sad wonders of my life? Or will societies and scholars come to study me, to peruse my insurance policy and read the marginalia in my volumes? Will they seek to retrieve me in future séances? Or ask Sally Ritchie to recollect, to salvage memories and anecdotes?

The Cape Girardeau High School band plays "Columbia, the Gem of the Ocean," and down I go. I melt, going away, all gone, never to explain myself or my miracles again, not even these words that vanish now—poof!—upon this mysterious page.

The Makeup Man

A new fad was "in": Everyone was mutilating himself. There were famous actors who had actually removed their ears or eyes. Executives had cut deep scars into their faces. Plastic surgeons on Wilshire or Sunset—for their usual high prices—were turning teenage girls into monsters: both eyes on one side of the nose, say, or lips severed from the mouth, or the skin drawn like awful cellophane down the cheek and neck. Those who could afford such alterations were envied most.

An old makeup man lived in Beverly Hills as this new hysteria began to ride the air. The palm trees in his front yard had withered, but he kept trying to revive them; earthquakes had left raw openings in parts of his city; food supplies were sufficient and everyone still had a car, but the new fad dominated every conversation and newscast.

In the old days of glamour and good looks, the makeup man had had shops everywhere, private offices in two of the major studios, and a fine laboratory in his home. He had serviced the stars on their yachts and soundstages, and it was agreed he was without equal in the industry, a magician. He was known in the business as Mr. Byron or the Fabulous Byron. Naturally, he had many lovers. He could invent faces so beautiful that his clients wanted never to be without him.

Now he stayed home—a less expensive place—trying to revive his withered palm trees, taking his pills, and listening to the distressing news of The Rovers or The Fad on television.

One morning, just before his early lunch of oatmeal and juice, a girl came to his front porch.

"I'm Sylvia," she said through the screen door. "I don't have enough money for anything permanent. But—you're the Fabulous Byron, right?"

He nodded yes. Nobody had called him that in years.

"Make me ugly," she pleaded with him.

Byron held the door open as she stepped inside. He reached out his gray hand and turned her head slightly so he could see the curve of her cheekbone. Sylvia was gorgeous, easily the most beautiful girl he had ever seen.

He felt his lips pronounce her name.

—

Sylvia remained with Byron in that small hillside house above a darkened neon valley while he tried to decide what to do about her. She was broke and lost, another waif of the city, yet had that natural indifference only the truly beautiful or gifted possess.

"Why do people do this thing?" he asked her about The Fad.

She shrugged the question away.

Nakedness suited her. She shucked her clothes and curled up in his den during those soft warm mornings, combing out her long hair, munching fruit, and watching TV. Every afternoon, she stretched out on his patio cushions like a lioness, casual and dazzling, sunlight glowing on the tiny blonde hairs of her torso and turning her arms the color of caramel. At night, she slept in his bed. They lay apart. He ruminated on times past, and she suggested ways they might go about ruining her face. He was ancient and undemanding, so she allowed him nearness as they talked.

One morning, he observed her watching a TV program about The Rovers: those gangs of marauders roaming loose in various parts of the country. In obscure parts of Wyoming or the Carolinas or Arkansas, they had attacked farm communities, cleaned out supermarkets, or held public executions. Sylvia held her breasts and padded around his den in a frenzy as she watched. Her excitement filled the room with a strange electric pulse that caused his gray hands to tremble.

After this, he gave her his first makeup job. He opened up the holes of her face: made her eyes bulge, her nostrils flare, her mouth open in a drooling fall. He pulled back the skin and pinned it so she seemed caught in a hideous and terrified scream.

"Ghastly!" she cried. "I love it."

—

While Sylvia went out into the city to make her fortune, the makeup man drove out beyond Malibu to an abandoned beach house he owned. He hadn't stayed there in years, not since the mistresses and parties of his heyday. In his early retirement, the house had been rented, but soon tenants had written on the walls, ripped out fixtures, and chopped up the deck for firewood.

Slowly—working mostly in the mornings—he made repairs. When he grew tired, he strolled the beach. Cries of gulls. Odors of an air blended with salt and oily rot. Distant hulls of empty marinas.

The inland is a waste, he decided, and the last life is at the shore again, all the creatures crawling back toward the sea in a last primeval moment. He thought of the fierce crustaceans. Only guarded things survived: wrapped in their sorrowful armor, turned in on themselves.

In the evenings, he went home to fix supper for Sylvia.

Soon she had two bit parts and her newly styled face adorned a local commercial. With this small success she became petulant and difficult, and little that Byron did pleased her.

"More oatmeal?" she shouted at him.

He jerked out his false teeth and exposed his wrinkled gums. With his finger hooked into the corner of his mouth, he yelled back at her.

"Look, all slimy!" he said, spraying her with his words. "You've got those perfect white teeth, but I've got these—ancient and soft and slimy!"

"Sorry," she said, relenting.

He learned to be occasionally repulsive. It was clearly the way to deal with her.

—

The Fad seemed to energize people.

It was as if in all nature beauty sat still, languishing, content with itself, while ugliness became dynamic. Those thorny, pincer-fingered, nightmarish crustaceans endured, evolved, fed on the lovely soft flesh of the landscape and multiplied.

Sylvia too: Her new faces made her bold. She no longer draped herself over the furniture of his den or patio. Instead, she paced in his rooms. More often she didn't come back in the evenings. Her career included strangers, dinners, weekends down in Baja, parties in the hills, and in the end Byron was forced to create new distortions for her, each more sickening than the last, just to ensure her frequent visits. Anything to keep her near.

He loved to talk with her when the makeup was off and postponed doing new faces for her as long as possible.

"There were great beauties," he told her as he worked. "Garbo, Bergman, Taylor, Christie! Sensuous, luscious! And the size of their faces up there on the screens! Bigger than anything living, large as the Sphinx, as huge as the Colossus of Rhodes!"

"I do like to sit down close at movies so things look big," she admitted.

"A beautiful human face in gigantic proportion," Byron went on. "That's the mystery and power of the medium!"

"Can you extend my ears now?" she asked.

"Sure, anything, Sylvia."

"I want my ears wrapped around my face—like tentacles. As though—these—tentacles—are choking me."

—

Sylvia won a part in a monster movie. It was set during the period of the Spanish Inquisition. The picture was shot in Barbados and Texas with a British camera crew, an Arab producer, a Danish director, Latin hairdressers—everything normal—except that it managed to catch the spirit of The Fad at the height of the craze and became a box-office sensation. As a consequence, Sylvia was offered dozens of films and Byron, given his due credit, was brought forth successful out of retirement. In only a few short weeks, he opened Byron's Fabulous Emporium in Palm Springs.

All was well, except he was losing her.

An academy awarded him a medallion on which was inscribed:

beauty is only skin-deep

ugly is to the bone.

beauty always fades away

but ugly holds its own.

With his new wealth, Byron ordered a first-class renovation of the beach house and went into seclusion behind a high fence, three Dobermans, and a brace of guards with brutally scarred faces.

He ate his oatmeal, watched TV, and thought of normal times. Sylvia, he reminded himself, was from Ohio. Byron's father was once employed by the Department of Sanitation of Phoenix, Arizona, in days when there were families, hourly wages, ball games, anthems, and carburetors.

Feeling not at all fabulous, Byron stared into the depths of his television set one whole afternoon and evening, witnessing more than he could assess.

One team had won, another lost.

The number-one hit song of the season was the one about the exciting adventures of The Rovers.

A strange disturbance at a remote edge of the galaxy had been recorded on instruments but not fully identified.

Tattoos were the coming fashion.

Light, scattered earthquakes were predicted from the West Coast to the Rockies.

Sylvia's horrid face was part of an award-winning advertisement for handguns.

Food supplies, analysts insisted, had dwindled only slightly.

In some parts of the South Pacific and in the middle jungles of the African continent, palm trees still thrived.

—

At the Palm Springs Emporium, a shiny laboratory awaited the master's touch. When Sylvia became one of the all-time great movie monsters, ranking with Dracula, the Creeper, and the Beast with Five Fingers, she became too busy for Byron, so he began to play around in his lab.

He went back to an old experiment: devising a youth cream.

The base compound of Byron's Fabulous Youth Cream over the years had always been sulfonmethane—which produced a hypnotic effect. But Byron, by his own admission, wasn't a scientist, just an artist, so his test tubes and flasks were always filled with fluids that looked good but did little.

His new effort was less a cream than a handsome milk.

In despair, he poured it over his oatmeal and ate it.

Not much taste, but his eyes fastened on the bright spoon in his bowl and he sat there in a trance for sixty hours.

—

Byron went to a party hoping to see Sylvia.

For the floorshow, the hosts presented a philosopher who was reluctant to speak. After a brief and futile interrogation, the master of ceremonies put the philosopher's feet into a vise. The philosopher, an old bearded man who looked wise, writhed in pain as the emcee tightened the vise, but he confessed no secrets.

After a buffet supper, some men beat on a 1976 Chevrolet with old pole lamps. They banged out an effective rhythm and everyone except Byron danced.

Later, the emcee announced in a panic that Rovers had surrounded the estate, so the guests fled in every direction. They dived through windows, hid in pantries, and sprinted off into the night toward the beaches, but it all turned out to be a hilarious practical joke.

—

When Sylvia finally came to visit again, she still wore her famous tentacled face.

The air sang with nervousness that night. The restless ocean pulsed into the shore below the beach house, far off in the darkness the Dobermans were beginning to bark, and Sylvia's laughter was false, a performance. She was happy about The Fad's passing, she told Byron, tossing her head and laughing, ha-ha because the required makeup, ha-ha, was beginning to irritate her skin. She seemed desperate and unnatural.

Soon she began to shed her clothes in the old way. Her fingers—silvered, Byron noticed—trailed over his new couches, the brass telescope aimed out at the ocean, and his warm television set as she moved through his rooms.

"What do you want?" he asked, following her.

Byron felt both annoyed with her and sorry for her because she had lost that magnificent indifference.

She wore a tattooed wildflower below her navel.

She danced through his place, dropping her gossamer blouse here, a shoe there, touching things; she draped her clothes over his furniture and knocked ever jeweled bottles of cosmetics on his mirrored worktable, trying with all her might to bewitch his rooms and his life again, the crude charm of her brown body against all his powers.

Her wretched face distracted him. He couldn't help it, but she just wasn't the same as that first time she came to him.

"You'll make me beautiful and splendid now!" she sang to him, dancing away.

"I can't do it!" he called, his breath growing short as he clumped upstairs after her.

"Oh, yes you can! You can do anything!" she reassured him, whirling. She moved out onto the deck under the stars, back into his bedroom, across the hallway, her arms beating like wings.

Byron also wanted to say that she didn't love him or appreciate his achievement but knew that would sound childlike. She was still doing her pathetic dance.

"Only our art and the industry matter!" she called to him, spinning out of reach. "You'll find me another fad, then another!"

"No, you don't understand," he wheezed.

"Trick after trick, Byron, you're a genius!"

"The fads kill us!" he yelled at her. "They're real! You just don't know!"

"You're going to make me lovely now! You're going to!" she insisted, and she let him catch her. He grabbed her and they wrestled each other down on the thick, creamy rug before his hearth. The flames crackled beside their faces as she began her desperate seduction, pulling his scrawny weight on top of her, laughing in his ear, opening herself to him.

"You don't know what you've done!" he said breathlessly, but she laughed and nuzzled, entwining him. Her hands caressed him as he reached for her face and began to tear her latex mask away.

He was the master, the supreme artist, destroyer, and creator, but his talent sickened him now, for it made all passing fashion real, as always, and every fad part of the true texture of the soul.

The sea and the dogs were howling as he pushed his fingers into her makeup. He felt her body relax as she let him work. But then she suspected what she saw in his eyes.

"What is it?" she asked, and she tried to crawl out from under him. They struggled, rolling and falling, until she saw herself in the broken mirror of his worktable, which lay tipped on its side at the far end of the room.

Her faces were coming off one after another, caked artifice and flesh, each more wrinkled and horrid than the one before. He dug into the sockets of her eyes and peeled back another fistful.

Her screams and cries grew louder and darker than the night surrounding them.

Beneath it all, deep down, like the makeup man himself, the famous Sylvia was only a skull.

The Good Ship *Erasmus*

This is one of those cruise ships dedicated to helping people. These ships embark every day now from all over the world, some of them stuffed with psychiatrists trying to help the passengers forget their troubles, others with physical-culture experts trying to beat the blubber off a fat clientele, others with religious leaders trying to purge or mystify those who are aboard.

Our ship, the *Erasmus,* has a somewhat less complicated mission: theoretically, at least, it is just a ship that will hold us captive on the high seas until we have all stopped smoking. We sailed from Amsterdam a few days ago, puffing like mad on the dock before the horn sounded, and in a few short weeks we will be around Italy, the warm Mediterranean waters soothing us—one hope being, I assume, that craved minds will turn away from nicotine to romantic lust—until all lungs are healthy again.

My game is smuggling thousands of cigars and cigarettes on board.

By the time we see the French coast I'm largely in control of many of the three hundred lives around me.

It is enough to make me slightly melancholy, philosophic. I stand here at the rail gazing into the calm summer waves, ruminating on the nature of evil.

—

The *Erasmus* has twin stabilizers, a cruising speed of twenty-six knots, lounges, shops, bars, a gymnasium, swimming pools, dining rooms, and an optimistic staff. Perry Cheyenne is the Passenger Host who directs our seminars, offers encouragement to those in withdrawal and despair, arranges parties and games and contests. He wears tennis clothes and a yacht cap, grins, bounces as he goes.

Our captain is never seen, just this happy Passenger Host. The captain is far away, up there somewhere on the bridge, steering us onward.

—

Shopping for clothes, I buy tennis wear just like Perry's and give serious consideration to a maroon tuxedo. I boarded with four oversize suitcases and a trunk all stuffed with everyone's favorite brands, domestic and foreign, so had only my one business suit.

I do all this because of the character of our age. It grows difficult to find a situation in which one can be clearly immoral, in which one can be sure of his wicked deeds.

"I'd *give* you the tux, mister, for one lousy cigarette, believe me," sighs Ramona, the salesgirl. She is working her passage on this expensive cruise here in the men's shop.

"I have plenty of cigarettes in my cabin," I disclose, admiring the cut of the jacket.

She eyes me wantonly.

"What price you asking?" she blurts out, incapable of coyness.

"There are many prices," I tell her. "The cost isn't always the same."

—

There are deeper elements in all this beyond the fact of its being a simple tobacco-curing sea voyage. There is the death of God, the tides of history, my own somewhat complicated personality. It's very confusing, sorting it out, which accounts for the choppy style of this report. Also, not only do I lose track of the exact philosophic flow, but my attention span, like yours, is short.

On deck, naturally, we passengers exchange personal information.

My father was from Chicago, my mother from Geneva, and I was born in the skiing village of Igls above Innsbruck as an American citizen. Father was an author and consumer of thick books, and in his library I spent my asthmatic adolescence, ducking out of boarding schools to sit among his volumes instead. Once, six days into my puberty—I knew you'd want this incidental and inevitable note—I seduced our young Austrian housekeeper. I traveled and studied. Soon I knew many things, and some of these which I tell my fellow passengers are:

The earliest cavemen lived in caves on the French Riviera very near the beach and sunshine.

The poet Rilke died from being pricked by a rose thorn.

The population of the world now doubles every thirty years.

Scheherazade's erotic *Thousand and One Nights* ends with a prayer.

The only place to get a drink on Sunday morning in Rome is inside the bar at St. Peter's.

Choose one.

—

Sitting in deck chairs together, Mrs. Murtaugh and I discuss our separate problems. She is already beginning to resist therapy and sits here sucking a dummy cigarette, a little wooden Tinker Toy.

"My seminar group is meeting right now," she wails, "but I just can't go today. I don't like my hypnotist. If you don't respond to your hypnotist, he just can't put you under so you might as well quit."

"This is a degrading sort of troublemaking," I complain, "coming on board a sailing vessel and peddling smokes. In another age I might've been a satanic figure, my life a tragedy of corruption. Now look at me: I go around letting those of weak wills sniff the nicotine on my fingers and smell my brown breath."

"Worse yet," she continues, "I can't make love without a ciggie. I *have* to catch a smoke before and afterward or I just can't go for sex. I told my group leader that and I told that insensitive hypnotist, too!"

"The world is too libertine," I muse aloud. "In another age I could've been Iago, but not now. I take the whole reckless curse of human history back to its cosmic roots, too, and the lost sense of the divine."

"So here I sit in a dowdy deck chair! A deck chair! I'm only fifty-six years old! I'm a warm-blooded woman, let me *tell* you, and a cruise is a cruise!"

"One could blame God, of course, for making man finite. A really benevolent God would've made man his equal—been a sport about the creation, I mean—but no, man is a weak hybrid, lower than the angels. And so it was certain to come to this: a time when the moral distinctions completely blur. Man adrift in a sensual sea. Perfecting the rhythms of pandemonium."

"What'd you say you peddled? Did you say ciggies?"

"I once wanted to be really evil. For instance, I thought of things like murder. But the whole world has thought of things like murder. But the whole world has too strong a death drive on its own—nothing very original can be done even with murder! And sex criminals can't get a headline because their perversions are so everyday. I spent my teen years practicing lots of nasty habits, I mean, but now there're movies and songs celebrating these things! I'm trying to get across the point, Mrs. Murtaugh, that all my life I've dreamt about doing people in, but fortune has only left me a few petty hustles."

"Did you say you actually have ciggies?"

Clearly, Mrs. Murtaugh isn't quite on my frequency as I describe the final indifference of the Greeks to their gods, Dante's rejection of religion in favor of secular politics, the Renaissance, growth of the factories, Einstein. Her eyes fasten on me as I talk and gaze out toward the Spanish coast, but she hears little.

At last, yes, I say, yes, Mrs. Murtaugh, I'll take your BankAmericard.

—

Everyone scampers ashore at Bilbao, the Bay of Biscay glistening in the hot sun around the *Erasmus* as I wait on board. By this time those who have resisted me run boldly toward the nearest cafés, where they pay outlandish prices for packs of Pipers, Celtas, and other mediocre Spanish cigarettes.

Perry stands astride the gangplank, meanwhile, with his good-natured shakedown crew. When passengers return with bulges under their sport shirts and Bermuda shorts, the crew searches them and laughingly tosses their goodies into the bay. I look on with approval. A mere twenty-dollar bribe passed my contraband aboard without the slightest inspection, and I disdain the lack of

foresight and these clumsy attempts on the lone returning gangplank.

Perry gives the fallen few pep talks, making a fist as he lectures
like a determined prep-school coach. Both his teeth and his shoes
glisten white.

—

Two of my customers are caught smoking in one of the
cramped hatches and Perry and his crew suffer doubts over their
effectiveness at the gangplank. Perry shames the offenders in
front of a Combined Seminar Meeting in the auditorium, shred-
ding their cigarettes in public. One of them, a civic leader from
Palatine, Illinois, nearly weeps. I respect Perry's zeal.

After this spectacle there is a speech by the ship's doctor, who
says things like, "Please, *folks,* don't poison your body!" Then we
have a demonstration by the hypnotist whose victim is a long-
legged girl named Daphne. When she swoons many in the audience are visibly moved.

There aren't enough chairs and the room is crowded, so I move
among the throng like a savage force. Here and there I catch a
knowing eye.

—

The famous Danish porno cruise ship, *Flicka,* passes us after
we turn back into the Atlantic. Dedicated to orgy-minded travel-
ers, it flies a single red flag and moves by us slowly on the hint of
music.

Erasmus lists to port as we pass, my envious fellow passengers
out there clutching the rail for a good look. Soon it is beyond our
wake.

—

Pensive, my philosophical mood hanging on, yet talkative, I
consent to my assigned session with one of the psychiatrists-in-
residence, a Doctor Gonatt. He is impressed by my Austrian background and remarks that he once tried to read one of Father's
novels.

Gonatt strives to comprehend me and suggests an arrested

moral growth brought on by culture fatigue, and I have some difficulty explaining, no, I am actually an advanced and complex monster, and dedication to evil usually has curious and subtle side benefits for mankind anyway. We all know the evil that good men invariably do, I point out, but we must also consider the ironic value of the deviate. The sheep is not truly itself without the wolf, I explain, fetching an illusion that escapes him.

We talk and talk.

Gonatt has a drinking problem, I learn, and is trying to recover financially so he can reopen his clinic near San Diego. He used to smoke a pipe, he recalls: a big, curve-stemmed meerschaum with a bowl like a factory chimney.

As he prattles his hands begin to tremble, so I can do no other than offer a menthol filter, which, naturally, he accepts.

—

Here I sit in the Desiderius Bar, the ship's plushest lounge, with the keys to my closet and locker safely rattling in my pocket, content that the stewards who clean my cabin will never find anything, but one of my best customers comes over and informs me that Perry Cheyenne is onto somebody. Paranoid, I consider returning to B Deck and checking my hoard, but I calm myself.

"Watch your step, pal," my customer advises. His name is Mr. Branch, a successful food expert from Brussels, and he has never indulged in such side-of-the-mouth dramatics before.

I offer the next barstool. "Steady now. Tell me what's happening," I say evenly, trying to reassure him.

He insists there are high-level meetings involving Perry, the captain, the ship's doctor, and certain spies. Perry is furious. There have been butts in the public rooms and telltale holes burned in a few of the bed linens.

I buy poor Branch a drink and promise an extra pack for his loyalty, but inside me I feel a stirring: a tingle of excitement, a new pulse. Deep down, perhaps, I crave a confrontation.

I wear my maroon tuxedo to the evening dance. I know that Perry watches me as I make the rounds talking and laughing. The game seems to be on.

Later, back in my cabin, I can't sleep. I know that a showdown with Perry might be inevitable, yet it isn't what I want. Specifically, I need an intellectual adversary—not just some giddy zealot.

The captain: one wonders what or who he is.

—

Beyond Gibralter the nights turn suddenly hot and life on the *Erasmus* grows intense. Pairing off seems to occupy everybody's time, and the ship begins to rock with new diversions. Girls in bikinis, laughing, spring from one deck to another; the men are brown and strangely healthy in spite of my booming business, their coughs lessened, and all the meals and games are attacked with gusto.

At the pool there is hardly room for me to splash around. One of the major lounges has been converted into a lively casino, games in every corner, and the Desiderius is packed with roaring drunks.

Perry seems content that such revelry excludes smoking, but a few of us detect his almost imperceptible discontent. Perhaps the slant of his yacht cap. A bounce slightly lessened.

However, before the floor show and dance he leads us in our nightly deep-breathing exercises, slapping his hands loudly and giving off his familiar "Hey, everybody, now!"

Afterward the usual crowd of female enthusiasts is around him, gushing, admiring his stamina.

Out on deck I stroll along moodily until my shopgirl, Ramona, comes and takes my arm. I speak of the ancient Roman mentality which resulted in Nero, the acute aesthetic awareness of certain high Nazis, the occasional meditations of de Sade, which, in my opinion, soared beyond his more frequent banality.

Meanwhile, Ramona nuzzles my neck.

From high on the bridge comes a green glow from the captain's window.

The sea is moderate.

Mrs. Murtaugh and Dr. Gonatt pass by holding hands.

—

We anchor offshore at Cannes. Everyone pours down into the awaiting launches to go ashore and visit the film festival, shop, strut around the promenade, and of course steal a few drags.

Near the beach just outside the Hotel Martinez photographers encircle a movie starlet who tries to contain herself in a peekaboo swimsuit. As I linger near this confusion, my thoughts momentarily meandering on to the nature of publicity and its role in the world's present corruption, I find Perry beside me. He makes a tsk-tsk at the proceedings, appears friendly, but I take this seemingly accidental appearance as ominous.

"How's everything going?" I query him.

"Not awfully well," he admits. "We should have many more passengers cured by now than we do."

"Oh? How many do we have?"

"At last night's staff meeting we estimated 15 percent—far below normal. I've been ramrod on cruises where we got 50 percent."

Now I make a tsk-tsk.

We exchange a few minutes of smalltalk there on the promenade until the starlet backpedals into the hotel with her fixed smile. Then Perry excuses himself and ambles away and, yes, I see that his bouncy walk has modified.

No doubt of it: he's worried and this banter was an ill omen. Why me?

In the cover of darkness, later, I transfer my diminished stock into the locked cabinets beneath the hand-painted ties and initialed handkerchiefs in Ramona's men's shop. For a mere pack a day, she is now my dealer and accomplice, and it's none too soon.

—

Sicily is admired for its lovely cliffs above the sea, its hearty peasants, its wines, but I admire it for its history of violence.

As we pass by on a sunny noon, I cease whittling my Christian name into the rail and salute with my pocketknife.

—

The captain asks to see me.

When Perry presents himself at my cabin door with this message I feel excitement. Do they have evidence, I wonder, or are they bluffing? Will the captain be a worthy adversary? Even if I'm caught dead to rights with Ramona as the unshakable witness for the prosecution, what could they possibly do to me?

I dress slowly in my all-whites. Take, I caution myself, every possible psychological advantage. My thoughts spin like dervishes.

They're just no match for me, neither Perry nor his eager scouts. Also, I've committed no crime and at most they can only put me ashore at one of these lovely southern ports. And what could they possibly say? I'm intellectually stockpiled to parry their pious thrusts.

Perry waits smugly for me in the corridor and escorts me up to Deck AA. Every step I'm practicing my argument.

Society has gone mad, so that as the man of reason tries to apply his reason to madness he is being absurd. He thinks he is doing good as he uses his wit against the world's puzzle, I'll tell them, but he's actually trying to ponder the unfathomable. Not only is he a useless dolt, but he's even harmful because he misleads others. The true monster, however: ah, he goes his wicked way, attracts constant notoriety, and possibly teaches mankind a hard lesson in morality—in spite of himself.

We reach Deck AA. A long walk to the bridge.

My lips move as I practice my lines.

Perry, straight of back, knocks with authority on the door, opens it, and ushers me inside. Before us is the helm of the ship— a big wheel just like in swashbuckling movies—and the luminous green eye of a large compass. The walls are dingy white, and beyond the wide, salt-sprayed windows the bow breaks the waves.

The captain isn't present.

Nervously, Perry announces that we should wait.

As we stand in silence I take a good look at the bridge. It seems vaguely familiar—although I've never been in such a place before—yet also personalized and different. The captain, wherever he is, is clearly a man of reading habits: paperbacks, a few antiquated leather-bound volumes, magazines, and newspapers are stuffed into the shelves behind the desk. There is also a narrow, uncomfortable-looking bed.

When I inquire, Perry admits that sometimes the old man sleeps up here and doesn't bother to go below.

A variety of clothing is strewn around. Not a very neat man, I surmise, and I count two frayed naval topcoats, a rain slicker, a few discolored turtlenecks, underwear, socks, and, curiously enough, a shawl.

Perry shows his discomfort as I observe all this.

Soon there is a whistle, a cough, and another whistle from an instrument near the compass, and Perry dashes over there. A man from the boiler room—I can hear, in the midst of his profanities, talk of gaskets and seals—says that the captain is down there, grease up to the elbows, yes, dammit, and, no, there's nothing seriously wrong, but the captain can't make it. I'm to come back later, the voice says, because the captain has the opinion that the appointment isn't urgent.

This frustrates us. Primed for accusation and argument, I start to protest. Perry, his smugness gone, sputters and asks if he shouldn't remain and steer the ship, but the voice answers hell no, naturally not, the ship's locked on course.

Embarrassed, Perry says he must attend to his many duties and offers that I'll have to find my own way to see the captain.

"No problem," I say, "Get on with your business."

He's visibly shaken. His yacht cap sags as he tells me that Deck AA is often closed to passengers, that I should probably seek written permission, that, er, perhaps another crew member could escort me.

"You heard the man in the boiler room," I answer. "It's nothing big. I'll stop around again when it's convenient for everyone."

—

The cigarettes are untouched, safely there underneath the counter in Ramona's shop. She doesn't understand why I kiss her cheek.

Later, alone, I probe the aspects of my new advantage. Either they were bluffing or they have the barest suspicion. At any rate, now I'm free to make this a real intellectual rendezvous, a true confrontation: I'll bring down the weight of Nietzsche, Machiavelli, and all the obscure Mongol thinkers on that innocent captain's arguments.

The best time to catch the old sea dog, I reason, will be in the evening, so I wait until the day's seminars finish and the dances begin before making my way to the bridge once more.

Empty. The ship is still automatically fixed on course. I peer through the window at the green glow of the compass. Eerie.

Feeling odd, I go back to my cabin, slip into my maroon tuxedo, and take refuge in the music of the Desiderius.

—

The next day I make frequent trips up to Deck AA, but the old boy is never there.

On one of my visits I try the door and find it open. Inside, I casually grip the wheel. On the nearby desk are charts—an outline of the Italian coast around Amalfi. I exchange stares with the omnipotent compass, gaze off at the horizon where, dimly, far away to port, lies the coast.

The wheel, yes, is fixed on course. Comforting.

—

Days pass.

Perry is deep in a frenzy of work now, seemingly having forgotten me. The seminars are booming therapy sessions with the members shouting obscenities at each other, vomiting up their private lives, accusing and demanding, and Perry is there, I learn, orchestrating all of it. When I see him on deck his clothes are soiled and wrinkled, his hair is long and hanging from his yacht cap, his eyes weary.

I hear of a bloody fight in the casino lounge.

Beside the nearly empty swimming pool—one fat man lolling on his back—I take a glum stroll. After a while I sit down on the tile, deciding not to take my swim.

Where, I wonder, is our elusive captain?

Tonight after checking the bridge again I visit the boiler room, but the engines are purring unattended. There seems to be no one above or below, just Perry and his bedraggled crew working amidships with an increasingly restless cargo of passengers. The voyage is too long for us, I tell myself.

Toward morning I wander back toward the vacant bridge. Prying, I rummage around in the captain's desk—paper clips, parchments, a service medal, the passenger list, a quill pen—and pull a few books off the shelves. A few first editions nobody would ever read. Magazines: popular European gossip items, nudist-camp publications, occult periodicals, journals on sports, wildlife, travel, cuisine.

And who is my eclectic adversary? An ordinary escapist, the Flying Dutchman, some alienated intelligence, just a shy and simple pilot?

Before departing again, I trace my finger over the charts. Not too difficult reading charts, I conclude; the deeps and shallows are clearly marked.

—

The scent of the Greek isles rides the wind.

At times, now, I forget exactly where we're putting into final port.

My mind is on last diversions—parties, another amateur night, my shopgirl who insists she has fallen in love with me, testimonials in the Desiderius for those few who have actually kicked the habit—and I am still playing hide-and-seek with the old sea wolf upstairs.

Disheveled, a mere wisp of a smile left on his face, Perry goes around patting everyone on the back and making the best of a cruise low on converts.

A few brave passengers grin sheepishly, shrug, and light up the last of my dwindling supply in public.

—

On the bridge again.

Once more I take a grip on the helm and peer out over the bow, but this time I'm surprised to find that we're not on a fixed course and that I'm alone at the wheel. The locking device: yes, here it is. I see, it must be part of an automatic system with the compass. Sure.

The compass illuminates the darkened room in a cozy green glow, my charts curl, and I slip into one of the turtlenecks.

Long days and nights.

Far out now, no sign of land.

We have a westerly course, a good barometer.

The new Passenger Host pops in, salutes, makes happy smalltalk, and reports that the new passengers are settled into seminars. His name is, I think, Jerry, and he asks if I'll have my meals up here today and I say, yes, please. I watch him bounce away in the whites, calling and waving to someone below as he descends.

Later he returns with a crisp new passenger list, the mimeograph ink hardly dry. I read over it wondering if any of these passengers might be capable of philosophical discussion.

My Ramona is gone.

We made a stop somewhere, exchanged everyone, took on supplies, set forth again, and the most curious thing about this is that my new quarters are filled with cigarettes.

Weatherman A Theological Narrative

In his seventieth year a strange foreboding comes to Mr. Pollux, the old meteorologist: he begins to understand that he is the God of the Universe.

Certainly, his place is imposing: he is the sole occupant of a gigantic tower, not unlike a fire watcher's perch, high in the Ozark Mountains. The tower is one of nine Mid-America Storm Towers (Operation MAST, project of the National Weather Service) in which skilled weathermen scan the horizons and charts and computer tapes for signs of tornadoes and major disturbances.

In his busy loneliness in the tower, Mr. Pollux eventually faces the vexing evidence: he knows that the weather follows his direction, that it obeys his every projection and mood.

He wonders if his long experience in the business has finally made him especially sensitive or if he is just having a run of lucky coincidence with his forecasts. Yet, testing himself, he finds he can invent the most fanciful or the most oddly precise bulletins which come true down to the last curious detail.

He has two tornadoes bump together, say, near Eureka Springs, Arkansas.

—

He also tests his mortality by remembering.

Yes, he had a family: parents, long ago, and a sister who married and lives in Toledo.

Also, a favorite nephew, little Cappy.

Cappy came to visit the tower—let's see, he can't quite recall—five summers ago. They went out on the deck that encircles the tower, and on the night of the Fourth of July Mr. Pollux produced a fantastic electrical storm: bolts and explosions and everything his nephew could want.

"You're not really making all that thunder and lightning," little Cappy said with a knowing smirk. He was eleven years old that summer.

"Yes I am," Mr. Pollux told him, pointing a finger and making a great fork of electricity.

After his nephew went back to Toledo there were lots of candy and chewing gum wrappers lying around the laboratory and no one ever came to see him again.

—

Surrounding him are his instruments: hygrographs, radio-sondes, microseismographs. His computers rasp and whisper, the radar antenna atop his tower squeaks with every rotation, and the big brass barometer keeps sinking below 29.80.

Every morning he sends up weather balloons.

Twice each day he phones in his reports, which are taken by one of the recording machines of the National Service. Not even a human voice to say thanks.

At night the National Service sends out his bulletins to airports, TV stations, newspapers, corporations, and private meteorologists everywhere.

He imagines millions of people bending forward in grim reverence before their television sets, listening to tomorrow's sunshine or rain.

You know you're God, he decides, when you're no longer in contact with people, but have magnificent power.

—

In April he phones his sister long-distance, but there has been a freak late-season blizzard up in Ohio and the lines are down.

Annoying, but far away where even the powerful have no control.

—

He thinks up all of the old theological puzzlers and makes up answers to each one, answers he'd give, say, if anyone ever came to his tower to interview him.

1. If God is good, why does he allow suffering?

Answer: He is only pretty nice. And whimsical.

2. Is God simply the Prime Mover? Did he create the world and then bow out of its operation?

Answer: Yes, God retired and was given a gold watch and fob for his services by the eleventh-century theologian Anselm.

3. If God is all-powerful, can he then make a rock so heavy that he can't lift it?

Answer: Yes, he can make such a rock—and this confuses him. But, then, the essence of the Holy is loneliness and confusion.

4. If God loves mankind, why did he create man finite and even lower than the angels?

Answer: It is man's lot to sit apart, like an audience.

5. If God is a personal God, where does he sit? And isn't the order in which he is contained greater than he is?

Answer: A good tower keeper is a daydreamer and all reality is imagination.

Mr. Pollux feels most powerful and important when he makes tornadoes.

This is the great tornado belt of the planet, so everyone expects catastrophe—though not, perhaps, with such frequency as Mr. Pollux provides this spring and summer. Except for a rare cyclone in such faraway places as Pakistan or Turkey, the middle United States has a virtual monopoly on tornadoes. In one weekend in the month of May, Mr. Pollux creates 267 separate twisters in the four-state area.

He feels sorry for the victims, sure, but a first-rate tornado is hypnotic and its vortex is a masterpiece.

—

Back to the telephone.

Mr. Pollux calls around to the other tower keepers in Project MAST. They're all lonely, eccentric types, and most of them have weird, unscientific notions of how things work. The guy in Oklahoma believes that inside dust devils are real devil spirits—mean, dirty monsters just like the Cherokees used to believe in.

"Nuts," Mr. Pollux tells him on the phone.

"I'm writing down my theories in a book," the guy explains, and Mr. Pollux wants to hang up on him.

—

Mr. Pollux remembers hard, trying to recall as much of normal life as he can. One day he thinks about all the girls and women he has known and about how he enjoyed kissing them. He didn't care much for those open-mouthed, sloppy, overheated kisses, but liked the old-fashioned sort with the lips in tender use. How far back, all this? How long since the last kiss? Straining for recollection, he gets the Roaring Twenties, the Merchant Marine, New Year's Eve in 1949, then primordial images assault his brain and he sees a landscape of volcano, a red sky, the bones of dinosaurs among the ferns and ridges of an ancient jungle.

—

Animals amble and scurry around the bottom of his tower: bears, raccoons, squirrels, deer.

"My job is statistics!" he calls down to them. "An average of two hundred and thirty-five clear days in a year around here! Stupid piece of information, right?"

He also yells down special weather terms. "Prevailing westerlies!" he calls. "Occluded front!"

Then he goes to sleep and dreams odd nightmares. A strange storm erupts, a rain of fire, and both the forest animals and a mob of people come and rattle his tower trying to climb up. In the dream he comes on TV like the hick weather commentator from Joplin and points with a stick at a weather map. He explains the holocaust to his audience.

"A God who is accessible," he adds, "would not be God."

—

The computer breaks down and spews out hundreds of feet of tape—data that doesn't even make sense to Mr. Pollux, who puts up with everything. He gathers up the pile of tape, tears it in little bits, goes out on his deck, summons up a strong wind, then pitches the tatters out over the Ozarks like confetti.

—

Memory, knowledge, everything in the head is a form of madness, Mr. Pollux decides.

The month is June and the horizon is a pavilion of stately thunderheads. He drinks iced tea and contemplates.

God, the mind of all existence, the great perceiver, is a madman. Madness is a holy state. And destruction is the primary form of creation. And God, naturally, as Mr. Pollux knows too well, is suicidal.

—

In the early autumn Mr. Pollux makes a tornado the size of the city of Wichita, Kansas, and it churns across the helpless prairie, dancing like a fat cobra in the fields. Clouds boil over all mid-America.

Senile and lost in his meditations, Mr. Pollux still won't surrender such ecstasy.

—

Last mortal efforts.

Mr. Pollux calls the national headquarters in Washington, D.C., and they fail to locate his service record in the Merchant Marine. Honorably discharged, he assures them. Gives his rank, serial number, and ship. Then he calls Toledo. Disconnected. He leaves a message in the recorder at the National Weather Service: "Two-week notice. No more bulletins from me after December." Writes a note, then, on his weekly grocery list and drops it down the mail chute: "Forget the soup this week. Send doctor and priest."

—

He prepares a great blizzard. Canada is snowed under even as he considers how to phrase his bulletin.

Winds a hundred miles an hour, temperatures sixty below, and frozen tidal waves slam into the cities of the Great Lakes. Another Ice Age arrives: fresh glaciers advance, new matterhorns are gouged out of the midwestern plains, the people of Omaha and Des Moines and Denver are sealed in the frozen flow, and in the

Ozarks the blizzard collides with the lingering zephyrs and a calamity of storm erupts. Mr. Pollux watches from his tower. The skies boom with thunder, ice breaks down the trees, and the animals shudder by, moving south into oblivion.

He sees his death from a great height, far distant, as if he stands beyond the coldest star, his tiny and silly loneliness a sacred and private pain. "Ouch," he tells the cosmos. "Ouch, ouch, ouch." And he flaps his arms against the relentless chill.

Cold: so complete that the metal girders of the tower grow brittle and snap. And the world is as blue and silent as a story in which a single man goes down to death.

About the Author

William Harrison is the author of novels and short stories that have been filmed for movies and TV, as well as screenplays, essays, and travel pieces. He is perhaps best known for *Roller Ball Murder*, in print and in film, and the recent novels *Three Hunters* and *Burton and Speke*.